CLAUDE MERCOEUR'S
REFLECTION

Borgo Press Books by FRÉDÉRIC BOUTET

The Antisocial Man and Other Strange Stories
Claude Mercoeur's Reflection and Other Strange Stories
The Voyage of Julius Pingouin and Other Strange Stories

CLAUDE MERCOEUR'S REFLECTION

AND OTHER STRANGE STORIES

FRÉDÉRIC BOUTET

Translated by Brian Stableford

THE BORGO PRESS

MMXIII

CLASSICS OF
FANTASTIC LITERATURE
NUMBER TWELVE

CLAUDE MERCOEUR'S REFLECTION

FIRST EDITION

Published by Wildside Press LLC

www.wildsidebooks.com

CLAUDE MERCOEUR'S REFLECTION

CONTENTS

INTRODUCTION

This volume is the third of a set of three showcasing the work of Frédéric Boutet, the other two volumes being *The Antisocial Man and Other Strange Stories* and *The Voyage of Julius Pingouin and Other Strange Stories*. Viewed as an ensemble, the collections illustrate the range and development of Boutet's early work, and provide a few representative samples of its later evolution. Although several stories by Boutet were translated into English in the 1920s, mostly in America, they were selected from his later works, when he was mostly writing sentimental stories and crime fiction for popular magazines; no examples of his early work, most of which consisted of offbeat supernatural fiction, have previously been rendered into English (although his work of that sort became quite popular in German translation, where it retains a higher reputation than it does even in France). This set of three volumes will hopefully serve to introduce the work of a highly distinctive writer of weird and baroque fiction to a new audience.

A brief account of Boutet's life and the overall shape of his career can be found in the first volume of the set, which contains translations of the contents of the 1903 collection *Contes dans le nuit* [Tales in the Night], featuring stories originally published in 1898-99, plus the novella "L'Homme sauvage du Quai Bois L'Encre" (tr. as "The Antisocial Man of the Quai Bois-l'Encre"), written in 1901 and first published in *L'Homme sauvage et Julius Pingouin: Deux petits roman fantaiststes* (1902). The second volume features the second novella from that collection,

"Le Voyage de Julius Pingouin" (tr. as "The Voyage of Julius Pingouin") plus three items taken from the 1899 collection *Drames baroques et melancoliques* and a dozen items originally published in the evening newspaper *Le Français* in 1903 and reprinted in the 1908 collection *Histoires vraisemblables* [Plausible Stories].

The present collection opens with a translation of the longest story from *Histoires vraisemblables*, the striking supernatural comedy "Quand nous avons passé," translated as "When We Have Passed On," for which I have not been able to identify any previously publication, and then completes the set of stories from the collection in question, adding one extra item published in *Le Français* in 1903 that was not included in the 1908 collection because it is an adaptation of an episode contained in "Le Voyage de Julius Pingouin." It was, however, added to a 2004 reprint of *Histories vraisemblables*, and I thought it worth including here in spite of the fact that the earlier novella is include in the second volume of the set, as an instance of adaptation. Boutet frequently readapted motifs and stories in that fashion.

The present collection continues with a translation of "L'Expérience" [The Experiment], which first appeared in book form in *Aventures sombre et pittoresque* (1921), and seemed worthy of inclusion because it shares a character with "Le Meurtre de l'Américain," here translated as "The American's Murder." Both stories are examples of Boutet's rare excursions into science fiction. The latter story was included in the collection (incorrectly advertised as a novel) *Le Reflet de Claude Mercoeur* (1921), all of whose contents are translated here, concluding the volume. Although the latter collection contains no supernatural fiction, the novella is interesting as a sample of Boutet's offbeat crime fiction and the short stories illustrate his sophistication of the ironic *contes cruels* that he had began producing nearly two decades earlier for *Le Français*. The last item "Lenoir et Keller" tr. as "Lenoir and Keller), originally published in *Je Sais Tout* at the height of the Great War in 1916, is particularly interesting, not merely because it illustrates the adaptation of his typical themes to the context of the conflict but also because it extrapolates the antisocial tendencies celebrated, illustrated and dramatized so extravagantly in his early novellas.

The translations of stories from *Histoires vraisemblables* were made from a copy of the reprint edition published in Rennes in 2004 by Terre de Brume. The translation of "L'Éxperience" was made from the version reprinted in the octobre 2002 issue of *Le Visage Vert*. The translations of the stories from *Le Reflet de Claude Mercoeur* were made from a copy of the 1921 Flammarion edition of the book in question.

WHEN WE HAVE PASSED ON

A viscous warmth still seemed to be lingering in the great cemetery, like an equivocal vestige of the ardors of summer, in the November night. The sky was drowned, the horizon livid, the silence muffled. The last perfumes, like withered leaves, were swirling in the sultry nocturnal air. An insidious mist coiled over the ground, hanging like scarves from the branches of sculpted yews, padding the arches embroidered in the stone and the artistic lintels of narrow perpetual swellings.

The paths were tidy, the lawns green, and the trees neatly-pruned. The aspect of the ensemble, comfortable and plush, was a pleasure to behold. Only a few neglected tombs offended the gaze with their plaintive dilapidation.

A clock in a veiled bell-tower, in the pale fog and the deadened night, chimed.

"Finally, we can come out," murmured a skeleton, opening the door of a little chapel with violet stained-glass windows. With his right hand, on whose bones a signet ring glittered, he arranged his shroud elegantly over his clavicles, and with a discreet rattle he went along the aristocratic pathway where he dwelt. "I have a desire," he continued, stretching himself with an air of satisfaction at being in the world, "to go see dear Saint-Firmin. Since he lost his iliac bone at that party the week before last, he's been vexed, and one doesn't see him anywhere. My visit…why, what's that?"

He stopped, amazed. He was at the foot of the great outer

wall, and over that wall the leg of a human clad in black trousers had just passed, next to two hands grasping the summit. The rest of the body completed the climb by means of a readjustment, with a dull rustle. A young man dressed in mourning, sitting on the top of the wall, looked down without seeing the skeleton, who had hidden himself, and then leapt down. He got up again, seemingly uninjured.

The skeleton had no hesitation in grabbing him by the collar. "What are you doing here?" he asked, severely.

The young man in mourning-dress started violently, opened his haggard eyes, tried to cry out, could not do it, and fainted.

"Why, what's got into the imbecile now?" muttered the skeleton, embarrassed. "Ah, there's water in that urn."

He sprinkled water on the young man, and slapped him vigorously with his hands.

The other came round, got to his feet, and made as if to run away, but the skeleton's fist held him in place.

"No, Monsieur," he said, dryly. "Stay there, if you please. Do you think you can introduce yourself in that fashion into private property, albeit in joint ownership. What are you doing here?"

The young man's mouth was open, but no sound came out.

"Come on, Monsieur, answer me!" ordered the skeleton, conscious of his rights and getting a little heated. "Don't oblige me to hand you over to the law! Confess! Why did you introduce yourself here by climbing over the wall? Is it to burgle our dwellings? Has the love of money brought you to this venerable enclosure to rob us? Or has some disrespectful curiosity regarding your superiors driven you to disregard peril and propriety alike? Speak up—are you a spy? That would be even more infamous! Isn't it enough that you have the liberty all day, you and your kind, to come and annoy us here, at home, and prevent us from coming out with your adipose presence? Can't the night, at least, belong to us? Can't you leave us tranquil, you living wretch? Do you have any right, you plump barbarian, to climb over walls to disturb the thin folk? Do we come to violate your homes, you lump of flesh? Come on, speak up! Answer

me! Quickly—or I'll clout you over the head with this urn."
And he shook the vessel.

"Mercy! Have pity on me, Monsieur!" stammered the young
man in mourning, throwing himself at the severe skeleton's
kneecaps. "Don't throw me out—be merciful! I didn't know!
Have pity on me, a desperate unfortunate! I have a fiancée, the
light of my life, an adored young woman…dead, Monseigneur!
Dead before the wedding! And me, mad with love, intoxicated
by grief, wanting to pray on her grave, far from profane eyes, to
kiss the earth where she lies…have mercy, good skeleton, I kiss
your feet! Take me to her—My God! My God!—in order that I
might sob over her grave!"

And he sobbed over the bones of skeleton's feet. The latter
seemed to be moved to compassion.

"Come on, come on, calm down, my poor boy," he advised.
"I forgive you. Yes, I forgive you…for love…obviously.… It's
not worth the trouble, but it's serious, damn it, is love! Come on,
come on, I'll take you. Come on, my friend…damn it!"

He coughed as if to clear his throat, doubtless to hide his
emotion.

"Thank you, Monseigneur, thank you!" sniffed the prostrate
and tearful unfortunate.

"Calm down, calm down." The skeleton gently lifted him
up by the arm. "I consent to take you, but I'm failing in my
duty and breaking my promises, you know. It's not permissible
to introduce a living person among us. In general I ought to
tell you, your society…well, frankly, it disgusts us.… You lack
boundaries—the flesh, you know…pooh! But I'm moved by
your grief, and, with a little cleverness, by passing you off as a
newcomer.…"

"A newcomer?" stammered the young man. "What do you
mean, worthy skeleton?"

"Why, someone recently buried, who still has his…his
habit…his envelope, his shell…in sum, his flesh! Usually, the
people who find themselves in that state, especially when they're
a little advanced, scarcely show themselves. It's not good form.

One waits to be proper, to be elegant, to present oneself with all one's advantages, and not leave one's relations a grotesque memory.... However, it's admissible that one might go out on the first few nights, while one is still presentable, to make acquaintances and leave one's card. Afterwards, well, one stays at home.... Oh, one gets bored, it's true. The hours go by slowly when one's in one's bier, and the rain, the winter evenings, also go by slowly, and come to soak or shrouds, while one hears the wind moaning in the branches.... Oh no, it's not cheerful, damn it! And one wishes that *they*'d make haste!"

"Who's *they*?"

"*They*...you know...the ones who occupy themselves with a fellow when no one else occupies themselves with him. The little workers of the final hour, who sculpt our lines by shaping them neatly. The true undertakers, who feed on us while there's something there....

"One wishes that one could say to them: 'Get a move on, then,' but it's impossible. They go their modest little way without ever making haste or sleeping. One feels them tunneling through a muscle, swarming in the cavities, gnawing on a bone, and they tickle you, and one doesn't dare move for fear of disturbing them.

"In life, it makes one feel sick just thinking about them, but believe me, once one's here and once can appreciate their services, one ends up getting attached to them and one is glad to see them getting big and fat, for it's a sign that the work is making progress."

"My God!" the young man groaned. "What horror!"

"Not at all," said the skeleton. "They're the ones who get us out of the ambiguous situation in which one isn't oneself...when one's neither flesh nor fish, if I might put it like that...without which, one would never become respectable. And as I've just told you, when one understands them properly, one ends up getting fond of them....

"One follows their labor, one calculates the progress they've made, always nibbling without ever hurrying...and I repeat that one gets impatient to be finished, because, throughout that time, it's customary not to go out. Some of us don't observe that esthetic regulation, and they walk around all the time, even in their worst modifications—but we close our eyes, so to speak. Generally, they're the passionate—like, for instance, Monsieur Honorus. Do you know him?"

"No," said the young man.

"Honorus, of the great factory of Honorus, Wey & Co., the iron-founders—very plush monument, large chapel, magnificent candelabras, gilded doors, sumptuous decoration: terrible taste, but very rich. Well, Monsieur Honorus came here eight months ago, and he's outside every night. He's not pleasant to see, mind, but his behavior's scandalous. One only meets him in the young women's pathways...."

"What?" the young man exclaimed.

"Exactly—that astonishes you, but that's the way it is. There's an individual who can't wait to be like everyone else before resuming his debaucheries. I pity the unfortunates who... anyway, society always treats him a trifle coldly, for he's too attached. We long-dead folk who constitute the aristocracy, owe our status to being reserved. To be sure, we don't shun pleasure, but we observe a certain moderation....

"But I can see you're a little calmer now, my dear Monsieur, and my loquacity had no other purpose. We can go. Permit me, first, to introduce myself: Baron La Rose, second pathway on the left, violet stained-glass, hereditary chapel, reconstructed in 1820...oh, modestly, because of the Revolution, you know...I'll introduce you as one of my young relatives."

"I'm Vicomte Adhémar de Léonce," sighed the young man.

"Delighted," said the Baron. "Delighted, my dear Monsieur— we are, if I'm not mistaken, related on the distaff side. Well-died people—pardon me, for you I ought to say well-born—always find one another...now, if you want...."

"To weep on her grave—oh yes, that's what I want!" And poor Adhémar sniffed again.

"Then I'll ask you...which person is in question?" the Baron interrogated, gently.

"Oh, forgive me—that's true!" moaned the young man. "Louise...Louise de Rivière. My God! When I think that she's prey to the horrors of the tomb!"

"I know," said the skeleton. "I know where she is—in the southern pathway, near the yew cross. Very honorable family, tomb in perfect taste, Vosges granite and porphyry.... Let's go...but, oh, damn it! Your outfit...bah! That happens sometimes. One piece of advice, though! Keep your eyes half-closed. They're too bright...."

They went off along the main pathway.

They walked slowly through the small white city, cheerful and animated beneath its beautiful veils of insulating mist. Around them, skeletons were hastening to some rendezvous of pleasure or business. Others, smoking and dreaming, were idling nonchalantly or sitting and chatting on old worn headstones, their polished skulls gleaming softly in the uncertain light, through the soft mist blurring their silhouettes. Games of baccarat, poker and bridge were in progress here and there, followed by galleries of attentive gamblers.

Amateur runners were doing laps around a large clump of bushes. On the thresholds of sumptuous monuments, decorated by evergreen plants, the masters of the houses, crowned with immortelles, draped in their finest shrouds, were welcoming the elegant groups of their guests courteously. Intimate soirées and family gatherings cheered up the most modest concessions.

In front of one mysterious vault, a few people sitting in a circle, phalanges united, were turning a slab and evoking the living. Children, watched by their mothers or nursemaids, were amusing themselves here and there. A troop of joyous companions went by, humming and rattling, while a violent altercation and domestic dispute rose up between the co-tenants of a temporary vault surrounded by a circle of idlers.

Far from all that agitation, near the cypresses and their propitious shade, on the lawns and between the clumps of bushes, amorous shadows enveloped in shrouds the color of the wall were hastening and meeting up furtively, without the slightest sound of conjunction...and couples, side by side and intertwined, were plunging into the protective mystery of the pathways, or closing the discreet door of some inhabited chapel or isolated cenotaph.

The young man in mourning-dress seemed impressed by so much civilization, and the obliging skeleton, in order to inform his protégé as much as to sustain the plausibility of his role as a newcomer, amicably gave him explanations while saluting friends he perceived.

"The quarter we're going through," he said, "is the chic, fashionable and rich neighborhood to which strangers come. There, on the left, is major commerce, banking and industry. The quarter we're coming to, and which I inhabit, is the aristocratic quarter, naturally stricter and more exclusive: the Faubourg Saint-Germain of our old cemetery. The inhabitants recognize one another by a dignity of manners, their finesse and there distinction. We put a high value on the delicacy of extremities, you see. That's how one discerns nobility. The Comtesse de Talk, who lives near me, is justly celebrated for the divine lightness of her small bones. She's an exquisite woman, and has the most beautiful teeth in the world, but her hand! Oh, my dear chap, that hand! It's a dream! Undulating articulations! The primness of a perforated gem! The whiteness of fresh ivory! We're intimates, and I glory in it! The dear Comtesse has told me that her sympathy for me was born in the contemplation of my foot! Yes, my dear chap."

He smiled, with a self-satisfaction full of implication. "It's true, of course, that my foot...well, breeding! The foot of a cavalier, you know!" And he extended an irreproachable metatarsal, finely encased, with elegant and neat phalanges.

"Yes, yes," said the young man in mourning, who did not seem to be in full possession of his faculties

"Here, too," the skeleton continued, "status is everything. We conserve the status we possessed before, that our larva—

don't take that ill; you seem to me liable to make a distinguished corpse—had among the living. An aristocrat is an aristocrat forever, a rich man remains a rich man. Democracy, I beg you to believe, does not infect us unduly.

"Naturally, I'm talking about respectable folk. In the plebeian population over there"—jabbing a disgusted thumb over his shoulder-blade, he vaguely indicated the northern part of the cemetery—"it appears that they form insurrectional organizations and hold anarchic meetings, declaring that social class ceases with life, that all men die equal and a thousand other nonsensical slogans of that sort. It's of no importance, because individuals of that kind are of no account. If you could see them! They're frightful! Ignoble! One could almost prefer the living! They revel in dirt and ignominy. They haven't even found a means for each one to have his own dwelling. They live in holes, in heaps, can you believe, without observing the slightest decency, getting drunk, fighting and stealing bones from one another to complete their skeletons.

"There are old ones who are so wretched by virtue of being patched up here and there that hardly a single piece of their original carcass remains. It's no longer one skeleton, it's twenty of them; one never knows who one's talking to—every bone has a different origin. And they spend their time whining, recriminating and protesting about everything. Either that or they're making speeches standing on their little mounds, proclaiming the sovereignty of the people, declaring that we're oppressing them, that we take up too much space, that their existence is becoming impossible and it would be better never to have died!

"In the meantime, the young women prostitute themselves in corners and the children play bowls with skulls that might perhaps have belonged to their ancestors. What profanation! It's true that those people have no ancestors! Fortunately, an extensive authority keeps them in place, otherwise there'd be everything to dread! Sometimes we go among them in disguise, in order to accompany ladies—the caprices of pretty women are the scourge of Grand Dukes, you know! But truly, it's too infamous; I shan't go again. It dishonors one to think that one is made of the same bones as such brutes....ah, *bonsoir*, my dear Saint-Firmin! So you've decided to come out!"

The Baron stopped to shake the hand of a stout skeleton with a sympathetic appearance and a comfortable shroud, who was trotting along, smoking a cigar, on the heels of a pert individual whose shroud, coquettishly tucked up, uncovered a slender fibula.

"Yes, yes," replied the stout skeleton. I manage to find my iliac—it's that little minx Clara who had hidden it." He dabbed his parietals with a flap of his shroud, and added: "It's warm this evening."

"And what a mist! If one had bronchi, eh!" the Baron remarked, wittily, making his stout friend burst into immoderate laughter, which made his entire solid carcass rattle. Monsieur La Rose continued: "But permit me to introduce a newcomer to you, who is a relative of mine, Monsieur Adhémar de Léonce, an accomplished young man."

"Delighted, Monsieur," said the stout skeleton, recovering his composure and bowing courteously to the young man while holding out his right hand, a set of knucklebones, which Adhémar shook, not without a certain frisson. "Delighted to have you among us. My dear Baron, I hope you'll bring Monsieur along to the Comtesse de Talk's twelve o'clock; he'll see all of society there, and we'll meet again."

"Yes, undoubtedly," the Baron replied, "but I don't want to keep you, my dear friend...."

"Hmm...I'd like to stay, but excuse me...a find, a marvel, my dear chap, a little charmer—plebeian, no doubt, but slim, light, clean, polite...and coy...I fear that she might escape me...."

And bidding farewell with a gesture, he drew away hurriedly on the track of the pert shadow, which seemed to be taking pleasure in allowing that pursuit, doubtless not being as coy as Monsieur de Saint-Firmin would have liked to think.

"What a charming man," said the Baron. "Ever young, ever amorous, always in quest of new adventures, but obliging and courteous too. Oh, he takes death cheerfully, that one—long and good, he says, and my word, he's right. In accordance with his advice, my dear chap, I'll take you to Madame de Talk's soirée, and you'll see that we aren't boring...but forgive me; I'm talking about pleasures when you have an affliction of the heart...."

They took a few steps in silence. The skeleton seemed quite satisfied with himself and others, although he seemed sincerely sympathetic to his companion's pain. As for the latter, one could not begin to fathom his thoughts, but they were somber—that was obvious.

"Forgive me," the skeleton said, suddenly, "if I'm stirring up your grief, but has your fiancée been among us for long? I don't remember her."

"Twelve days," moaned the young man. "The misfortune happened while I was traveling. I learned of it when I returned. I thought I would go mad, and I was closely watched. This evening, I was able to evade the surveillance. But why do you ask?"

"Oh, no reason, but you know...women...and as she can't hope to see you again very soon...."

"What are you getting at?" the living man interrogated, in anguish.

"Well, my God, it's delicate.... I might be mistaken but I'd like, out of friendship, to avoid the overly rude blow of a new dolor. And the demoiselle, of course, must have thought that if you'd wanted to follow her, you'd already have done so, and not having done so, would sooner or later console yourself with the living, your peers.... And it might be that she...one gets bored when one has nothing to do, and there's no lack here of... consolers who know their business, especially with a pretty newcomer."

"What horror! What an idea! I'm sure of her," the young man declared, peremptorily.

"So much the better, so much the better," said the Baron, who seemed skeptical. "But I thought I ought to say something." He pointed to a melancholy young skeleton wandering in a deserted pathway around a little chapel that was closed. "Look, there's a poor fellow who, like you, is suffering from love...."

"Oh," said the young man in mourning-dress, sympathetically, darting a glance at the unfortunate who had been indicated to him. "Has his fiancée left him?"

"No, not exactly, but it's a sad story, which shows how sentiments can be modified by a separation. It's him who left his fiancée, in ceasing to live a few years ago. So he was here, lamenting, full of love and thinking about the one he left behind in the degrading and transitory jail they call the world of the living, and he was jealous, suffering a thousand lives at the thought that she might have forgotten him and fallen in love with someone else. Those sentiments are terrible here, you see, for they're so impotent.... I'm sure that if he'd been able to do it, he'd have gone to kill her, in order to have her with him....

"Fortunately, newly-arrived relatives told him that the little one had remained faithful to him and gone into a convent. That was a great relief for the poor fellow, and he continued to wait, passionately, but suffering less intensely. That didn't last very long, because she came here not long after him. When he saw the funeral procession arrive and found out that it was her, his joy scared us all...but the young woman had been seriously touched by religion, it appears, and never wanted to return his love on seeing him here. She loves him like a sister, she says, and not otherwise—so he's fallen into a frightful despair from which nothing can extract him. Every day, he comes to prowl around her chapel. She never opens the door, perhaps for fear that she might weaken, and they talk through the little grille, him begging her to have pity and love him a little, her exhorting him to tame his passions and lead a resigned and virtuous death...but shhh! Here he is."

The young skeleton had, in fact arrived close at hand in the course of his mechanical wandering.

"Well, my poor friend," said the Baron, sympathetically, gently putting the tips of his phalanges on his ulna, "are you still as unhappy?"

"Oh, I'm going out of my skull!" replied the poor young skeleton, dejectedly. "I love her too much, you see! I adore her with all my soul, madly! I spend hours, prostrate and tortured, at that dear accursed door, which never opens to me! I burn, I beg, I suffer…oh, how I suffer! And she…never a word of love, never a surge of emotion. Always calm, always cold, always insensitive…and so lovely, so lovely!

"Sometimes, through the grille, in the mauve shadow projected by the stained-glass window, I catch a glimpse of her, upright, elegant and proud, finely outlined in her light form by the rays of moonlight that kiss her little polished bones so amorously! Oh, I'd give anything in the world to touch the hem of her shroud!

"Her teeth shine and drive me mad, and the mysterious hollows of her wide orbits seem to me to be a divine and deceptive abyss into which my passion plunges, is lost and is reborn, a thousand times more ardent, returning to envelop me like a seething, furious, devouring sea!

"I can't forget her, nor flee from her, nor bend her will. What torture! She has no heart, I tell you! And me, me…!" He gripped the left side of his thoracic cage despairingly. "Oh, I'd rather be back in the time when I was alone here, when I was awaiting her coming, when I still had hope…I have no more strength, no more courage, no more hope! The day before yesterday, I tried in vain to hang myself. Oh, I miss life—at least one could die!"

The unfortunate fellow's agitation had declined. He drew away, dejectedly. He went to sit down on a black tomb and, detaching his left tibia, which he had pierced like a flute, he played a melancholy, soothing and amorous tune on it.

"That's the song they once both loved, in the time of their love and their life," murmured the Baron to his companion, who was moved to tears.

They drew away, and the plaintive sound floated after them.

"Are we nearly there?" asked Adhémar, in a faint voice.

"Yes," said the Baron. "The yew crossroads is at the end of

that path to the left."

"My God, my God!" moaned the young man. "To see her tomb!"

"Be careful," said the skeleton, suddenly. "Quick—let's hide in here!"

The young man in mourning-dress allowed himself to be dragged into the shadow of an old chapel. From a side-path, a tall, frantic half-naked skeleton emerged into the pathway, brandishing an iron bar, which he was whirling around, shouting furiously.

"I'm alive," he howled. "I'm alive, for God's sake! Help! Help! I'm alive!"

He disappeared at top speed, brandishing his weapon. His cries became inarticulate. Two other skeletons launched in pursued, passing by at a run.

"What's going on?" asked Adhémar, trembling.

"He's a madman," said the Baron La Rose. "A dangerous madman, that his guardians are trying to recapture. Let's go...."

They advanced rapidly along the pathway.

"As you heard," said the Baron, "his madness consists of believing that he's alive. We all dream sometimes that we're alive, especially in the early days, and believe me, it's a frightful nightmare—meaning no offense. But he, poor chap, believes it all the time, and he's completely insane. It's true that he's gone through a rather harsh ordeal. He was brought here and buried alive."

"Alive!" said Adhémar, with a start of horror.

"Yes—he was cataleptic. Once buried, he woke up. You get the picture? He was in his coffin for seven whole days, howling. The living couldn't hear him, but we could hear him very clearly. He howled as he was howling just now, and its was enough to chill your bones. He ate his entire right hand before...before becoming tranquil...."

"But why didn't you rescue him?" Adhémar exclaimed, alarmed by his companion's calmness.

"My God," the skeleton replied. "That's nothing to do with

us. We don't like getting mixed up in your business, in general; we're afraid of being betrayed. And really, once one's here, one might as well stay. A little sooner, a little later…we never intervene in such cases."

Adhémar flinched. "In such cases?" he stammered. "You mean it happens often?"

"Often enough," said the Baron. "It's easy, you know, to bury someone alive. Obviously, it's not very pleasant for the individual concerned, but when the painful moments have passed, they generally don't regret it—on the contrary. As for that one, we liberated him as soon as he was one of us, but it had gone on too long and he was a nervous type—he was raving mad."

"I can understand that, poor fellow!" stammered the young man in mourning, who plunged into meditation.

"We're here, my dear chap," said the Baron, suddenly touching his arm.

"My God, my God!" moaned Adhémar, putting his hand on his heart and stopping. "We're near to her.…"

"Lower your voice," instructed the Baron, "and if you trust me, let's approach without being seen. The Larivière family monument is over there, behind that bush—let's slip into the shadow of the yews without making any noise."

Stifling the sound of their footsteps as much as possible and ducking under the branches of evergreen foliage, they advanced to the vicinity of the monument. Then, without being able to make out the interlocutors, they heard two voices whispering in the shadows.

The young man had a spasm. "It's her voice," he whimpered, panting. He seemed to be on the brink of dying.

"Shh!" breathed the Baron, supporting him; he seemed keen to see the investigation through to the end. Without being able to retain a muffled snigger, he added: "There's also a man's voice. Let's get a little closer; they won't hear us."

Silently, with the prudence of a serpent, they crept closer.

"Stop here," murmured the Baron. He recognized the masculine voice "Ah! That's Henry de Livry, one of our best Don

Juans."

"It's her, it's her," moaned Adhémar, feebly, perturbed to the utmost depths of his vital spirits.

"Shh! Listen!" the Baron ordered, almost imperceptibly, lying flat on the ground and obliging his companion to do likewise.

"Henry," murmured the feminine voice, which was soft and musical. "Why are you here? I begged you not to come back."

"Forgive me, Louise. I love you so much. I thought I could, for one more night...."

"But I'm becoming ugly, and I don't want you to see me like this."

"Ugly! You, my love? But you're more beautiful than ever. Less beautiful, to be sure, than you will be later, but already so beautiful. Your skin is taking on charming tones, your eyes are more profound, your silky golden hair...."

"Soon I won't have any. It's already going...."

"You'll only be more beautiful. My love, since the first evening I saw you here, in this poetic and deserted spot, since the first evening when I fell in love with you, every evening, I've followed the exquisite marks of transformation on your face passionately. What I see in you are not the gross charms that pleased the living, which I see coming to an end. What I love in you is the promise of your true beauty, which I sense ready to emerge, to blossom, to shine radiantly in all its elegant purity. Beneath that flesh, which I hate because it is delaying the hours of our happiness, because a man has loved you in it, beneath that flesh, which is ceasing to be yourself and which you are allowing to fall away like an excessively heavy cloak, I divine your real, adorable personality, as indestructible as our love...."

"You're sure of that, Henry? It astonishes me so much."

"It's the last memories of the errors of life that are still troubling you. Look at me, my love, am I not as you will be, and don't you love me thus?"

"Oh yes!"

"Would you love me more if I had flesh, hair, all the bother of a weighty, thick, suffering body, becoming more dilapidated every year as it approaches its end?"

"No, no, Henry! I understand very well. But what do you expect? It's been such a short time since I changed. I'm still almost alive."

"Yes, that's true. My God, it will be a long wait...."

"Alas, Henry—how long?"

"Oh, that depends. One can't tell in advance...."

"Oh, I'll hurry...it doesn't do any harm, does it?"

"No, no harm. One gets bored, that's all, but one interests oneself in the work that liberates us...."

"Of, if I could beg them to make haste...so many long hours without seeing you...."

"You'll think about me?"

"I'll only think about you. The memory of your love will never leave me. My God, when I think that, as soon as I'm free, beautiful, like you, I'll be able to throw myself into your arms. You won't forget me for someone else, between now and then? I'll be here, alone, shut in, while you...."

"My beloved...."

"Henry.... But go—it's late, my grandmother might come back...."

"No, my darling, you know that she's in the chapel, and that she'll stay there until morning."

"Yes, but I'm in haste to begin my reclusion. I'm in haste to surrender myself to them, in order to resemble you sooner."

"They take hold of us even before the funeral, my love, and as soon as we're here, we belong to them and their work begins...."

"Oh, my God, Henry, go! I don't want, before you...."

"One more word, Louise: that fellow, that living man—your fiancé, in brief—you no longer love him, do you? You no longer think about him?"

"Henry, I've already told you...."

"But I need to hear it again! Especially at the moment of such a long separation.... I'm jealous...not of the kisses he's been able to give you—your flesh isn't you—but I'm jealous of your love, of your thoughts. You no longer love him, do you? You no longer love him, that gross human larva, lumpen, stupid, adipose and hairy?"

"No, I swear to you, since I've seen you, the memory of his gross face is repugnant to me...."

"Oh, Louise, let him never attempt to dispute you with me!"

"You're mad! He's a robust and healthy man. He'll fall in love with someone else who's like him, and continue his dirty living existence with her. May he become very old, and never come here...that's all I wish for him...."

"Is that really true, Louise? You don't want to see him again? If he were to die, that wouldn't change your sentiments for me?"

"Oh, God no! I scarcely loved him, without knowing anything, like a crazy living little girl—but you, Henry, I love you profoundly, like a woman, like a dead woman...."

"Louise, I adore you!"

The voices melted away, becoming lower still, and tender, in amorous whispered endearments that were suggestive of speech and kisses.

That was too much for poor Adhémar. With a sigh, he collapsed on the Baron's hospitable clavicle.

"Damn!" muttered the other. "He's got worse! It's true that it's a rude blow for the poor fellow." He shook him, tapped his hands, and having brought him partly back to his senses, with a strength one would not have suspected in such a thin being, muffling his footfalls, he carried the unfortunate man outside the clump of yews in which the blackest of treasons had just pierced his heart.

"My God, my God, the vile woman!" moaned Adhémar dully, dazed by dolor.

"It reminds one of life, eh?" observed the Baron, with a bitter smile, forgetting that his companion was not entirely like him. "But don't attach too much importance to that, my friend. Have courage. It's a hard blow, but take it like a man."

"My God, my God!" moaned Adhémar, spasmodically.

"What horror! And her grandmother, who goes to the chapel instead of watching over her! My God, my God, I'm choking!"

And suddenly, letting himself fall on to an old mossy slab at the corner of a deserted pathway, he burst into convulsive sobs.

"Weep away—no one can hear you, and it'll soothe your pain," murmured the Baron, sitting down beside him. "Weep, poor childish heart, broken by the cruel heart of a woman." Pensively, he added: "It's a long time since I've seen real tears wept. We sometimes sweat when the weather's damp, but it's not the same....it's very moving and a trifle ridiculous."

Adhémar wept for a long time.

The Baron remained sitting by his side, without saying anything more, until he saw that his companion's sobs were diminishing in violence. Then he got up and, with gentle firmness, constrained him to straighten up and listen to him.

"My friend," he said to him, "you've wept as much as a man can and must when he's sensitive and great suffering strikes him for the first time. I've respected your grief. But it's not appropriate to yield to your sentiments like a child devoid of energy. Envisage the situation frankly and accept it. That young woman no longer loves you, and if you want my opinion, which is only what she said herself, she never loved you, even when she was alive."

"My God," moaned Adhémar.

"No, for sure," said the Baron, forcibly. "It's necessary to cut to the dead—pardon me, to the quick—and not cradle oneself with illusions. We're going to leave this deserted and not very comfortable place without further ado. We'll take a little walk, to enable you to pull yourself together, and then I'll take you to the Comtesse de Talk's."

"To a party! Never!" said Adhémar.

"Yes," said the Baron. "Do that for me. It will change your ideas and bring you back to yourself. Afterwards...."

"Afterwards?" stammered the comatose Adhémar.

"You can do as you wish," said the Baron, negligently, who seemed to have a thought at the back of his skull, "but let me tell you right away that I consider you to be a gallant man, for whom I experience a keen sympathy, and whom I'd be happy to have as a best friend."

"I too like you very much, and I'll do as you wish," sighed Adhémar, shaking the worthy skeleton's phalanges feebly.

"No more sighs, then," said the Baron. "Be sad, but don't show it. Anyway, damn it, at your age, when one loses a woman, one finds ten more...."

"Oh no!" Adhémar protested. "Women—I hate them!"

"That's because you love them too much," said the Baron. "Or, rather, because you only love one of them. Love several at the same time, and...tell me how it works out... But let's go. We'll call in at the great market, which is a curious thing to see, take a turn down below and then go see the dear Comtesse. We'll arrive just as the party's warming up."

They left, the Baron cheerfully whistling a funeral march and, from time to time, making a witty remark, a pun or a deft and mordant quip to distract his companion, who was walking with his head bowed and shoulders slumped, depressed as he was by dolor and the dark thoughts he was mulling over.

At a junction of the path, in a large isolated crossroads near the enclosing wall, they saw several skeletons together, conferring gravely. Two of them, separated from the group and from one another by the whole breadth of the crossroads, seemed to be waiting with a slightly feverish dignity. Another was measuring distances on the ground, Long hard objects wrapped in green serge were lying on the ground.

"Look," said the Baron in a low voice. "They're making preparations for a duel. One of the gentlemen—the tall one with the embroidered shroud who's standing apart on the right—has been accused by his companion of cheating at cards. He's just had an extremely fortunate bank at baccarat—too fortunate, it appears. Anyway, he's a sort of flashy Brazilian who poses as a man of the world and who never ought to have been allowed into a respectable club like *Les Racines*, where the quarrel took place. His adversary had some sorry adventures in his youth, and isn't much better than him. The duel will be serious because there are scores to be settled. They're caught by the hair, if I might use the expression, and no one's more jealous of his honor than someone who has none. But let's make ourselves scarce— reporters are arriving, by invitation, and photographers, and I don't want to be recognized, because I refused to serve as a second. It's a shabby affair, in which a real man of the world can't get mixed up."

"With what weapons will they fight?" Adhémar asked, who was visibly thinking about something else.

"Flat swords," the Baron replied, drawing away with him. "But please, my dear chap, pull yourself together and make an effort to shake off your sadness. You're getting deeper into it by the minute and chewing it over. It's true that it's very recent and that, before having seen your mistress again—or, rather, having heard her—you were only suffering in your heart, whereas now it's your self-esteem that's afflicted.…"

"Perhaps," said the young man. "My suffering is certainly more painful now. Just now, I was able to weep for my lost love and that adored woman, whom I believed to be pure and sincere, without any further thought. Now, you see, my injury is crueler, my wound more envenomed, for not only has the woman I loved been stolen from me forever, but I can see her in the arms of another, I know that she didn't love me, and shame, scorn and bitterness are rendering my tears more scalding."

"Undoubtedly," observed the Baron. "Nevertheless, a little while ago you were able to believe that you had lost the exquisite exception that one never finds—a loving, frank and faithful woman—whereas now you know that her soul was the eternal feminine soul, flirtatious, fickle and capricious, which enjoys doing us harm and laughs at our avowals. Let's not be hasty to condemn, though…she was very young to be in love when you knew her, and perhaps she really has encountered in Henry de Livry her predestined amour."

"Ah!" the young man exclaimed, "I should have killed myself when I learned of her death. I would have come here. I would have been ready, later, at the same time as her…and she would still have loved me. It's my fault.…"

"Undoubtedly," said the Baron, with a smile. "You seem to me to be one of those true lovers who don't want to see the defects of their lovelies, and who always accuse themselves of the sins they've committed. But let's pass on. It's too late now. You'll never be able to efface from your memory what you heard just now, and she'll never love you again. Shake off the memory of that lost love, accept the inevitable and be a man.…"

"You're right," said Adhémar. "Excuse my weakness. I'm going to get a grip on myself. I'm very lucky to have found, in my misfortune, a friend like you.…"

"Very good," said the Baron. "I'm glad to see you like this. We're going to distract ourselves."

"Yes," said Adhémar, who seemed resolute. "We need distraction. But explain to me, I beg you, something you said just now. You mentioned reporters. Is there a newspaper here, then?"

"There are three," said the Baron, "and naturally, each one has a different opinion. The issues are written in chalk on slates, which are passed around and fixed outside. First, to begin at the bottom, we have the organ of the common people: an infamous, pretentious and bilious rag that devotes itself, under the pretext of denouncing abuses, to the most atrocious blackmail. It's stupidly entitled *Le Corbillard des Pauvres*, and delights in dragging the most eminent dead through the mud. Its editor is an ignoble individual who signs himself Le Mort Maigre. He's a universally-scorned renegade who poisons the people with criminal slanders and invites the communal graves every evening to rise up *en masse* and march against us to claim their mortal rights. Pooh!

"Next, at the opposite end of the spectrum, is *Le Monitor des Os Blancs*, respectable, to be sure, but unbearably tedious. Only the staunchest conservatives read it. I must confess that, for myself, I don't have the courage. It's edited by a kind of historic ruin who dates from the *ancien régime*, and prints any tedious and stupid tidbit to please his clientele of dowagers and backward curés.

Finally, there's *L'Écho de Minuit*, the only readable paper, which reports society events and parties, the night's news, and the names of new arrivals of note. In its supplement, *Le Mort Pour Tous*, it also publishes articles signed by the most notable literary and political celebrities we have among us, and who obtain glory by contributing to it. The paper is very interesting and its editor, who's a friend of mine, is a remarkable intelligence, fond of art and letters. He's thinking of founding a theater, using the great public cenotaph as an auditorium, but he needs subscribers. The great artists who are resident here would like nothing better than to lend their collaboration, in spite of the jealousy that they experience for one another...."

The Baron interrupted himself, for they were leaving the narrow pathways, propitious for conversation, and emerging into a vast artery that was almost tumultuous.

"What a crowd!" remarked Adhéma, astonished.

"Let's join in," said the Baron, "and observe what's happening around us. It's very busy tonight. The majority of the merchants you see are Jews—their cemetery's over there to the north. They maintain the traditions of their race intact, I can assure you. Here's one—you see, that old man with the sordid shroud who's scarping dried mud off his ankles with a fibula. He's one of the biggest capitalists we have here. He's made a veritable fortune solely by selling metal plates that he hammers himself. It was fashionable a few years ago to line one's lower jaw like that. It was all the rage for a long time. According to one's fortune, one employed gold, silver or lead. The lower class, always ambitious to ape the ridicule of superiors that they imagine they can equal in that way, made use of the lids of sardine-tins on a massive scale. The vogue passed, as all vogues do, but a lot of merchants got rich on it."

Adhémar listened to these explanations while making his way, with some difficulty, through the dense crowd surrounding him. On each side of the avenue there were displays, behind which, squatting like tailors, were merchants fashioning articles animatedly and agitating all their bones wildly over the slightest objects. Save for rare exceptions, the merchandise was not very attractive, and would doubtless only have been considered by the inhabitants of living world to be junk, only good for putting in the cellar or throwing into the gutter, but it was hotly contested nevertheless.

Adhéma observed, regretfully, that the transactions were not all made in entirely good faith. One skeleton especially, who seemed to be drunk and was accompanied by a young woman of loose morals, was odiously deceived by a young dealer in detached bones. The latter, before Adhémar's very eyes, robbed the drunkard of his own clavicle and then sold it back to him at an exorbitant price, with the manifest complicity of the girl, who protested to the poor soak that she could not love him much because he was incomplete. Indignant, Adhémar wanted to intervene, but the Baron dissuaded him urgently.

"Be careful not to get mixed up in anything whatsoever," he told him. "These are the dregs of the population and you'd be looking for trouble. Let's remain spectators, as prudence demands—and it might be better for us to retire. We've come a little late. At this hour, roguery rules and prostitution triumphs in these ill-famed locations. Let's go; I wanted to show you a gracious child who's usually here, selling fire-follets or glowworms, which ladies buy to make into ornaments, but her place is vacant already, so we'll have to leave it for another time."

As they withdrew, they were subjected to tenacious propositions from low-class hetairas and the insulting remarks of several skeletons of shady appearance. The Baron's firm attitude imposed itself upon them, and Adhémar, who was beginning to feel some anxiety, breathed more freely when he and his companion turned into a tranquil pathway.

"What villainy!" said the Baron. "It was time to go. That's how riots start. Let's go to the Comtesse's—her luxury and grace will seem all the sweeter after that ignoble spectacle."

Without further discussion, they hastened past neatly-formed chapels and regular gravestones. The denser mist limited visibility and stifled footfalls.

"Oh!" Adhémar exclaimed, suddenly. "A Man!" his arm indicated a fleshy apparition emerging from a chapel.

"Could it be a burglar?" Monsieur La Rose advanced swiftly. "Oh, no," he added. "I recognize him. He's one of ours—but what is he doing?"

"What am I doing?" replied the individual, angrily, in whom Adhémar was able to recognize a body that was still almost entire, and not even too dilapidated, but was visibly as dead as anyone else. "What am I doing? That's none of your business, is it?"

"Monsieur!" protested the Baron.

"Ah, it's you, Baron!" And the dead man assumed a less hostile attitude. "Pardon me—I didn't recognize you...the fog! And I'm annoyed. For an hour I've been working to clear my chapel of the funerary ignominies with which my wife stuffs it every year under the pretext of souvenirs. It's not enough that she poisoned me...."

"Poisoned!" said Adhéma, terrified, paying no heed to the nudge in the ribs that the Baron gave him. "Your wife poisoned you!"

The dead man looked at him. "Indeed," he said, dryly. "She poisoned me in order to marry my best friend. That's the way of things. It makes me mad! I'd rather she hadn't employed, under the pretext of caring for me, that filthy arsenic, which has conserved my flesh for years without me being able to lighten myself like everyone else. But all in all, I could let that go, having never had any disposition to play the rake. No, what disgusts me is these wreaths, which she persists—God knows why—in sending me every year. If they were even something artistic, with natural flowers and nice ribbons, but look at this! Look at this cheap rubbish in iron wire and glass beads! Every year it's the same. She gives the job to that drunkard François, my former valet, and he buys filth to his own taste and hangs it up all over the place, sobbing, too drunk to see clearly any longer! For God's sake!"

"Calm down, now," said the Baron. "You're expressing yourself rather violently. Distract yourself rather than shutting yourself away—go out, see people. That will change your ideas."

"Pooh! With the face I have? Go out? No thanks! I look like a spoiled mummy. I'd prefer not to show myself. Then again, I'm too old for partying. I prefer sleeping or reading peacefully. I wouldn't have got up, except for these infamies, of which I had to rid myself as soon as possible. What do I look like, I ask you, when I have this on my grille?"

And with a kick, he sent a wreath flying twenty meters.

The two friends bade him farewell and went on their way. "His wife never poisoned him, you know," said the Baron, when they were some distance away. "One of his cousins told me the whole story. The unfortunate woman suffered ten years of marriage and martyrdom with that misanthropic and alcoholic old fool. He did indeed take arsenic medicinally, and that's what conserves him, but he died quite simply of his illness, and if his wife has remarried and tasted a little happiness, it's only just.

"I hope the unfortunate woman never comes here—he'll resume tormenting her, and he'll reproach her all the time with that fantastic tale of murder, which he's invented wholesale, but which he's ended up believing to be true. It wouldn't be a death for the poor woman. But we're getting back to the classy quarter now. What a pleasure to find oneself at home, in the comfort of one's habitual environment. Will you do me the honor of coming to my place when we leave the Comtesse's?"

Suddenly a cheerful voice broke in: "Here you are, then!"

They turned road and saw the stout skeleton that they had run into at the beginning of the evening. A middle-aged dead man, who seemed to have quit life only a few days previously, clad in a beautiful brand new shroud, was walking beside him, seemingly prey to an ill-concealed alarm.

"My first cousin," said the stout skeleton, making the introductions. "He hasn't been here long, and it's his first outing.

"I've only just gone to fetch him, and he's still half-asleep."

Adhémar seemed interested by this cousin, who was fairly similar to him, save for the bagatelle of the change of state.

"Have you...slept well?" he asked, for something to say.

"Yes, yes," murmured the cousin. "It's good to sleep as one does here—my God it's good...."

"Isn't it?" remarked the Baron. "Especially after all the bother you've just been through. All the bustle of funerals wears you out with fatigue and annoyance!"

"Did you suffer much before? Did the thing itself give you a lot of trouble?" asked Adhémar, with an ardent and tremulous curiosity.

"Shh, my dear chap!" hissed the Baron, digging him in the ribs. "One doesn't ask that sort of thing; you'll give yourself away."

"I d...don't really remember," stammered the cousin, who seemed anguished. "My daughter wept so much..... I've left her alone down there, and that torments me...."

"Come on, come on—the Comtesse will think we've abandoned her!" To break off the conversation, the stout skeleton pushed him forward. "We're very late," he added. "I was held up. Delightful, believe me, delightful...such grace and charm... ha ha!"

They soon arrived. The party was in full swing. The Comtesse's monument was very elegant, decorated with perfect taste, as were the vast vaults where a soft phosphorescent light reigned.

The mistress of the house welcomed the newcomers with a marked favor. Her capacious silk shroud, slightly low-cut, allowed her pearl necklace to be seen, and fell in broad pleats around her slender form. Very gracious, coiffed with chrysanthemums, gloved in white to the elbow, she took a step toward her guests that revealed the fine phalanges of her child-like feet, laden with rings.

"I was almost despairing of seeing you, Baron," she said, with a delightful amiability, playing with her fan while Monsieur La

Rose leaned over to kiss her hand. "You and Monsieur Saint-Firmin are ever faithful, though." Welcoming the newcomers, she added: "In any case, the presence of these gentlemen explains and excuses your lateness."

"A thousand thanks, Madame," stammered Adhémar, bowing deeply.

The stout skeleton and his cousin, who still had a rather sad expression, also presented their homages, and then went to mingle with the guests, who were not very numerous but all individuals of the highest society. Adhémar, somewhat out of place, moved a few paces away and leaned on a marble column, pensively.

"What a charming fellow," said the Comtesse to the Baron, who had remained beside her. "He's well worthy of being your relative, but why has he maintained those hideous vestments of existence?"

"He didn't know that he'd have the honor of being introduced to you, my dear Madame," the Baron replied, a trifle embarrassed. He lowered his voice: "But allow me to tell you that I've never seen you looking so lovely...."

"Bah!" The Comtesse seemed to smile softly. "You say that every time we meet."

"Doubtless because it's true every time," said the Baron, amorously, leaning toward her. "You headgear this evening suits you delightfully. Those heavy flowers, on the polished white of your temples! My God, you're seductive!"

The Comtesse seemed to smile again, and, turning toward him, with a movement that was simultaneously chaste and provocative, she opened the top of her shroud momentarily. Through the fine trellis of ribs, the intoxicated Baron saw a fire-follet glowing in the location of the heart.

"It's burning for you," she said, with adorable coquetry.

"My love, my queen," murmured La Rose, transported.

"Shh! Someone will hear you. Let's go rejoin your young

relative. That terrible Vidame[1] Hilarion is going to bore him with his stories of the other world."

"Let's go—but I beg you, tomorrow night at my place?" pleaded the enfevered Baron.

"Perhaps," the Comtesse murmured, softly.

The Baron offered her his arm, and they both advanced toward Adhémar, who was, indeed, the prey of the Vidame Hilarion, an old skeleton dressed in the antique style, finicky and passionate, who had been introduced to him by Monsieur Saint-Firmin, doubtless desirous of getting rid of him.

"Yes, Monsieur," he was saying to the young man, in a shrill voice, holding on to the lining of his jacket. "Yes, it's incredible, and yet I affirm it to you! I read it in a newspaper of the living, which had been forgotten near my residence, the inept opinion of one of their doctors regarding our modifications. Well, would you believe that the donkey with a soft brain and dirty skin dares to write that *they* don't exist! That they're a legend! That we disaggregate on our own without anyone undressing us! What stupidity! What impudence! What blasphemy! Does he think, that shameless idiot, that we're disposed to retain indefinitely the ignoble charnel burden that makes us resemble larvae like him! Which dishonors us as much as if we were wearing a rag! Which buries the nobility of your physiognomy, Monsieur, and will deprive us for a long time of the pleasure of seeing you! *They* don't exist! Truly, it's revolting! And do you know what they're doing at this very moment?"[2]

Adhémar started. Fortunately, the Comtesse, on the Baron's

1. Vidame, from the Latin *vicedomus*, was one of the more esoteric titles in the French feudal system, originally referring to an official appointed by a bishop to further the Church's worldly interests. The rank was equivalent to the secular rank of Vicomte, and was eventually absorbed into it; the character's retention of it would have been an anachronistic affectation even in life.

2. This joke assumes a pun that does translate into English although the relevant terminology is less esoteric in French than in English, linking the insect larvae that devour the flesh of dead bodies to the "larvae" [ghosts] whose existence is denied by living skeptics.

arm, arrived beside them.

"Come, come, Vidame," don't get angry." Madame de Talk had a ironic expression. "What is it now?"

"The living, Comtesse! The damnable breed that's always making things up about its superiors, and leaving infamous newspapers lying around in our abode expressly to insult us."

"That's of no importance," said the Comtesse, negligently. "Don't forget, Vidame, that we descend from the poor living...."

"Alas," groaned the Vidame, "it dishonors the dead, to be produced by the living."

"Bah!" said the Comtesse. "I don't feel dishonored, myself. And I don't deny at all what I was before coming here. But how are your charming daughters, Vidame? I don't see them this evening."

"My God, Comtesse, the older one was obliged to stay at home to keep my son-in-law company; he had a dorsal fluxion— I'm instructed to give you're their apologies and regrets—but Adrienne's with me; here she is now."

And the Vidame indicated a young person of virginal appearance, whom Adhémar, his esthetic sentiments being strangely modified, found utterly charming as she came forward, gracious and, it seemed, blushing. The Comtesse kissed her tenderly on the forehead and sat her down beside her.

A conversation was engaged, becoming lively and animated. The Baron was the soul of it, by virtue of the finesse of his remarks and the witty charm of his repartee. Adhémar sat down next to the young Adrienne and, from time to time, made some banal remark to her, obtained at the price of a furtive emotion of which he was unable to take clear account. The child's timid and simple responses and the sincerity of her youthful voice, however, made an increasingly deep impression on him, and in his heart, wounded by the recent and cruel disappointment he had suffered, a kind of tender seduction blossomed, like a balsamic flower whose fresh perfume put pain to sleep....

There was dancing toward the end of the soirée, and when Adrienne placed the light bones of her little hand on Adhémar's shoulder, and when he felt, in the grip of his arms, the flexible vertebrae of a wasp-like waist fold softly, a strange intoxication invaded his entire being, and he shivered profoundly, agitated by a passionate emotion that the circumstances rendered very curious. Then, forgetting a great many things regarding himself and the world, just as he had once looked into the living eyes of his first beloved in search of her dream, he leaned tremulously toward the timid and troubling companion enlaced by his arm, and in the profound orbits, full of a great shadow unknown to mortals, he dared to pursue, with a bewildered ardor, a similar and new dream.

He thought he saw in that shadow a response to his desire; an immoderate joy saturated his feeble heart, and, abandoning himself to the whirlwind of unconsciousness that carried him away as the autumn wind carries away a willow-leaf, he murmured phrases passionately, which were no longer phrases of indifference but which strongly resembled, although they were more ardent, the phrases of love with which he had once captured, during his terrestrial interval, the heart of the girl with long hair and supple skin who had betrayed him, and whom he was betraying in his turn....

His tender words doubtless found some echo in the new object of his desire, for Adrienne, now, no longer dared raise her forehead toward him, which seemed to have reddened, and she trembled with emotion in his arms. Such symptoms delighted Adhémar and increased the strength of the sentiments as well as giving free rein, fervently and persuasively, to their expression.

However, the soirée was reaching its conclusion; the majority of the guests had already retired, and the final refreshments were being handed out.

"Tell me, Baron," remarked the Comtesse, who, while leaning on her faithful friend's arm, was observing with interest the smiling Adhémar and Adrienne, now sitting side by side pensively, exchanging long troubled glances, "don't you think that your young relative seems rather taken with my young friend Adrienne?"

"But…it doesn't seem to me…," stammered the Baron, who had indeed noticed it, and was as astonished by it as he was annoyed.

"Come, come, Baron, there's no need to be disturbed by it," protested the Comtesse, mischievously. "It's perfectly evident… and it's very good. Your young relative is accomplished, that's obvious at first glance, and as for my little Adrienne, she's worthy, as you know, of being loved by a gallant man."

"Yes, certainly," murmured the Baron.

"She's as virtuous as she's beautiful," the Comtesse continued, "and has never lent herself to those girlish flirtations that sometimes go a bit too far. It's obvious that Monsieur de Léonce has made a deep impression on hr. Anyway, here comes the Vidame—who, in spite of the habitual blindness of parents in these matters, must have noticed it. Isn't that so, Vidame?"

"Comtesse?" The Vidame, who was a trifle deaf, turned round.

"Doesn't it seem to you, as it does to me, that your daughter and that charming young man, the Baron's relative, are getting along very well?"

"Oh! So much the better! I don't mind at all, to tell the truth." The father, who had not noticed anything, seemed perfectly content. "She doesn't want to accept the homages of anyone, the silly girl, and whenever I press her to make a choice among her suitors, of whom there's certainly no lack, she refuses squarely, under the pretext that she doesn't love any of them, and wants to wait for the chosen one, who'll certainly come along. I no longer know what to do. If Monsieur de Léonce is the chosen one, I'll be delighted. He's the Baron's relative, and that says it all from the viewpoint of rank and fortune. I also remember that I knew his great-uncle, the general. Adrienne de Léonce! A fine name, to be sure! So much the better, so much the better! It's an embarrassment, you know, to have a daughter to marry off."

"Don't go too quickly," the Baron protested, seriously alarmed by the turn the adventure was taking. "Nothing's happened yet!"

"Bah! We'll fix an engagement tonight!" And the Vidame Hilarion rubbed his phalanges joyfully. "We'll go quickly and true—here, we know how to take advantage of good opportunities. We're not like those imbeciles the living, who use up their dirty little existence speculating about a future happiness that they never attain. We have the time to wait, and that's why we don't!"

Thinking that he had said something profound, he laughed like a creaky church door.

"Although," the Comtesse remarked, "Monsieur de Léonce won't be ready for some time. But I know Adrienne and the rectitude of her sentiments. That delay, far from diminishing her love, will increase it.

"Indeed, indeed—and it will be a great marriage," the father remarked, proudly.

Baron La Rose no longer knew what to say. "Permit me to go talk to Monsieur de Léonce," he stammered.

He went to join the amorous object of his concern.

Adrienne and Adhémar were still sitting side by side, their voices stifled by the timidity of passion, exchanging eternal oaths. Monsieur La Rose sent the young woman to speak to the Cometesse and took Adhémar's arm.

"My dear chap," he asked him, rather abruptly, "have you any idea what you're doing?"

"I'm in love," Adhémar replied, seemingly in seventh heaven and smiling with interior joy.

The Baron was flabbergasted. "Word of honor, you're admirable! What! Two hours ago you were sobbing on my sternum because of your lost love, and I had all the difficulty in the world sustaining your despair, and now I find you smiling, drunk with joy, and when I ask you to account for the compromising follies you're in the process of committing, you reply: 'I'm in love!' with an ecstatic expression, as if it were the most normal thing in the world!"

"I didn't love the other one," replied Adhémar, calmly, still in the bosom of his enchanted dream. "I thought I loved her but I see now that I was mistaken. Don't remind me about those moments of gross dementia. I've banished them from my memory forever. Adrienne, I adore! I adore her, I tell you! Celestial angel, river of delights, intoxicating soul, divine purity! I adore her! How feeble and insufficient that word is! You can't understand...."

"Naturally!" The Baron seemed furious. "Love, in truth, renders people idiotic. But have you thought about the person with whom you're in love, the unfortunate child? Have you thought about that?"

"I love Adrienne!" Adhémar replied.

"I know that. You've already told me that. But do you know what Adrienne is? Do you know that? She's one of us. One of us! Do you understand? Get a grip on yourself! She's one of us! And you're alive, damn it!"

"What does that matter?" the imperturbable and ardent young man replied. "I love her!"

"What does it matter? Word of honor, it's stupefying!" the exasperated Baron almost shouted. "It wouldn't matter at all if you loved her without her suspecting it—that wouldn't worry me at all—but it also seems that she loves you: that's the problem!"

"She's been kind enough to make that sweet admission to me," Adhémar replied, proudly. "That was a divine moment for me, and my happiness is complete."

"But what about the situation, wretch!" groaned the Baron. "The situation! Your situation! Mine! What are we going to do? What am I going to do? Me, who was mad enough to bring you here! Me, who's responsible for you!"

"You'll have no reason to regret it, Baron," Adhémar put in, with a noble expression.

"But what do you expect me to do? Think for a moment, will you? If I tell the truth—and how can I not tell it?—I'll be dishonored in the orbits of our entire society, which I've betrayed out of weakness for you. All doors will be closed to me, and I'll have to fight twenty duels with the Vidame and all his relatives. That's nothing, though—how will the Comtesse take it? What will she think of me? And that poor little Adrienne, whom you love! Who loves you sincerely, as her first love! Poor child, compromised by you! By a living man! With my complicity, for I'm an accomplice! What a situation! What am I going to do?"

"Tell the truth," replied Adhémar, tranquilly.

"Tell the truth! Yes! It's necessary! And without further delay. But what shame for me," murmured the Baron, disheartened.

"Not at all," said Adhémar, serenely. "Let's go!"

He shoved the Baron toward the group that had formed confidentially around the Comtesse and Adrienne, with the Vidame not far away.

The latter, on seeing the two friends approach, could not contain the delight caused in him by the thought that he was about to get rid of his daughter. "Very glad to see you, my dear Monsieur de Léonce," he said, coming forward and taking Adhémar's hand, which she shook cordially between his hard phalanges. Astonished, he remarked: "Why, how warm you are—and how your eyes shine!"

"That can be explained," Adhémar replied, politely. "Monsieur le Baron La Rose has something to tell you."

"Very good!" said the Vidame.

"Any communication on the part of Monsieur La Rose will be very agreeable to us," said the Comtesse, taking a step forward, while Adrienne, who seemed confused, stayed behind. Madame de Talk added: "In any case, my young friend has allowed us— the Vidame and myself—to anticipate what it might be."

"I...I don't think...." murmured the Baron, who had a light sweat on his forehead, so anguished was he.

"Yes, yes, I believe...." The Comtesse put on a cheerful expression. "Come on, Baron, speak—you can do so freely. All my guests have gone, and we're all family now...."

"Yes, speak, Baron!" said the Vidame supportively, striking the pose of a noble father—which, of course, he was.

"Oh well...well...I don't know how to confess...." Monsieur La Rose truly seemed to be suffering. "Well...I've betrayed you, Madame! I've betrayed our entire society! Monsieur de Léonce"—he pointed at the individual in question—"is alive!"

"Alive! O horror!" cried the Comtesse, with a spasm of disgust.

"Alive! One of those wretches among us! With my daughter!" roared the Vidame. "Baron, you'll reckon with me!"

"Alive! Him! My God!" sighed Adrienne, in a desolate voice.

That was the only one that Adhémar heard. He leapt forward to catch the poor child in his arms, as she sagged like a flower whose stem has been broken by a hurricane.

"Back!" cried the Vidame, launching himself forward. "No living person shall touch my daughter!"

"Calm down!" Adhémar, whose left arm was sustaining the fainting Adrienne against his heart, made a gesture with his right whose dignity imposed itself even on the furious Vidame. "Calm down," he repeated, with all the honest frankness of youth and with honor on his brow and in his eyes. "Alive? I certainly am! It would be bad form to deny it, and no lie has ever soiled my lips. I'm alive, but, if the Baron is guilty of introducing me among you, be sure that, in accordance with the grandeur of his character and his virtues, he has been guilty of nothing except nobility of soul and generosity. He has put his faith as a gentleman in a gentleman who is not undeserving of it, believe me! I am now alive, but that's of no importance, for right here and at this very moment, I shall cease to be!"

"What?" said the Comtesse. "You want to…?"

"Generous friend!" cried the Baron. "I hoped so, but my delicacy forbade me to mention it to you."

"Good, young man!" said the Vidame, blowing his nose.

"My noble Adhémar," sighed Adrienne, who had partially recovered consciousness

"Angel," said Adhémar, with infinite tenderness, amorously pressing the charming child's flexible ribs against him, "Angel, to win you, it's the only thing I can do. Anyway, the sacrifice isn't one—far from it. I've had enough of life and its gross treacherous women! Here, I've found honor, love and friendship! I'm staying!"

"What joy it will be to keep you!" exclaimed the Comtesse.

"Your entry among us is truly romantic, and you will do us honor, Monsieur."

"My friend, I weep!" The Baron kissed Adhémar on the cheek, and the Comtesse too, in the midst of his disturbance.

"My son!" And the Vidame kissed Adhémar on the other cheek. "Those imbeciles," he added, "wouldn't want to be alive any longer, if they could see the happiness we enjoy here."

"I love you," murmured Adrienne, so softly that only Adhémar's heart could hear it.

"Let's act without delay!" cried the intoxicated man.

"Perhaps it would be better if the ladies retired," the Vidame suggested.

"You can't be serious," protested the Baron. "It can't happen in Madame de Talk's residence. Propriety demands that it take place outside. We'll go out."

"Indeed," said Adhémar, utterly excited. "Let's go out!"

"*À bientôt*, Monsieur de Léonce," said the Comtesse, emotionally, to the young man. She added: "Let him go, my dear Adrienne," for the young woman, clinging to her beloved's neck, did not seem to be able to tear herself away.

"One kiss," Adhémar begged, holding her back. She allowed him to take it with a sob of delight, and the Comtesse drew her to her side.

"Is it going to hurt him?" whispered the tender child, in a voice full of anguish, as she let herself fall, swooning, upon Madame de Talk's clavicle.

"No, it's nothing," the latter stammered, supporting her, deeply affected herself and going pale.

Adhémar, Monsieur La Rose and the Vidame went outside. As morning approached, the fog had become glacial and its heavy folds were trailing like a livid crêpe. Adhémar shivered slightly.

"An old residue of the infirmities of that dirty life!" the Vidame muttered, between his false teeth.

They arrived at a comfortable bench at a little crossroads that was entirely deserted, and sat down.

"What means are you going to employ, my dear friend?" asked the Baron, affectionately.

"I brought various different things," Adhémar replied, "for I have no intention, when I came here, of leaving again. The cowardly despair that drove me then appears very undignified and ridiculous now, but at least, in consequence of it, I have everything that I need."

He took out of his pockets a revolver, a dagger, several small phials and a letter. "This piece of paper," he said to his companions, "contains what the living call my last will and testament. In it, I order that I should be placed here, in a monument, in perpetuity. As I'm rich and have no close relatives, that will not encounter any difficulty." Speaking to the Baron in confidence, he added: "The world can believe, if it wishes, that I'm quitting life in despair, because of the little slut whom you know, but that doesn't matter to me."

"The opinion of the living is of no importance," the Baron declared. Aloud, he added: "With regard to your habitation, though, right next door to me, a little way from here, there's a property for sale. Specify, then, path D, number 28. It's very well accommodated, and will be perfect for a young couple."

"And order two coffins, lead and oak," remarked the far-sighted Vidame. "One sleeps better—but not quilted; it frays and makes one cough."

"Good," said Adhémar. He reopened his letter, and, although scarcely able to see it in the soft and livid light, resting it on his knee, he traced a few lines in pencil. When that was done he stood up, resolutely, but a trifle pale and shaky all the same.

"Now, friends, I'll become one of you!" he said, emphatically, putting the revolver to his forehead.

"Not like that!" exclaimed the Baron, grabbing his arm. "You're going to shatter your skull! Adrienne would be desolate!"

"Oh, of course!" said Adhémar, redirecting the weapon toward his breast.

"Be careful of your ribs!" remarked the Vidame in his turn. "It spoils the look if they're broken."

"What shall I do, then?" asked Adhémar, troubled, looking at the revolver as if asking its opinion.

"My dear chap, are you particularly enthusiastic to make use of that brutal and noisy implement?" asked the Baron. "I saw a certain little phial in your hand a few moments ago...."

"Poison?" said the Vidame. "That causes suffering, is rather disgusting and can go wrong. No—believe me, young man, employ the clean weapon—the dagger. That's the only one, you see. The pure and faithful blade of our ancestors! One slices through the heart frankly, and that's it!"

"You're right, Vidame!" the Baron exclaimed. "The dagger! It's noble, and one knows what one's doing!"

Adhémar unsheathed a charming little dagger with a sharp blade and a coat of arms on the hilt. "Do you think," he interrogated, with a slight spasm, "that I'll be able to do it? All alone? At the first thrust?"

"I'll gladly render you that small service," the Vidame proposed, hastily, taking possession of the dagger, whose point he tested on the first phalanx of his thumb.

"Choose the place carefully, and plunge it in with a single thrust, while I support our dear friend." So saying, the Baron stepped behind Adhémar. He told him: "We'll place your testament beside you, on the bench, and the groundskeepers will find you when they make their first round. We'll doubtless have the pleasure of seeing you again in two days, for you'll surely be put here provisionally."

"Let's get on with it—dawn's approaching," said the impatient Vidame, brandishing the dagger.

"Yes, let's get on with it," stammered Adhémar, nervously, whom the Baron was holding under the arms, firmly.

"With your permission, I'll move the garments aside," said the Vidame, unbuttoning the jacket and waistcoat. He took up a comfortable position and placed the point of the dagger on the uncovered breast level with the heart. "Whenever you please!"

he said, with a courteous politeness that was not exempt from a certain unconscious ferocity.

The living man swallowed his saliva convulsively.

"G…go!" he said.

"Aah!" he groaned, having been obeyed, with a vain twitch and a final hiccup. "Aah—life!"

As he quit it, a cock crowed.

THE REPENTANT THIEF
A MEXICAN TALE

The man in question lived in a town in Mexico, where he exercised his profession successfully.

He had no name, but because of the frankly carrot-colored tint of his hair, he was known as El Zoro, and was proud of it.

He was a past master in his art and devoted himself to it with passion and discernment, neglecting none of the methods that had been taught to men for the plunder of his neighbors. He stole everywhere, always and in every way. It was the pleasure of his life and the sole source of the income he had to sustain him. Happy are those who, like him, obtain their daily bread, and even a little more, by following the vocation that Providence has given them.

El Zoro lived content with his lot, and all his friends liked him and held him in high esteem for his frank character and his cheerful temperament. With terrestrial happiness he had the peace of the soul, for he was a sincere Catholic, accessible to good sentiments and careful to fulfill with all exactitude, so far as his work permitted, the duties imposed on him by religion.

In the thirty-second year of his life, he suffered an accident.

It happened one evening in June, in the course of a *volerio*—which is the feast given, in Mexico, by the parents of a child who has died in the age of innocence. It happens in the lower classes. There are flowers, dancing, games and debauchery around the exposed cadaver, and everyone is invited.

El Zoro, installed on the first floor of the house, was passing the time agreeably by playing cards and drinking *refino* with a few distinguished people of his acquaintance. Everyone was a trifle excited, but El Zoro, as was his habit, was enjoying considerable luck. Perhaps, under the influence of strong liquor, he took that luck a little too far. At any rate, after one especially fortunate and profitable hand, there were protests, and a tumult, and El Zoro, sweeping up the stakes on the table, leapt backwards.

"Who dares," he said, "cast doubt on my honor?"

"Me!" said the hoarse voice of one of his fellow players. And he explained, a trifle confusedly, that El Zoro had been cheating, that it was appropriate to search him in order to recover the money that he had fraudulently won, and then to hang him outside, in place of the lantern that would be unhooked in order to make way for his rope.

To this proposal, El Zoro preferred to make himself scarce, by jumping out of the window.

"Seigneurs," said the person who had already spoken, casting a dignified glance over the assistants that had gathered around him, with a bag and a rope, "El Zoro is vermin, unworthy of frequenting decent folk. I propose that we expel him from our society and our friendship."

This motion was carried, and they resumed the game. Meanwhile, El Zoro went home, consternated.

"What's happened to me?" he said. "What could have happened to me? They were all drunk, except me, and I've got myself pinched like a debutant—me, El Zoro! Oh, God has abandoned me, along with the Most Pure Virgin!"

That thought was a revelation to him

"It's my punishment," he said to himself. "For many months, prey to a life of debauchery, I've been getting closer to the tribunal of penitence! This evening's accident is a sign for me, an appeal from Heaven, I need to wash myself of my sins. I've been living like a pagan for too long. From tomorrow onwards...."

He went to sleep, appeased.

Early the next morning, he went to the nearest convent. He made a generous offering under the eyes of a sympathetic fat monk and threw himself at the feet of that holy man begging him to hear his confession.

The holy man took him to a little chapel and, having sat down, made the penitent kneel at his feet. Then, leaning forward, he deployed his large cape and covered his head and that of El Zoro, in the Spanish manner.

When the liturgical preliminaries were more or less complete, the monk said, unctuously: "I'm listening, my son."

"I have sinned, Father; I'm a great sinner!" exclaimed El Zoro.

"Repentance washes away all sins," said the monk. "What have you done?"

"I've stolen, Father," El Zoro confessed, spasmodically.

"Many others would hang you," said the monk. "That's a great sin, my son. Have you stolen much and often?"

"All the time, Father, everywhere and as much as I could."

"Be specific, my son."

"Impossible, Father; I've done nothing else. I've stolen from everyone, the old and the young, the virtuous and the wicked. It's me who robbed the town lawyer when he opposed your convent in court, and I was the cause of his death because he lost his case and was dishonored. I have all the papers…and he died of yellow fever in Vera Cruz."

"He died as a punishment for having opposed the convent in court," the monk murmured. "That was just, and this worthy rascal was the instrument of God." Aloud, he said: "Go on, my son."

"Well, Father, the magistrate was in court in the process of interrogating one of my best friends. I was there. I saw the magistrate make the gesture of checking the time, but he couldn't find his watch. I thought that he'd forgotten it, and was seized by an inspiration, for I have an inventive mind, Father. I left the court and went to buy a turkey, which I took to the magistrate's home. His wife let me in.

"'Seigneur Callientes,' I said, 'has bought a turkey in order to throw a party, for he's had some good news today.'

"'He's been appointed principal judge!'

"'Perhaps,' I said. 'I don't know. Undoubtedly, if one considers his merit. At any rate, he's sent the turkey and wants me to bring his watch, which he forgot this morning.'

"'That's true,' said the woman, who was joyful. And she gave me the watch, and some money for a reward....naturally, Father, I sold the watch, and in that I was surely guilty."

"Certainly," said the monk, "For a turkey isn't worth as much as a watch."

"Especially as the turkey didn't stay with the judge, because it was hung before being cooked and I had it stolen by my cousin. What do you expect, Father? One doesn't like to lose...."

"You were very guilty," murmured the holy man, suppressing a smile.

"I was even more so yesterday evening, Father, after an unfortunate incident in a card game." He described it succinctly. "I let myself become angry."

"Were you really cheating?" asked the monk naively.

"Of course, Father. There wouldn't be any pleasure in playing otherwise. But after jumping out of the window...I allowed myself to blaspheme against the Most Pure Virgin...."

"Wretch!" exclaimed the monk, horrified. "Wretch! Do you not have black shame in your heart? That sin is a thousand times more abominable than all your other sins put together! Don't you know what punishment you were risking?"

He continued, but El Zoro was no longer listening. As the holy man had moved, one of his wide black sleeves had opened, and at the bottom of the fold that is a monk's pocket, the penitent saw an attractive gleam, which his experienced eye recognized as that of a gold snuff-box.

Immediately, instinct and habit spoke. In the course of a speech consecrated to the glory of the Most Pure Virgin, the monk had closed his eyes unctuously. In the shadow of the cape, as rapid as lightning, El Zoro's hand plunged into the hollow of the sleeve and took the snuff-box, which immediately passed into his own pocket. The thing was accomplished with the surety of gesture and inimitable sleight of hand that characterizes a master. Immediately, however, the horror of the sin that he had just committed saturated the soul of the guilty party, and he burst into sobs.

"Father" he cried, "that's not all! I've sinned even more odiously! Have pity on me, Most Pure Virgin! I've robbed a holy man!"

"You've robbed a holy man?"

"Yes, Father! A holy man! I've robbed him, while he was in the holy and sacred exercise of his ministry, I, miserable reprobate that I am, reached out my hand and stole! A gold snuff-box, Father!"

"Wretch!" groaned the monk. "You're robbed a priest in the exercise of his holy ministry! Wretch! Criminal! Don't you know that it's a sacrilege, a mortal sin that burdens your immortal soul, which will drag you down into the depths of Hell, into torment!"

"Mercy! Pardon! Have pity on me!" yelped El Zoro, in the convulsions of repentance. "Forgive me, Father! I repent! I'll give you the snuff-box to expiate my crime! Will you please take it, Father? That would unburden my soul...."

"Take it? Me!" the monk reclaimed. "What are you thinking, wretch? Nothing in the world would make me soil my hands with the contact of something stolen!"

"Take it, Father! Take it and absolve me!" begged the desperate El Zoro. "I'll put it into your holy hands. I don't want it any more! I'm suffering too much. Take it, Father!"

"Enough!" the monk interrupted. "Not one more word on the subject, I command you. You're a miserable sinner, but your repentance seems sincere. Find the owner of the stolen object. You know who it is, no doubt?"

"Yes, Father," stammered El Zoro, steeped in tears.

"Well, give it back to him and beg his pardon. Then you'll be washed clean of your sin."

"I've already offered it, Father," sobbed El Zoro. "I offered it to him two or three times, but he refused in spite of my insistence."

"He refused?" said the monk, astonished.

"Yes, Father. He refused—I swear it to you on the sacred blood of...."

"No unnecessary oaths," said the holy man. "I believe you. Well, since the snuff-box has been refused by its legitimate owner...."

"Take it, Father, take it!"

"Enough," said the monk. "You're mad, I think. Since the object has been refused by the person to whom it belongs, well, keep it for yourself, but don't make evil use of it. Perhaps the owner, in refusing its restitution, wanted to show you what scant value it's necessary to attach to worldly things, to these vain baubles of gold and silver of which men are so desirous."

"You think that's the reason, Father?"

"Yes," said the monk, "certainly. The moment he becomes a holy man, he is capable of any disinterest. Meditate upon the lesson he has given you, my son, keep that stolen object, which you wanted, by virtue of a laudable sentiment of repentance, to place in my hands. Keep it, meditate your contrition, give alms and pray."

Thus absolved, the pious El Zoro, in the quietude of his conscience washed clean of all sins, in the joy of his heart, enlivened by a significant profit, went away with the snuff-box—and the holy man never saw him again, in this world.

THE NENUPHAR

This story unfolded in the burning month of August, in a beautiful park, toward dusk.

The innocent Amélie was going to see a young man.

As can happen in such circumstances, the languorous vertigo of sounds and perfumes was drifting in the evening air, fiery vapors were putting the leaves of the trees to sleep, and along the broad pathways, the enervated statues were stretching on their plinths.

Amélie was eighteen years old. Her hair was blonde and her eyes flaxen. Her dress was muslin and her straw hat had a white ribbon. The park belonged to Amélie's mother.

Amélie was innocent, although she was going to see a young man. Innocence is subordinate not to the actions one accomplishes but to the spirit in which they are accomplished. Now, it was ingenuously that Amélie was taking a step that might seem risky. In fact the child had been promised in marriage by her mother to a worthy and good man who loved her very much, but who was odious to her because she had a beloved, the unfortunate result of romantic reading.

The beloved in question was a predator of young women of scant interest, whom she had met at a ball—a warpath on which he was in pursuit of victims. Amélie's Mother did not want to hear mention of him, and had in his regard—as in the regard of every suitor other than the one she had chosen—the heart of a saurian. The name of the beloved, for that lady, was An-Other; for Amélie, it was Him; and for himself, in his own esteem, it was Don Juan—which was exaggerated.

It was Him that the innocent child, at that crepuscular hour, was going to meet, as she did as often as possible, on the bank of the river that flowed through the park. That explains why she had an iris in her hand and the expression of an anemone cut by the cruel scythe on her face. She was convinced, in fact, that her heart would be reduced to dust and her life to shards if she were not united with her beloved. She counted in advance on the latter's dramatic suicide in that fatal event, and a brief and languishing existence for herself, soon limited by liberating death.

She arrived at the river bank and, like a stature of melancholy clad in a muslin dress and a straw hat, she sat down on the stone bench where, four or five times already, she had waited for the beloved. He was on holiday, not far away, staying with friends of his, and came by water, in a motor boat that he piloted with an enchanting grace.

Above the bench there was a marble Ceres, with her attributes.

Thus, Amélie waited, gazing at the river and the nenuphar water-lilies. Mayflies were dancing over the water, which swallows snapped up on the wing. "Such will be my life," Amélie thought.

The minutes went by, the blaze of the setting sun darkening the trees, and the first star twinkling in the green sky.

"My God, it's getting close to dinner time," said the desolate Amélie to herself. "He's not coming…just as long as nothing's happened to him.…"

"So, my poor child, you really imagine that you love that imbecile?" asked a voice behind Amélie.

She turned round, and saw that it was the marble Ceres who had spoken.

"Yes, Madame, I love him," replied Amélie, indignant at such a question. She added: "He's not an imbecile."

"Yes," said Ceres, "he's as much an imbecile as anyone can be. He's also a pretentious fop. Furthermore, he doesn't love you. He's distracting himself with you to pass the time and practice his charms, but he isn't serious."

"That's not true!" said Amélie, irritated.

"My poor child," Ceres continued, "it pains me to see you compromising yourself with such a puppet! He doesn't love you. He's incapable of loving anyone except himself, and you'd do well to marry the worthy man that your mother has chosen."

"I'd die of it," sobbed Amélie.

"No," said Ceres. "One thinks that at first, but it soon passes. In six months, you'll be wondering how you were ever able to look at such a ridiculous creature. It's necessary not to spoil your life or torment your mother. I remember how I suffered when my little Proserpine was stolen from me by Pluto. It's necessary not to play fast and loose with the heart of a mother, you see; it's necessary to be good and submissive...."

"But we love one another," Amélie moaned.

"Not at all," said Ceres. "I'm sure that you don't love him. But he came along at the right moment, and he knows how to play the comedy by which we've always let ourselves be taken in. He's abusing it. He's making fun of you, deep down, and would murmur endearments just as easily to anyone else...."

"That's not true!" said Amélie, indignantly.

"It is true," said Ceres, "and I'll prove it to you. I don't want you to be compromised any further; the fellow isn't worth the bother, and a young woman's reputation in a serious thing. Listen: you're wearing a new dress that he hasn't seen you in. Give it to me and take my place on this plinth. I'll welcome him on your behalf; I'll tell him that you weren't able to come and...you'll see whether he pays court to me. I'm a little old, but still...." And she smiled with a certain self-satisfaction.

"I'll do it," said Amélie, confidently. "I'm sure of him."

The exchange of positions was effected, although Ceres experienced some difficulty in putting on Amélie's dress, and the latter's modesty was alarmed by the state of partial nudity in which it was necessary to stand on the plinth.

"Silly girl," said Ceres, to make up her mind. "Since you'll become a statue, that's nothing. Hurry up—he's coming."

Indeed, the ladies' man, who had been delayed by an inopportune visit, was arriving at top speed in his motor-boat.

Ceres, sitting on the bench, and very pretty in her broad-brimmed hat, welcomed him very nicely. She explained to him that she had arrived the previous day to spend a few days with Amélie, and that the latter, prevented from coming by a bad stomach-ache, had delegated her, her best friend, to tell him, her beloved, that news, in order that he would not wait in vain.

The beloved received this news with an insouciant lightness that chilled poor Amélie's tender heart. Her pedestal was making her feet cold. The seducer, who had dressed up as a young Antinous—an intoxicating cravat and pink cambric shirt, framed in a sports-jacket in exquisite taste—was in full possession of his faculties and fancied himself even more a Don Juan than ever. In consequence, anxious that no opportunity for seduction should go to waste, he immediately set out to fascinate the new victim offered to him by fate, in order to pin her, if he could, in one of the showcases of his collection.

Imbued by this idea, he sat down with a propitiatory air and commenced by declaring that he did not regret the absence of the young woman at all, since that circumstance had put him in communication with a messenger so full of grace. The declaration having been well-received, he pounced and, rolling his bulging eyes, began sighing without further ado the coaxing phrases of which he made use in such circumstances. The consternated Amélie recognized the majority of them. He mingled them, besides, with mocking and condescending appreciations of the innocent child who was taking note of the experiment, convinced that he would thus give pleasure to her best friend.

"Oh," said Ceres, negligently, "she's a good little girl—she's very loving."

"Yes, naturally," replied the beloved, in a detached one, "but there's a lot more than that, which she doesn't have...."

And, encouraged by the malicious goddess, he explained that

the said little girl might be very agreeable for passing the time and distracting oneself, for want of anything better, but that she had amazing pretentions, especially if she hoped to marry him, Don Juan, the key to hearts, the boulevard of love and the reef of grim virtues. He followed up with comparisons that were all to the glory of his present companion, whose beauty was well made to inflame a great heart and to make the hot sun of passion radiant.

Ceres not seeming too refractory, without waiting any further, he attempted a few gestures.

Amélie could not believe her eyes, and wept hot tears on her plinth.

The goddess, however, under the pretext of the hour, cut short the conversation, which was becoming menacing. The predator of young women asked for a rendezvous for the following day. Ceres granted it and gave him to understand that she would love to have a flower plucked by the beloved's hand—a poetic memory that would render the hours of waiting less bitter.

Delighted, for he gladly worked with the romantic, he made haste to reach for a nenuphar blooming on the water.

The object was distant; the beloved, leaning over the river-bank like a frog, extended a prudent arm.

"Go on, then!" cried Ceres, impatiently, and shoved him in the back.

He went into the water head first. A convulsive rear end emerged momentarily, crowned with red socks in white shoes.

"He'll drown!" cried the sensitive Amélie, from her plinth.

"No," said Ceres, "don't worry. He's climbing out now."

The predator of young women, who had lost all right to public admiration, was indeed climbing out, splashing and snorting like a seal, with rage in his heart and his hair full of mud....

Two minutes later, the boat carried the seductive young man away forever.

"Well," said Ceres, returning poor Amélie's dress to her, "are you convinced? Are you going to do as your mother wishes?"

"Yes, Madame," said Amélie. And she went back in, weeping,

because the dinner gong was ringing.

GORDON AND THE
LONG-HAIRED STAR

Last year, I spent the summer in a little village where there is, among other things, a church, and a large square in front of the church.

One Sunday in September, at about midnight, I arrived in that square, coming from the railway-station in a cab. The weather was fine and the night dark; everything was asleep; we were traveling at top speed.

"Be careful of my face, I beg you," said a voice from the ground, which chilled us with terror—the driver, me and doubtless also the horse, which, with a desperate sidestep, stopped dead two paces away from a human being lying flat on the ground.

I had, however, recognized the voice of my friend Gordon.[3]

Gordon, who was born in America, in Wisconsin, has been a Methodist pastor in his youth, and has carried Bibles to the indigenes of Central Africa, who received them with gratitude, but sent the pages back to him, in the wake of political complications, in the form of rifle wadding. Gordon was disgusted and

---

3. Gordon features in other stories contributed to *Le Français* by Boutet, including one included in the previous collection in the present set, where further comment was made on his eccentric way with the French language, and a footnote observed the difficulties of translating those eccentricities into English other than by suggestion. This is the earlier of the two stories in question, published in February 1903; as there was no comet visible to the naked eye in the summer of 1902, it presumably recalls the Great Comet of 1901, also known as Comet Viscara.

went to Australia, where he devoted himself to trading in race-horses. Afterwards he returned to America, where he did God knows what.

Now he's in France, and occupied with a curious science, which he calls "medicine" and which he alone knows; he combines that with playing the clarinet, to distract himself. I'm one of his friends, and he had come that summer to take up residence in the same little village as me, with the result that I was exposed to the risk of meeting him anywhere and at any time—but I wasn't expecting to find him there that Sunday evening.

I got out of the cab and sent it away. Then I went over to Gordon. He was lying full length, with his back on a rubber blanket. Beneath his head was a pneumatic pillow and in his hands was a telescope, which he was aiming at the starry sky. He seemed, moreover, to be ignoring my presence, and I concluded that he was in a bad mood.

"What are you doing there, Gordon, old friend?" I asked, astonished.

"I'm searching the firmament for that pig of a comet," Gordon told me, in an irritated tone.

He has, I must admit, learned French partly with a professor of the École Normale and partly in the cabarets of Montmartre, which has equipped him with a picturesque and personal language.

"What comet?" I said. "Oh yes! The newspapers have been talking about a comet. Why do you want to see it?" I added—rather stupidly, because when one wants to see a comet, it's for the sake of seeing it, and that's all.

"To satisfy my passion," said Gordon, "but for five nights now I've been squinting at the temperament without discovering the camel, and with diabolical torments."

"Five nights," I said, leaning over him. "And have you...?"

"Oh! I see it!" he howled. "Oh, how monstrous and rutilant it is! My dread was entirely justified! But where's it gone now? It's gone...."

My friend had made an error. I perceived it instantly. "You're mistaken, my dear Gordon," I said, softly. "What you're mistaking for the comet is only the glowing end of my cigarette, which happened to be in the visual field of your telescope, and...."

"If it's that dirty cigarette that misled me," he said angrily, "I say that it's truly boarish"—he doubtless meant boorish—"of you to play such a joke on an old friend like me and give him a heart attack...."

"I didn't do it on purpose," I said, to soothe him, "but I think you're looking in the wrong direction...."

"No!" he said. "There's the décor of the firmament"—he handed me a piece of paper—"and with my silent lantern, I've consulted my direction with care. Only it takes time. I began searching for the comet on Wednesday evening, from my window, but I couldn't pick it out. Then I went down into my courtyard—but no more means there, because of the walls. I couldn't get a reference-point in the sky. Impossible even merely to discover the...the mountain beasts that climb trees... you know...of which they say in Montmarte that the theaters don't want to play...."

"The mountain beasts that the theaters....oh yes! Bears![4] The constellations of the Bears. And then?"

"Then I went back in to drink whisky for consolation. And as I was tired, I went to bed. Thursday evening I didn't accomplish anything, because it was raining and the sky was black. Then I played my clarinet for consolation and went to look for you for a game of billiards, but you were away, as you are every time I needed you. Friday it was fine and I went up on my roof, but policemen on horseback came, whom that old woman my neighbor had sent for because she hadn't been able to make me out and thought I was burgling my house. Then I came down. Yesterday, Saturday, I spent all evening in this square without discovering anything and I almost broke my back standing up to

4. *Ours* [bear] is use colloquially in French to mean an ill-bred and riotous person—the kind of heckler that the artistes in Montmartre cabarets would not want to have in their audience.

see in the air with this filthy telescope, as heavy as anything... then, this evening, I made my reparations to be more comfortable, and decided to stay as long as the discovery took."

"I assure you," I said, "that when it was shown to me the day before yesterday...."

"Oh, you've seen it?" he said, setting his telescope side.

"Yes," I said, confidently. "I've seen it, and quite clearly. Let's go back to your place. I'll show it to you if I can. It ought to be directly opposite your windows."

"And what does it look like?" he asked me, very seriously.

"What? Well, like something...bright...luminous...nebulous...long.... Well, like a red-hot gridiron, for instance, seen from a long way off."

I was a trifle embarrassed, for I had said that to Gordon to get him to come back in, and I'd never seen a comet, so far as I could recall. It appears, however, that my uncle—at least, he says so—had shown me one when I was still a wailing infant in the arms of my nurse. I had even laughed with jubilation. It's quite possible, but I've lost all memory of it. My uncle's affirmation remains integral nevertheless, but insufficient to furnish me with any sort of description.

"A red-hot gridiron," Gordon repeated, still lying down and pensive. He sighed. "I don't understand."

"Yes," I explained, "A gridiron...or a miner's lamp...."

At this point, I was interrupted. Out of the steep and tortuous little ditch known as the main street, into the square, at the double, came a group formed by two gendarmes, one of them a brigadier, and an indigenous inhabitant of the region.

They arrived beside us.

"Is this the cadaver?" asked the brigadier, pointing at Gordon, who was on the ground and not moving.

"What cadaver?" I asked.

"This fellow"—the brigadier turned toward the indigene— "told me that he's seen a frightful spectacle—a cadaver lying in the square in a pool of blood with a golden dagger sticking out of his breast. He came to get us out of bed and dressed for that.

The Maire's been informed, If it's a joke, we'll see...but...."
He looked at Gordon. "But it's you again, you brute, with your
damned telescope...."

The latter, still lying down, has picked up his telescope and
made no reply.

"Calm down," I said to the brigadier. "What's happened?"

"What! Me calm down!" he howled. "I am calm, by thunder!
But this is an imbecile for whom we've already been disturbed,
two nights ago, simply because it pleases the gentleman to
commit extravagances searching for God know's what that he's
lost in the sky!"

"I'm searching for the comet," said Gordon, majestically,
"and I'm elevating my soul at the same time...."

"Be polite, eh!" cried the brigadier.

In spite of my attempts at conciliation, a few lively retorts
were exchanged. Gordon, vexed by the epithet *loony*, proffered
by the brigadier, got to his feet, and the affair was threatening
to turn out badly when the arrival of the Maire caused a salu-
tary diversion, in the sense that, under his orders, six witness-
statements were immediately taken, relating to six charges: to
wit, three against Gordon—for insulting language, nocturnal
disturbance on the public highway and outrage against public
morals (?); two against the local man, who had gone to fetch
the gendarmes, and would certainly have done better to remain
tranquil, for manifest drunkenness and false witness; and one
against me—an innocent victim who had never ceased to agitate
the olive branch—for injurious rowdiness!

After which, he permitted us all to go.

In a bad mood I took charge of the pneumatic pillow. Gordon
picked up the mattress and the telescope. We walked for a while
in silence.

"And you say that it's a free country, French territory?"
Gordon demanded of me, bitterly. "Where an inoffensive citizen
is not his own master to live in tranquility, to go up on his roof
and lie down in a square without anyone in it, to study medicine
in peace! I'm certain that it's a peril for the world, this comet,

for it's in the Bible and also in the discoveries of scientists. Well, I want to see where it ought to be coming from because I firmly believe that it will fall on the terrestrial world and I want to travel to the other side in order to be underneath. And I'd have warned you—but it's finished. I give up. The comet can fall— I'm not looking any more. I'd have to suffer those diabolical policemen again, one night or another, and I'd rather receive the comet."

THE AUTHENTIC
ANTIQUITY

Monsieur Blaireau, the honorable and eminent curator of the well-known museum, the "Egyptian antiquities man," as he is known admiringly throughout Europe, was in his grandiose office in the very heart of the incomparable museum, his domain, his honor and his life. While awaiting the moment to leave the office in question, where he never did anything at all, Monsieur Bleaireau was dozing blissfully among the marvels of vanished ages that decorated the walls.

Monsieur Blaireau was content with life, more so today than usual, for he had just, in his own estimation, carried off a veritable triumph in a certain affair, somewhat disagreeable at first sight, of antiquities that had been recognized as not being such. The incident had been prompted by indiscreet publicists, who, under the pretext of telling the truth and informing the public, had informed the whole world of things that no one needed to know, thus making a fuss—which had caused Monsieur Blaieau to groan, and to curse his excessively clear-sighted eyes, people who got mixed up with things that did not concern them, and the newspapers—those who wrote for them and those who read them. Animated by the peril, however, he had demonstrated:

1. That the antiquities were authentic;
2. That if they were not authentic—not impossible—they were imitated as well as human hands could contrive;
3. That no museum in the world possessed antiquities, real

or imitation, comparable to those that could be admired at the Museum of X***.

Monsieur Bleareau had concluded by observing, as if by hazard, that, moreover, the aforesaid controversial items had been acquired under the reign and with the approval of the regretted and eminent Monsieur Douxamy, Monsieur Blaireau's predecessor, and that the latter had done nothing but record the aforesaid pieces in the catalogue and assign them a place in the exhibition, without permitting himself to question an authenticity admitted by his eminent predecessor....

That demonstration, in which Monsieur Blaureau dodged responsibility with an undeniable skill, had excited universal enthusiasm. Everyone had flocked to the museum to contemplate the controversial objects, and everyone everywhere had proclaimed the impregnable science and equally rare genius that the curator Monsieur Blaireau had shown, while casting a few rather bitter aspersions on the memory of poor Monsieur Douxamy, who was no longer here to defend himself. And everything was looking rosy in the curator's heart.

At the beginning of the present story, as I said, Monsieur Blaireau was in his office, somnolent and blissful.

Four o'clock chimed. In the empty and sonorous hall of the museum the distant calls of "Closing time" by means of which the attendants were hastening the flight of a few obstinate were resounding, and fading away. It was a spring evening.

Monsieur Blaireau, darting a glance out of the window of his office, smiled at the puerile leaves of a young chestnut-tree that was swaying in the fluvial breeze. Monsieur Blaireau was even happier to be alive. He washed his hands, lit his cigar and put on his overcoat, checking the creases. He was turning from the mirror toward the door in order to leave, when it opened silently, allowing the penetration of a vaguely human but very singular individual.

"Eh?" said the curator, rather surprised in considering a tall, slender brown figure clad in a painter's smock stained with colors, with his head in a tight round skullcap made of little strips of dirty cloth. "Who are you?"

"I," said the figure, who had closed the door, "am the Theban mummy from the main hall, and I've had enough!"

"You've had enough of what?" asked Monsieur Blaireau, almost unconsciously, his vital spirits congealed by stupor.

"I've had enough of everything, especially of being a mummy in your vile museum," said the other, sitting down in a green armchair and putting his meager left calf on his sharp right knee. "I've had enough, and more than enough! It has to end."

There was a silence. Monsieur Blaireau, the Egyptian antiquities man, glazed with his frightened bulging eyes at the astonishing antiquity that had come to pick a quarrel with him in this extraordinary fashion. Varied, but not very agreeable, sentiments conflicted in the curator's soul.

"You…you understand French, then?" said Monsieur Blaireau, finally, in a strangled voice.

"It seems so, imbecile, since I'm speaking it!" exclaimed the irritated mummy. "Now, stop looking at me as if I were a panorama—I don't like it."

Monsieur Blaireau turned deep red. "I beg your pardon," he said. "I was doing it unintentionally. But it's curious to see a dead man come back to life, isn't it?"

"Oh, don't be silly," said the other. "Everyone knows very well—except, perhaps, for curators of antiquities—that we've been embalmed alive in large numbers. The American master has proved it, and many others since. You don't have to tell me ghost stories. If I were dead, I wouldn't be here, I assure you; I'd have stayed at home."

"That's astonishing…astonishing," murmured Monsieur Blaireau, rubbing his nose. "But how are you able to speak and walk?"

"I move my tongue and my feet, like everybody else," the Egyptian replied, seemingly offended. "Are you trying to insult me by asking me that, idiot?" He reached over the table and pinched Monsieur Blaireau's ear maliciously, adding "I can also make use of my hands, you know."

"Monsieur!" cried the latter, in pain.

"Monsieur?" said the other.

There was a silence.

"That's enough," the mummy continued. "I've seen too much of you. I find you ugly. I want to leave. But as, after all, in spite of your ugliness, your avarice and your stupidity, you're the curator of the museum where I'm a mummy, before I go I want to do what I've come for—to wit, to hand in my resignation."

"Your resignation!" groaned Monsieur Blaireau "Your resignation from what?"

"My resignation as a mummy, naturally. It's too much. For years and years I've been awake, there, all alone in my case, and I've stayed very quiet, allowing myself to be looked at out of pure generosity, for I'm a polite man. But I've gradually become increasingly disgusted. Everything's going from bad to worse. The hall attendants wash the floors like pigs, the showcases are no longer dusted, and the heating is no longer turned on. The crowd's becoming insolent. The curators I've seen succeeding one another haven't done their job well, but never as badly as you. They've died one after another—as you'll die too—and others have replaced the dead, but I've never yet seen one remotely comparable to you. You surpass them all effortlessly. Douxamy, in spite of his deafness, his stubbornness and his senility, was a genius compared to you, refuse of the human species. That vexes me.

"And I'm bored—I'm telling you, frankly, that I'm bored. I want to go out, to see the world, to live modern life a little, have some fun in my turn. I want money, because I believe I perceive that, since the days of Egypt, that hasn't changed, and that to be comfortable in the midst of men and women one needs money. And your women are pretty, which necessitates more money. To think that it's four thousand nine hundred and forty six years since I had one... and I can't stand it any more...."

"Monsieur!" protested the prudish Blaireau.

"Well, what?" said the other. "There's no reason, because

you can't do it any more, to be disgusted with others." He went on: "Money—I would have got some by selling a few of the things that you call your treasures, but I've looked at them close up, and they're worthless...."

"What?" said the curator.

"They're worthless," the mummy repeated. "And that disgusts me. And now there's this dishonorable story of the apocryphal items that the newspapers have published. That's nothing yet, for they don't know...but if they take it into the heads to look closely...it'll be the end. I don't want to see that. In the early days, when I considered your antiquities, it pained me, that's all; but gradually, I've got used to it. I ended up admitting them, you understand, and almost believing that they were real...but with the papers, that's no longer possible; everyone doubts everything.

"They even doubt me—yes, Monsieur, me. There was one imbecile today who said: 'And that Chinaman there, it's a hoax; look at his face, it's painted wood.' And he said that to a pretty young woman, who laughed. Well, it's the last straw. I don't want people to make young women laugh by saying that I'm a Chinaman in painted wood. I'm an Egyptian, Monsieur, and alive, damn it! But it's over. I'm taking back my liberty. I want to write in the newspapers too, to earn money by recounting what I know—the truth—and people will see. And I'll talk about you, you old fool, who has attracted insults to me by posing as a man who knows everything when you don't know anything at all."

The furious mummy stood up.

If he goes, I'm ruined, thought the curator. "My dear...dear... friend," he said to the Egyptian, placing a hand on his arm.

"No, Monsieur," said the other, stepping away.

"Come on, my dear friend," Monsieur Blaireau pronounced, in a seductive tone. "Isn't there a way to work this out? Let's not get carried away. Let's be adult about this. First of all, I refuse to accept your resignation. A man like you has a duty to his fellows. To be sure, we have other mummies in the museum, beautiful and authentic"—the citizen of Thebes laughed sardonically, which induced a cold sweat on Monsieur Blaireau's back—"but you're the most admirable, the most necessary, the most intoxicating for the eyes."

"What's your point?" the Egyptian interjected, dryly, although he seemed somewhat mollified.

"What's my point? Keeping you. Come on, don't be difficult. There's always a means of sorting things out. Be reasonable. You want liberty, I understand that, but come to the museum every day, from nine to five—that's not long—and stay in your case in order to be seen. It's no more difficult than going to an office, and everyone, nowadays, goes to an office—it's a necessity of modern life, and since you want to live, there's nothing else to do. A man can't live in an office; he never does anything there but he needs to go there. He has to—it's as indispensable as bread. You'll be doing as everyone else does. You'll have your hours in the office—in the case, I mean. It's the same for all of us. You'll be standing up instead of sitting down, that's the only difference...."

"Yes," said the mummy, still peevish, "but all of you get paid...."

"Naturally, you will be too. You'll have...let's see...four hundred a month. That's nice, eh? And three hundred indemnity for accommodation. And in the evening, you can go out, live a little, have some fun...."

"Fun, fun...and my retirement. Will I at least be able to retire?"

"Retire, to do what? You'll be irremovable."

"That's true enough," the mummy remarked. "But after all, I've already been working for many years for nothing, so advance me ten louis is compensation for the past years. Then again, all your employees, functionaries or otherwise, are decorated—all of them, and lavishly; the attendants have badges or gold-rimmed hats, and that's good for obtaining respect. If that imbecile today had seen me wearing a braided helmet, or a kepi, he certainly wouldn't have dared to mock me...."

"Probably not," Monsieur Blaieau agreed, "but I can't give

you anything at all as regards a helmet or a kepi—it wouldn't go with your physiognomy. Would you like academic palms, though? That's an idea, eh? We could attach them to the case...."

"Go on then," murmured the mummy, visibly won over by that last promise. "Agreed. But let me have your overcoat and the key to the main door. I want to go out this evening, and this smock that I've taken from a painter really is too dirty."

"There you are," said Monsieur Blaireau, "Very glad to get away with it so cheaply. Don't forget the hours: nine to five. And above all, not a word to the papers."

"You can count on me," said the Egyptian.

And he went out. Sticking his head back through the doorway, he said: "Don't forget that I want silver palms on my case, not a simple ribbon."

"Agreed, my dear chap!" shouted the curator, putting on his hat.

A few moments later, as he went downstairs, he murmured: "It's obvious that fellow from ancient times doesn't realize how widespread that honorific distinction is. Thank the Lord, for that permitted me to win him over easily—and he's probably the only one of our antiquities that's genuine...."

THE TRAM-DRIVER'S TRAGEDY

The scene represents a tram progressing through the streets of an eccentric quarter on a winter night.

The tram is immense, yellow and electric. It moves surrounded by flashes; its voice is thunderous; and furious jolts agitate it on the bends.

The interior is occupied by passengers, who are:

To the right, commencing at the rear: a young shop-assistant; a man asleep; two nuns with their rosaries; a well-to-do fat lady who is picking her nose. (This deadly sport, once a repugnant prerogative of early and unconscious infancy, is becoming more widespread among adults, who indulge in it furiously in public places, and even in the best salons, thus scorning the laws of civilization and inspiring mortal disgust and irreducible hated in their neighbors.) The fat lady takes up a lot of room and covers with her thickness a timid man who does not dare to move or complain, and thus remains submerged on the right side, while is left side is bruised by the weapons of the soldier who is the seventh and last passenger in the right-hand series.

The left-hand series begins with a young milliner going home to her mother's house. Then there is a street-arab in rags plunged into reading a political newspaper of the lowest kind, and a mother with a basket and a four-year-old offspring. Beside the offspring there is the blockhead of the bus, and finally, an old gentleman ranting.

At the front of the tram, isolated on the platform by thick glass, and combating the elements, clad in animal-skins, sits the driver, on whom a heavy responsibility weighs. At the rear stands the conductor, a child of the people coiffed in a kepi and shod in galoshes. He sometimes circulates, distributing little pieces of paper, but more often stands still, exchanging meteo-rological opinions with an intrepid voyager smoking a cigar, and playing the part of one of those courageous people who take pride in not being afraid of anything inoffensive.

On the top deck, there are the top-deck passengers, a vague and disinherited collectivity, which sometimes reminds the world of its existence by tapping a timid foot. In addition to this intermittent sound, one perceives the muffled racket of propul-sive utensils, the purring of the nuns muttering their rosaries and the soft snores emanating from the man who is asleep, The child is being good.

It is very cold, and snow is falling in gusts.

Scene I

The tram stops at a station, an outpost situated at the limits of the inhabited world, before the suburban solitudes. An inspec-tor of antisocial appearance, drowsy and shivering, emerges angrily from his warm wigwam and comes to exchange caba-listic signs with the conductor, and to ask the soldier whether he really is a soldier. No one gets on or off. The vehicle moves off again. There is a pause.

Then the driver sings out.

THE DRIVER

"Forward ho! Forward ho! Forward ho! That's the last stop! Now I'll never stop again. I've had enough of always turning round at the end. Do they think they can keep me in slavery for a derisory salary? I've put the brake on my passions for too long, I want to enjoy life in my turn, in space and speed! I want to go to the ends of the earth in my tram! Forward ho! Forward ho! Forward ho!

He accelerates the velocity of the tram considerably. No one has heard him. The calm god named Security holds sway among the passengers, founded on faith in treaties. One of his arms rests on the confidence of human beings in their own inventions, the other on the unconsciousness of perils; his head leans softly on the bliss that one knows when one has surrendered initiative and responsibility to someone else.
Meanwhile:

THE YOUNG SHOP-ASSISTANT, *directing timid and ardent eyes at the milliner, aside*

How charming she is! Oh, those long brown lashes that cast shadows! Oh, that mouth! Oh, the grace of that bust! How I love her! Every evening for three months...will I ever dare to speak to her?

THE MILLINER, *aside*

He's nice...he's very nice...truly, he has a distinguished air...and serious too. Every evening for a long time...I'm sure that he can say lovely things...he has a fine curly beard and a beautiful cravat.... He daren't look at me. If he spoke to me, would I listen, in spite of everything Maman has said to me?

Slyly, she watches the young man. He does the same. Their eyes meet. Simultaneous sunlight.

THE MOTHER, *to her offspring*

Titi Tintin, dodo on Maman....

THE OFFSPRING, *whose name is actually Constantin*

Dodo Tintin…. *He curls up and goes to sleep on the maternal lap.*

THE MAN WHO IS ASLEEP

Snore….

THE NUNS

Rosaries….

THE URCHIN READING THE POLITICAL PAPER, *between his teeth*

Filthy government.

THE BLOCKHEAD OF THE BUS

I'm the blockhead of the bus! Idiotic and content, in a non-existence that nothing can perturb, bleak on my banquette, I'm the blockhead of the bus….

THE OLD GENTLEMAN, *ranting*

It's shameful! These trams have no heating at all. It's only in France that one sees that. (*He leans toward the blockhead.*) Observe, Monsieur, that this heater is cold. Oh, such things wouldn't be tolerated in America. The passengers would get together, and then…. (*Continuation of a speech devoid of interest and full of lies.*)

THE FAT LADY, *while picking her nose methodically and discerningly*

I'm a well-to-do fat lady and I take up a lot of space. I'm rich, certainly, and I could travel by other means than the tram, but money's money and I say that carriages scare me. I'd like to appear very rich, so that people will envy me, and very poor, so that they won't ask me for anything....

THE TIMID MAN

The fat lady to the right is covering me with the gelatinous cascades of her alluvial corpulence. The soldier to the left is bruising my tissues cruelly with his metallic harness, so my situation is detestable! In God's name! Why am I timid to the point of not daring to budge or change places!

THE SOLDIER

Bloody hell, it's nippy. If I only had a drink.... Just as long as I'm not late....

THE CONDUCTOR, *on his platform, to the intrepid voyager*

The snow's white; it's falling from the black sky. It's not good for the crops....

THE INTREPID VOYAGER, *lighting another cigar*

I've seen many other things in the course of my perilous explorations. Lions, tigers, hunger, thirst, cold, heat. Nothing can scare me—neither polar bears, nor ferocious Papuans....

THE PASSENGERS ON THE TOP DECK

We're the pale passengers on the top deck with the frozen feet? Oh, why are we in this wretched state? Why are we not high enough up on the social and monetary scale to allow us to share the delights down below, where it's dry, where one is under cover? O injustice of injustices, O inequality of conditions! O our fathers, was it for such results that you toppled kings?

Scene II

Darkness; squalls of snow; horrible cold. Immense speed of the tram, devouring the extent of unknown regions: plains, mountains and woods, white beneath the black sky.

THE DRIVER

Faster! faster! I shall vanquish the cold and the dark! Death shan't overtake me! Before me is the pathetic space that knows no limit; I'm racing into it. Behind me, bellowing in terror, are the ignominious passengers, the bane of my bitch of a life! I'm sick of them! Let them bellow, if they want to, a thousand times louder; I'm no longer paying any heed to them. At this hour, the sole desire of my existence, the obsession of my entire career—and I have seventeen years of service—is being slaked! My sensuality, retarded for so long, is going mad! Faster, faster, faster!

THE DEMON OF BLACK TERROR

His forehead is sweating and his eyes are full of tears. Convulsively, arms writhing and teeth chattering, he shakes the passengers, who are beginning to understand that things are not as they should be.

Murder! Murder! He wants to kill us! Conductor, stop! Terror! Terror!

THE CONDUCTOR

The driver, master after God of his tram, drunk or mad, is now juggling with our lives. No one can do anything to stop him.

THE SLEEPING MAN, *waking up*

What will be will be (*He goes back to sleep.*)

THE YOUNG SHOP-ASSISTANT, *to the milliner*

In this moment of peril, I'm burning my ships! O, Clementine, my name is Adolphe! I love you! Come to my burning breast, sweet angel! If we must perish, at least let us take advantage or our final seconds and let Death find us in the arms of Amour! With you, it will be sweet for me!

THE MILLINER

What are you saying, Monsieur? My God, how fast we're going! Maman, I'm scared! Save me, Adolphe! (*She throws herself into his arms.*)

THE MOTHER, *to her offspring*

Tintin, we're going to crash! (*Noise in the basket.*) There's my eggs breaking—it's the end of the world....

THE OFFSPRING, *fearless*

Dodo, Tintin

THE NUNS, *their teeth chattering*

Lord, Paradise, that's fine...but as late as possible! And we haven't been to confession.... Holy Virgin, the road is rough.... (*Frantic rosaries.*)

THE URCHIN

Filthy government! This is what you get with monopolies!

THE BLOCKHEAD

I can't say how little I care. I don't think about anything, I'm not going anywhere. My eyes are so stupid they're frightening. Spineless quivering lump, I'm the blockhead of the bus....

THE OLD GENTLEMAN

Damn it, I want to stop! Conductor, I'm making a complaint. It's truly extraordinary! In America....

THE FAT LADY

What use is it in this peril for me to be a well-to-do fat lady? Must I die, then, and leave everything behind? That driver is odiously criminal. That he might kill himself and the others is comprehensible, but not me, who has an annual income of sixty thousand! He's doubtless unaware of that, or else he's an anarchist. God, we're going faster. Soldier, soldier! Help!

THE TIMID MAN

The fat lady next to me is sweating with fear and her infectious juice is inundating me! The soldier, shaking with fear, is bruising me more cruelly than ever. I'm probably the only one who isn't afraid—I'm too timid for that....

THE SOLDIER

Bloody hell, I'd clap him in irons if I were his superior. I bet he's gone past the barracks, the Chinaman. And now the fat lady's making eyes at me. I need to run for help....

THE INTREPID VOYAGER

I'm scared! I'm scared! (*He hurls himself from the platform killing himself.*)

THE PASSENGERS ON THE TOP DECK

We've had enough of being on the top deck! In this race to death, it's still getting colder! Ice-cubes fill our tortured mouths, our feet are no longer our own, our noses, congealed promontories, are going to drop off like ripe fruit. It's too much! In Alaska, at least there's gold to find—here, nothing but starvation. It's too much! Before dying, let's get rid of vain social distances. If we have to die, let it be down below, in the warm, in the dry, in the light! We're going down! (*They start down the stairs.*)

THE CONDUCTOR, *picking up the iron bar with which, in normal circumstances, he switches the points on the tramway*

I'm here at the bottom of the stairs, my bar in my hand! No one will come down. I know my duty and I have my orders. By Heaven, I'll make a specter of the first one who tries to break through…and the second.…

THE TOP-DECK PASSENGERS

Harsh and brutal man, we'll get past anyway.

THE CONDUCTOR, *brandishing his iron bar*

Are you tired of life, then?

THE TOP-DECK PASSENGERS

He won't dare strike. Let's go down friends!

They go down. The first, struck on the head, dies and falls outside. The others go back up a few steps. Now they start begging.

You're the stronger, conductor, it's true! But come on! Recognize our suffering and observe our tears, frozen on our cheeks. We're in a glacial Hell up there. There's plenty of room down below. Let us come down. God will reward you!

THE CONDUCTOR

God has nothing to do with the regulations. You're top-deck passengers; you've paid three sous. Get back, immediately!

THE PASSENGERS

The contract you're invoking is bilateral. The tram, in taking us too far, is violating its terms. It's permissible for us to break ours!

THE CONDUCTOR

That's not my concern. You can write to complain. You don't have any right to be downstairs!

THE PASSENGERS

Have pity! Come on, we're like you, issued from the bosom of the people. Together, we've suckled the bitter milk of misery. We've been oppressed by the injustice of capitalists, bosses and managers. The same hovels are our lairs. On summer evenings, we chat together on our doorsteps. At the bistro, we drink wine together, then absinthe. Be kind! Let us come down! Have pity on your brothers!

THE CONDUCTOR

I'm not your brother. I have a cap with a badge. Get back up immediately!

THE PASSENGERS, *going back up*

That man has no soul. Honors have hardened his heart. We're going to die. (*They huddle together on the top deck, and are soon no more than an agonized block of ice.*)

Scene III

Tenebrous and unknown extents traversed by the tram, speeding like a bullet.

THE DRIVER

Faster! Faster! Faster! Hurrah! Hurrah! Hurrah! Everything gives me joy: speed, the cold, the wind, the snow, the dark, crime, death. I stroke it, I caress it, I brave it—what does it matter? I'll go all the way around the world! What glory! In a tram! Various fools, behind me, are being carried away in the whirlwind of my genius. How lucky they are! They're great deeds that I'm doing, and they're taking part in them, albeit without wanting to. That's the way destiny works, and the coming of a hero is a gift of the gods. Me, I'm the hero. I know, I want, I like! Faster! Faster! Hurrah! Hurrah!

In the tram, the good Angel of Habit, whose face is resigned and whose form is modeled on what surrounds her, has calmed the travelers by means of her blissful influence, and the travelers, once again, are taking an interest in their petty passionate affairs, or those of others, and vice versa.

Now, the young shop-assistant, uniting his overcoat with the milliner's shawl, with the aid of a few pins, has been able to extend an isolating curtain across the tram, which separates him and his beloved from contingencies, and makes the back of the tram into an inviolate nuptial alcove. Nothing can be seen, but they are audible.

THE VOICE OF THE SHOP-ASSISTANT, *ecstatic and incantatory*

Female flesh, ideal clay, O marvel!

THE VOICE OF THE MILLINER

Oh, that hurts! Maman! Maman!

The other passengers, paying no heed to that eternal and ever-recommencing drama, exist on their own account.

THE MOTHER, *having opened her basket to feed her offspring, awake and smiling*

Maman's little Tintin, eat sweetie!

CONSTANTIN

Tintin like sweetie! (*He seizes the said delicacy and swallows it.*)

THE RAGGED URCHIN, *excited by his newspaper*

Long live anarchy!

THE RANTING GENTLEMAN

Little wretch! In America, you'd be electrocuted!

THE URCHIN, *taking offense*

Hey, what do you take me for?

THE BLOCKHEAD

I'm the blockhead of the bus! The bus is going, everything's going. It's all the same to me!

THE SLEEPING MAN, *dreaming*

Green countryside…lovely sunshine…fresh grass…nice girlfriend…primroses for a pillow.…

In the unconscious and charming frankness of slumber, he slumps sideways, and his head weighs upon the bosom of his neighbor, the nun.

THE NUN, *timorously*

Charity prevents me from pushing away that forehead slumbering on my breast; modesty forbids me to keep it. What shall I do?

THE OTHER NUN

Vigil of important festival…abstinence and fasting…let us mortify ourselves, sister.…

THE FIRST NUN, *To herself, retaining the head of the young man, who is young and handsome*

Does this count as mortifying myself?

Rosaries.

THE WELL-TO-DO FAT LADY

I'm a well-to-do fat lady. That soldier seems ardent and vigorous, and I like handsome men. Besides, he's serving in the cavalry. I'll offer him a job as a gardener at forty-five francs a month, with the enjoyment of my person. That will be economical and sensual. Not to mention that, to stimulate his vigor, I'll also promise to put him in my will, and leave him the protection and care of my adored lap-dog Trou-Trou. Anyway, I hope to bury the pair of them, along with their successors in my favors....

She draws closer again, increasingly crushing the tortured body of the timid man, and surrendering her gelatinous corpulence to the embraces of the son of Mars, who is barely adequate to the task, but seems intoxicated by it.

THE SOLDIER, *exalted by his occupations*

Get in there, damn it! Get in there!

THE TIMID MAN

(*Nothing can any longer be seen of him but a twitching foot, convulsed by agony; his voice is a croak.*)

Are those two going to fornicate over my body? I'm dying of their shameful lust. O timidity! (*He renders up his soul.*)

THE CONDUCTOR, *to himself, meditatively*

Should I ask for supplementary fares, since the tram's going an extra distance? Why should they travel for free?

THE SPECTERS

(They are those of the passengers dead on the top deck, seeking vengeance. They surround the hard man who caused them to freeze to death in an infernal round-dance.)

Conductor! Conductor! Repent! We are your victims, and we shall make you expiate your crime. We are burning in Hell now, thanks to your ferocity—you've frozen us to death!

THE CONDUCTOR

What are these hideous phantoms? What do they want with me? I'm scared! My conscience is pricking, and yet I was doing my duty in being pitiless.

THE SPECTERS

Duty is not compatible with ferocity. It's necessary to be good and kind to your fellows.

THE CONDUCTOR

Duty is following the regulations…and nothing like that is inscribed….

THE SPECTERS

Come with us to the somber edge, to receive the payment of your crime and know the just law.

THE CONDUCTOR, *struggling, dragged feet first by the specters down into Hell*

Are there two duties, then?

THE SPECTERS

You're a soulless and accursed brute! (*They carry him off.*)

Scene IV

In the distance—in the snowy and terrifying night of that bleak unknown region through which the tram is traveling madly—the sound of the sea breaking on the stand can be heard, for all terrestrial roads lead to the sea.

An interval. The driver seems to be reflecting.

THE DRIVER

I think it's spoiled; I can't accomplish my desire to go to the ends of the earth, for my tram certainly can't travel over water. I didn't think of that. Anyway, it's all the same to me. Going to the ends of the earth—to do what? Not to mention that at every moment I'm violating my duty and the confidence of my superiors. Besides, as the world is round and has no ends, and, by going around it, I'd simply be returning to my point of departure, which would be ridiculous. The trip's been nice, but there's the sea a short distance away; it's singularly agitated, and the darkness isn't appropriate for swimming. Tram, let's go back!

THE TRAM

No! You've taught me what duty is worth! I too have suffered from always working under the orders of others, but I believed it was necessary that things were that way…. You've taught me liberty. I'm taking it in my turn. I'd rather die than live as a slave!

That said, and resisting the efforts of the fearful driver, the tram hurls itself into the sea, where it is swallowed up, with everything it contains.

THE HUMAN FISH AND
THE SOCIAL QUESTION

"What do I think?" said the intrepid voyager. "What do I think? Truly, you astonish me. I've always treated you as a friend, haven't I? Why, then, are you asking me such an odious question—such an odious and diabolical question? With no other interest, its seems, but putting me, immediately after my response—whatever it might be—at odds with all the gentlemen here present. Not to mention that they, after a short time, will all be at odds with one another. What do I think? But how do you know, first, that I think anything at all? How do you know that a single item of knowledge about this abominable and antihuman matter has ever contaminated the smallest fraction of my brain? What do I think? A curse upon your lugubrious curiosity. Listen, though—this will give you an idea of my opinion.

Five years ago, I was a member of an astonishing expedition of scientific exploration to Oceania, which Captain Altamont led, into the extreme South Seas and as far as the polar regions, to study the life in those regions—about which, truly, we don't know enough—and try to elucidate the question of the austral continent.

Well, I've undertaken a quite a few perilous and disappointing expeditions, but that one was the worst, I can assure you. None of the men composing it was a coward, believe me, and they were all used to the masks of death, but there, we had seen such odious and strange ones that we genuinely missed those which habit had rendered familiar. Altamont himself, who's cut out to do what no one else can, said that he had never lived such hard hours....

Furthermore, of the forty-two of us that set out, only seventeen came back, al the other having found their tombs somewhere in the deep sea or on some desolate islet, or in the belly of some voracious shark, or in those, more hateful still, of the cannibals native to those regions, where white men, as something comestible, are at a premium.

One morning—it was the nineteenth of January, I still recall—as we were in the open sea, we saw an individual in our wake, a human form, who was swimming at great speed, and we fished him out. Brought up on the deck, he was recognized as a man, but in what a state! Great God! Long hair mingled with algae and seashells, an entirely red and chapped skin, with scales here and there, and his fingers and toes connected by membranes.

He started jabbering in an extraordinary language, which included words from all countries, and we gradually contrived to understand him.

What he was saying was: "I'm a great hero. I'm searching for the truth. Do you have any in your cargo, by chance? No—I can see that you haven't. What a pity!" He sobbed, and went on: "For a long time, since my youth, I've been searching everywhere without finding it anywhere. However, I've studied, in my time—for at least a hundred and fifty years—with the most intelligent men, and also with the most idiotic, with all of them....

"I've been everywhere, from the top to the bottom, from right to left, forwards and backwards, crying to all the world: 'Give it to me!' But no one has given it to me. Perhaps they didn't have it, or wanted to keep it for themselves alone....

"When I was firmly convinced that I'd never discover the truth on land, I resolve to try to get hold of it at sea. Then I learned to live in salt water. When I'd got used to it, I set out, going straight ahead, facing the sun, led by the waves. I'm still swimming, I eat raw fish, and my hands have become webbed."

He raised his right hand.

"A superb example of transformism," said the ship's doctor, admiringly, who was listening and taking notes. It reminds me of the refrigerator rats."

"Yes, said the marine man, "I too know about the great Darwin and his theories; I'd like to believe that I'm a monkey, but I rather suspect that I'm a fish, and the doubt torments me. It's been many years since I cut my hair, because I've lost my pen-knife. It's frightful."

He paused, and went on: "So, for a long time, I've been floating thus, tossed by the waves of the powerful sea and exploring its abyssal depths in al directions. My heart is almost broken with despair, and my mind's coming apart by virtue of having thought so much, but I don't have the Truth. I haven't found it on any ship, either at the top of a mast, or in the depths of the hold, or in the souls of the voyagers. The stars haven't told me, at night, when I put my duck's hands together to implore them; the sun has dazzled my supplicant eyes cruelly, but hasn't told me anything, and the swell has sung that it doesn't know; and the flying fish fly by without replying…oh my God!"

He stopped again, resumed: "Can someone give me a plug of tobacco? Thanks." And he started chewing.

"I had an adventure a few days ago. I shouted at a big ship for someone to pick me up, thinking I might find the truth in the depths of one of its big cannons, but a fat man in a braided uniform stuck his detestable face over the stern and asked me what I thought about the social question, and where it was up to.[5]

"I couldn't reply, because I didn't know anything at all about the social question and I haven't the slightest idea where it was up to, as he put it…and I don't know if there's any Truth in it.

---

5. Up to this point, the story of the "human fish" has duplicated a passage from "Le Voyage de Julius Pingouin"—see the lead story in the second volume of the present set—almost exactly, but the question posed by the man on the warship is a different one.

"Then the fat man, maliciously, refused to take me aboard and withdrew his face from above the stern...."

The human fish paused for a moment to take a breath. We all looked at one another, fearfully. He went on: "So, there it is. Now, I wanted to come up here, in order to ask you: what's the social question, and where is it up to?"

"Enough!" cried Captain Altamont. "Not one more word! Get away, wretch. Overboard—and don't let me see you again!"

Four sailors jumped on the monster and, without precautions, threw him into the sea, so that he'd no longer infect the ship with his detestable presence.

"May he perish without remission, like a mad dog," Altamont said. "And may all those perish who are like him!"

Of all the perils that we ran and ever will run, he told me, wiping sweat from his brow, that was the worst and the most odious.

Such was the opinion of Captain Altamont, and Captain Altamont is no coward, I can assure you. And I, who haven't been created by nature to be afraid of anything whatsoever, shiver with horror whenever that incident comes back to mind.

And that might express for you—for you, Monsieur, whom I'm scratching out the list of my friends—*what I think.*

THE EXPERIMENT

Halpherson, the famous master of experimental physiology, standing with his hands in his pockets, tall and massive, with his back to the fireplace of his study, inclined his head, with its powerful clean-shaven features and short silvery hair, toward his listeners, the anatomist Jeffries and the biologist Moffat, both illustrious in America and in Europe, and fixed them with an obstinate gaze.

"I permitted myself to summon you this evening," he said, in his measured voice, emphasizing every word, "for a hazardous and sensational experiment that I did not care to undertake alone. Vulgar minds would have hesitated before its boldness, but its results might be so fruitful for humanity entire that they took priority over any other consideration. Shall we go into my laboratory?"

They followed him, anxiously. They were his intimates, as much as any man could be, and Halpherson had invited them that same afternoon, mysteriously, for ten o'clock, in a sudden and imperious fashion, with the result that they had dropped everything in order to come. However, his singular and daring genius always disconcerted them slightly; his lack of experimental scruples had already given rise to violent protests and this evening's preamble promised something exceptional.

In his vast, carefully sealed laboratory, the high electric lamps poured out their harsh light. There, the two scientists saw with astonishment, amid the habitual décor that was familiar to them in its scientific strangeness, an inexplicable bath that had just been filled with hot water, for vapor was still rising from it. Beside it, on a stool, a man was seated, clad only in a cotton shirt and trousers. He was livid; a tremor was agitating his back, and two slender chains shackled his ankles and his wrists. Nearby, seemingly standing guard over him, stood an athletic negro, Halpherson's personal domestic, who had served him for years with a dog-like devotion.

"Gentlemen," said Halpherson to his visitors, the man you see sitting there attempted to murder me yesterday evening, in the street, in order to rob me. This is the result he obtained." He opened his shirt, displaying a long deep cut on the left side of his breast. "I succeeded, however, with a blow to the chin, in putting him out for the count, as boxers say, and I brought him here with the aid of my domestic, for it happened almost on my doorstep. When he recovered consciousness, I got him to talk. His name is Wilson, and he's a rather famous murderer, already condemned to death, who has succeeded thus far in avoiding capture. My duty as a citizen is to deliver him to justice—which is to say, to execution...."

Those words fell into a heavy silence. The chained man was seen to shiver.

Halpherson went on: "I have another plan. You know the steps I've taken to have those condemned to death delivered to us for serious experimentation. Routine and prejudice have always prevented that proposition from being taken under consideration, and it has been so badly misunderstood that an inexplicable discredit had been reflected on my character and my work. Well, since chance has given me the opportunity to act freely with regard to this Wilson, I proposed a bargain to him: I would not surrender him to the police, would forgive his attempt on my life, would give him the opportunity to embark for whatever country he might wish, and would give him ten thousand dollars—enough to turn his life around—if he would agree to submit to an experiment in which he might lose his life....

"This is what it involves: I've discovered a serum, which, I believe, might replace human blood integrally—which is, so to speak, artificial blood, endowed, I hope, with vital properties equal, if not superior, to those of natural blood. I say that I hope, for I shall only be certain after a complete and definitive experiment, and that's the experiment that I want to make with Wilson. I shall open the veins in his arms in a bath. When his blood is entirely drained—when he has been dead for several minutes—I shall inject him with my serum, which will replace his blood and provoke the functioning of his organs. If my discovery is worth as much as I believe, Wilson will perhaps be resuscitated. Note that I say *if*, as, in the first experiment, there are doubtless more chances against than in favor, but there are chances in favor, for I believe that I can be sure of my discovery, which is as much as I can say. So, I proposed to this man, already marked for frightful legal death, that he should run those risks, perhaps to obtain a new life, which he will have gained by a gentle death devoid of suffering. Wilson understood and accepted. He'll tell you so."

The bound man made an effort to swallow his saliva. "Yes," he said, in a hollow one. "I accept."

"But it's impossible, Halpherson—you can't be thinking of it...." The biologist Moffat seemed astounded. "I can't be a party to it. You're going to render yourself guilty of murdering that man, or, if he gets through it, of releasing a dangerous criminal into society."

"If I get through it"—the condemned man's eyes lit up with a grim resolution—"if I get through it...ah, good God, I'll scrape the earth in the mines if I must, but I'll live peacefully!"

"Undoubtedly," said Halpherson. "After what he'll have undergone, he'll be too afraid of death to risk it again. And as for the responsibility...I don't think the police will worry overmuch about the disappearance of Mr. Wilson. That only leaves a case of conscience, my dear Moffat. Reflect and...you're free, naturally, to stay or go."

There were a few moments of silence. Moffat, who was pale, considered his options.

"I'll stay," he said, in the end. "All things considered, he's only risking a gentle death instead of a horrible execution."

"What about you?" the physiologist asked the other scientist.

"I'll say, naturally. That goes without saying. I'll never desert you, Halpherson, if you've found what you say...what a revolution in medicine! What consequences!" To Wilson, he said: "That ought to encourage you, damn it!"

"When one's where I am, one only thinks of oneself," the man relied dully. "But I have a chance...and then, electrocution....the chair...the helmet...." He shivered, looking haggard. "I prefer the bath...."

When the man was in the bath, with his hands untied, held by the wrists by the black colossus leaning over his shoulders, Halpherson came over to him, gripped his left arm, folded it and rolled up the sleeve.

"You're decided?" the physiologist asked again. "You're not going to change your mind? It will be too late. You're in the power of science and once the experiment has begun it can't be interrupted."

"Go!" said the man. He closed his eyes; his teeth were chattering in the silence. Halpherson leaned over, a scalpel in his fingers. The patient started slightly; a red thread ran down his forearm, but Halpherson had already plunged it into the hot water.

"You know what will happen, Gentlemen," he said, his voice as calm as usual. "The pulse will speed up; the arterial pressure will decrease; the subject will experience dizziness, dazzling and a sharp thirst; unconsciousness will follow soon afterwards."

He fell silent. With his thumb on the right wrist of the panting man, he counted the pulse-beats. Then, with the aid of an instrument with a tube and dial, he measured the arterial tension. A heavy emotion had gripped the two witnesses in spite of their professional habituation. The negro, standing upright, seemed an obedient machine. Halpherson remained calm. As for the subject lying in the bath, he was no longer breathing now; with his taut lips and closed eyes, he seemed to be dead already, and the water was gradually turning red.

"The pulse is accelerating and the pressure dropping," Halpherson murmured, after an interval.

"I'm thirsty," said Wilson suddenly, in a hoarse voice.

His lips were moistened with lemon juice. Shortly thereafter he groaned twice. Two more minutes passed, interminably.

The pulse is no longer measurable," said Halpherson. "The pressure's dropping. The instant's approaching."

"I have vertigo," stammered a tortured voice.

The condemned man had opened his eyes wide; in the waxen face, they were gazing without seeing.

"Take that away! he said, suddenly, with a movement devoid of strength. "I don't want to!"

"Falling unconscious," murmured Halpherson. "The end."

"No, no..." groaned the man. He made a desperate effort, as if to escape, but was scarcely able to contrive a convulsive twitch. The negro's heavy hands weighed upon his shoulders. He slumped back in the red water and his livid head rolled sideways.

"He's unconscious," said Halpherson, straightening up. "He's bled white...."

The anatomist Jeffries ran forward. "It's the end. Now take him out of the water, wait five minutes, and your serum...the poor devil had courage, all the same...I'd like to get him out of it. And what glory for you, Halpherson, if the experiment succeeds...."

The physiologist smiled strangely. "The experiment has succeeded," he said, tranquilly.

The other stated in amazement.

"Yes," said Halpherson, with his calm smile. "I haven't told you the truth, gentlemen. The experiment we've carried out isn't the one that I announced to you. We've merely carried out a study in autosuggestion...."

"Autosuggestion?" The two professors looked at one another in bewilderment.

"Yes. Your meeting in this laboratory, that bath, my scalpel and my speech were simply a stage-setting to impress the subject. I wanted to carry out an experiment in nervous impressionability, if I might put it thus. The man you see has not been bled, gentlemen. He simply believed so, and both of you believed it."

The physiologist took the left arm of the inanimate subject, damp with red water, wiped it, and held it up to the light. "Look—there's no trace of blood. I grazed him slightly with the point of my instrument, and crushed an ampoule containing carmine red in the same place—a simple means of progressively coloring the bath-water red. And I dictated to the subject his impressions of being bled white, which he reproduced one by one, according to the indications of my words, all the way to the profound faint in which he is now. It's a curious experiment...."

"It's even more complete than you think," said Professor Moffat, suddenly, who had just examined the subject, as he straightened up again. "The man is dead!"

There was a heavy silence.

"Bah! He was a murderer bound for execution," Jeffries murmured, between clenched teeth.

But Professor Halpherson was a trifle pale all the same.

CLAUDE MERCOEUR'S REFLECTION

I.
The Letter in Green Ink

Claude Mercoeur was alone and he was working. On a report that he had just scanned he wrote a brief note in blue pencil. Then he got out of his armchair and took a few steps in the vast and severe study; he went to one of the windows and, for a moment, gazed through it mechanically at the quay and the river, scarcely visible in the pale mist of the November morning. He returned to his desk, laden with the enormous stack of papers that constituted his personal correspondence, and began to open them.

Someone knocked. It was an usher. "Monsieur le Ministre, it's Dr. Vautier."

Mercoeur had looked up. "Well, send him in," he ordered, in his habitual brusque and authoritative tone.

The usher obeyed immediately. Mercoeur came to meet his visitor with an amicable urgency that he did not have for anyone else.

Dr. Vautier, tall and thin, clean-shaven, his face marked on the forehead and cheeks with deep wrinkles, his temples bare and his hair already silvery, seemed to be over forty-five, while Mercoeur scarcely seemed thirty-eight, with his solid frame, his chestnut-colored hair brushed back, his blond moustache and his aquiline, energetic visage with pronounced features, dark shiny eyes, sometimes almost ardent, beneath bushy brows. The two men were, however, the same age. They were former college friends. They shook hands with the frank and familiar cordiality of a profound and longstanding affection.

"Bonjour," said Vautier. "How are you? I'm not disturbing you?"

"You never disturb me, you know that. Sit down. Why haven't you come since Monday?"

"I've had too many things to do. You know that I'm one of the delegates to the Congress that will take place in America in two weeks. I have work to finish off, communications to draft. You know all that, since you're the one who got me selected for the congress, although other professors at the Académie de Médecine, older than me...."

"One doesn't have to be eighty years old to be one of the masters of French science," said Mercoeur. "You know full well that I say what I think...and what is. So, when are you leaving and how long will you stay in America?"

"I'm leaving in seven weeks and I'll be away for four or five months. After the Congress I'm going to spend some time with Carrel."

"That will be a long time without seeing you!" said Mercoeur, abruptly.

"I can come back immediately after the Congress...or not leave at all, if you think you need me," Vautier relied, calmly.

"Which is to say that for me, you'd sacrifice a voyage that will be a high point in your career, and which interests you passionately?"

"The sacrifice wouldn't be enormous. What one doesn't say at one moment one can say at another. Scientific truth, you see, inevitably comes to light. Besides which, you know, Mercoeur, that I could make sacrifices more important than that one, without hesitation, for you. Don't forget, I beg you, that if I am...who I am, it's thanks to you. If I hadn't had you for a friend when I was nineteen, after my first year of medicine, when I found myself without a sou to continue my studies following my father's death.... Yes, if I hadn't had the extraordinary, incomparable, incredible luck to have you for a friend.... When I think that you took the step, exceptional in a young man, of giving me a portion of your own income, which permitted me to live, to work tranquilly...."

An ill-contained emotion contracted Vautier's features. A smile softened Mercoeur's steely visage; an affectionate gaze came into his profound eyes.

"There's no need to keep recalling what we both know," he said. "I had money then that I didn't need—and I was already a good judge of men, presumably, since I took account of your value. You've always been my best—or, rather, my only—friend. With you I have the habit, as you know, of expressing aloud what I have in mind. I did so just now; obviously, going four or five months without seeing you, without telling you what I'm thinking, which I only tell you, won't be pleasant for me...."

"Me neither," Vautier observed. "That's why I'll...."

"Oh no, I beg you, no childishness, no silliness!" Mercoeur laughed benevolently. "You'll make your voyage, won't you? I demanded it! I was only teasing you by telling you that you were abandoning me, but naturally, you immediately replied that in that case, you'd stay...there's no means of joking with you, my friend!"

He had put his hand on his friend's shoulder, affectionately.

"Then it's all right," said Vautier, placidly. "I'll go." After a brief pause, he added: "Unless you're ill now."

"Why would I be ill? That never happens. My health is perfect, as you know, you who watch over me as if I were on my last legs."

"You don't look well, though. You work too hard. Why don't you give all that to one of your secretaries?" Vautier pointed at the pile of letters before which Mercoeur had sat down again.

The later shrugged his shoulders. "Because one never does enough things oneself. Because as soon as I entrust a job to someone else, I'm almost certain that the someone in question will make a mistake. Oh, with the best will in the world, out of zeal, haste, the desire to please.... Because everything I'm lazy enough to pass on to someone else is poorly understood and poorly executed. It's pride, a mania, whatever you wish, but I only have confidence in myself. I'd need two lives, you see, to get through everything. I scarcely sleep, never give myself an hour off, and have great difficulty facing up to the day's work. It's a perpetual torment, which obsesses me....

"I have a reputation—justified, I think—for indomitable energy. I'm ambitious, and my ambition has already obtained all reasonable satisfactions, since I'm a minister at forty, and two years from now, at the latest, at the first opportunity, I know, inevitably, that I'll have the Presidency of the Council. What I say there isn't vanity, it's the truth. With you, I have no vanity, as you know. Yes, it's all true—but there are moments when this life crushes me, when I sigh in cowardly fashion for a respite, however brief....

"But think of it, my friend: I no longer exist. I'm a machine for labor...and representation. And that's what wearies me more than I can say, because, fundamentally, it's futile. Do you understand? Utterly futile. Its décor and show, indispensable and vain....

"Yes, I know, it's the existence I've made for myself, but I repeat: it's not, properly speaking, existence. I don't know the meaning of words like idling, dreaming, relaxing, amusing oneself...living. Yes, living! Besides which, I have my reputation to maintain. I am, so far as the entire world is concerned, a serious, hard, austere man...that's my attitude, and I have an imperious need to continue to be exactly that. I find myself in the public eye, and, on the heights, as you now, according to Napoléon, one mustn't make any sudden movements.

"I'm suffering from ennui. It's implausible, isn't it? Claude Mercoeur suffering from ennui! But what do you expect? I'm not a statue made of stone or bronze; in spite of everything, at times, I want to live...."

He fell silent.

"Get married," said Vautier, suddenly.

"As if I had the time! Yes, perhaps I sometimes see woman who might please me. There's aren't many, but they do exist...."

"Gilberte Heurlize, for example. She's an intelligent woman, rich, good-looking; she's only thirty. She's been a widow for five years and has enough experience of life...."

"Perhaps. But she isn't in love with me. And I don't have the time, either, to make someone fall in love with me, or to fall in love myself. Yes, certainly she would please me. Among all the women I've met in my life, she is, I must admit, the only one that hasn't given me the impression that I'd be weary of living with her after three months of marriage.... Bah! Men like me aren't made for marriage. Complete independence is necessary for anyone who wants to work. I have to play my part; my life is my ambition, my career, my work.... However...however, it sometimes seems to me that a woman like her could help me...."

He remained pensive for a few moments. Then, with a habitual twitch of the shoulders that signified, in him, "What does it matter?" he lit a cigarette and resumed opening his letters.

"Excuse me," he said, after a moment. "It's virtually automatic work, which doesn't prevent me from chatting."

"There's never anything interesting in all that?"

"Hardly ever...anonymous slanders, nonsense, unjustified solicitations, the hallucinations of madmen....and nine times out of ten, the items that appear at first glance to be interesting are deceptive."

"You know," Vautier went on, suddenly, "you really don't look well, I assure you. If I hadn't checked you over three or four days ago I'd do so now, but as I've set my mind at rest, I know that it's just fatigue. So I advise you, as my sole prescription, but quite seriously, to get a bit more sleep. You could take a little strychnine."

Mercoeur shrugged. "If you wish—it's a tonic. But I'm quite well, you know...."

He interrupted himself. He was holding a commonplace

buff envelope on which his name and address were written, in primitive rounded handwriting, and above them, the word PERSONAL, underlined three times had been written in green ink. He opened the envelope and took out a letter, which he scanned.

"Again!" he murmured, with a hint of a smile. "He's stubborn!"

"What is it?"

"Perhaps something, but much more probably nothing at all. Here, read it!"

Vautier took the letter. It was written on lined paper and, like the envelope in green ink. He read:

Monsieur le Ministre,

This is the third letter. If it has no more success than the previous two I shall continue to write to you every week until I have achieved the result I desire: a conversation with you.

This evening I shall be outside Saint-Germain-des Prés and I shall be walking alongside the railings of the garden of the church, at the corner of the Rue de l'Abbaye and the square. I'll wait for you there between ten and eleven o'clock. It's a location that is busy enough that that hour for no appearance—however improbable it might be—of a trap to deter you, but sufficiently deserted for us to be able to meet without being overly inconvenienced by an excess of passers-by. I remind you that I shall be wearing a black hat, pulled down, and a large iron-gray overcoat with the collar turned up. I urge you with all my might to come. I cannot put into a letter what I have to say to you, which is of considerable importance, it seems to me, for you as well as for me—as you will realize, I'm sure, immediately. And you will also understand that it is impossible for me to act other than I am doing in order to meet with you. I know, as I have already told you, that these romantic and seemingly puerile precautions must seem ridiculous to you and that this meeting, requested by someone unknown to you, must seem simultaneously impudent, shady and extravagant. However, it's necessary that you come. I repeat, you will understand everything as soon as our conversation begins. I cannot act otherwise without our meting being futile. I assure you that it is essential that you come. I am not deceiving you and I am not deceiving myself; it's very important. You shall see.

I continue to employ green ink in order to write to you—one more eccentricity, very childish and vain, but the unusual color will attract your eyes, and that gives me the chance that you will read my letter every time, if your interest is awakened in the slightest. If it is not, it will permit you to throw the letter in the waste paper basket without reading it. Given what is known of your character, however, I think that you will read it, and I'm sure that one day, you will come. I hope that it will be as soon as possible. Why waste time? I even hope that it will be this evening.

There was no signature.

Without saying a word, Vautier handed the letter back to Claude Mercoeur.

"I'll go this evening," the latter said, suddenly.

"What! What an idea!" said Vautier, astonished.

"Yes, I'll go. Last Friday, when I received the previous letter—the second one—I was strongly tempted to go."

"But you're risking...."

"What? I have enemies, like all successful politicians, of course—but really, I don't know of anyone among them who can any serious hatred against me. They're rivalries, jealousies, resentments, which might lead to a few petty political treasons, that's all. But a trap, an attempted murder—no, old chap, I don't believe that. It's not my genre; I'm not melodramatic. And then, even if we admit the impossibility that anyone could have anything against me sufficient to prompt a criminal attempt on my life...well, rationally, instead of offering me such a bizarre rendezvous that either I wouldn't come or I'd arrive full of suspicion, he would purely and simply wait for me in the street until I leave here at night to go home, on foot, as I often do. Then again...no, it's implausible! Who could be determined to do me harm? For what motive? It doesn't stand up, I swear to you. This letter is...something else...."

"Perhaps it's some practical joker who wants to give himself the pleasure of mystifying then most visible of our politicians, of getting Claude Mercoeur going... In that case, either he'll try to continue to abuse your credulity by telling you some tall story, or, without showing himself, he'll watch with jubilation as you take your little stroll along the railings and your disappointment...which some journalistic humorist will report next week, with a commentary."

Mercoeur frowned. "A practical joker, you reckon. People aren't in the habit of playing jokes of that sort on Claude Mercoeur! I'm well-known, and any trickster I discovered would pay rather dearly, one way or another. Moreover, to forearm myself against the possibility of a trickster remaining in hiding, I'll go through the square first in a carriage; if I don't see anyone I won't get out and no one will see me. There remains the hypothesis of a madman...but these letters don't give the impression of emanating from a madman. And then, you see, I'm intrigued. I don't know why, but this seems serious to me; I have the impression of something interesting. A little trip to Saint-German-des-Prés, at ten o'clock in the evening, will be a change from my evenings of work or receptions. It's picturesque and romantic—it's a hint of life. I'm the opposite of naïve, I assure you, but something of the child probably remains within me by virtue of not living, of absorbing myself in relentless work. And what do you expect? The story might amuse me. And I'm not spoiled...."

Vautier stood up. "I have to go. I can see that you've made up your mind about this evening—but do you want me to go with you?"

"No, of course not! I'm instructed to come alone; I shall go. At the most, it will be one hour lost. Then I'll put in an appearance at the reception at Foreign Affairs. My carriage will come to wait for me there and I'll return to work at midnight. Come and see me tomorrow morning, and I'll tell you what happened—if anything happens worth telling. *Au revoir*, old chap!"

"Until tomorrow morning," said Vautier, smiling. "I'll come at ten o'clock, and you can explain the enigma of the letter in green ink."

They shook hands. Vautier went out. Mercoeur folded up the letter written in green ink, put it into his pocket and summoned his secretaries in order to get on with the business in hand. All day long, however, his singular rendezvous loomed over his quotidian labor, obsessing him.

II.
The Interview

The fog, which had partially dissipated during the day, had returned denser than before in the evening. Motionless, its soft and livid shadow submerged the streets, attenuating sounds, blurring the glow of the street-lights, which was amplified within it, diffusely, a specter of unreal light.

Quarter past ten was sounding when Claude Mercoeur had his carriage—an old fiacre that he had taken shortly after leaving the Ministry—stop at the corner of the Boulevard Saint-Germain and the Rue Saint-Benoît. The plan he had made—to pass by in a carriage in order to see whether anyone really was waiting for him—had proved impracticable, however; one could not see as far as five meters.

He got down and paid the coachman. He walked to the square at a rapid pace, crossed it and passed in front of the church.

He heard footsteps coming to meet him even before he made out the silhouette of a man through the fuliginous veil that was mingling its deception with the darkness. The man was wearing a long dark gray overcoat with the collar turned up over the lower part of his face, and a hat whose lowered brim shadowed his forehead and eyes—which were also hidden by round spectacles with yellow-tinted lenses.

Inexplicably, the curiosity that had driven Mercoeur to come to the bizarre rendezvous, suddenly vanished, and gave way to one of the abrupt fits of irritation that were habitual to him.

All this is grotesque, he said to himself, irritatedly. *Vautier was right: I'm an idiot to have come.* And to the man who stopped in front of him at that moment, scarcely a stride away, and whose features he tried in vain to see, he said, harshly: "Is it you who wrote to me? What's the meaning of this? What do you want?"

The man did not get excited. "I know that you'd come, eventually," he said, in a slow and muffled voice. "But since you've come, don't get annoyed. All this is obviously melodramatic and ridiculous, but I couldn't act otherwise...."

Where the devil have I heard that voice before? thought Mercoeur.

Meanwhile, the unknown man darted a rapid glance at the surrounding area. That corner of the square was deserted, and the fog enclosed both of then in its nebulous arms.

"Come under this street-light," said the man, "and you'll see."

Astonished by that composure, and intrigued once again, Mercoeur took a few steps with him. The man stopped under the street-light. Abruptly, he took off his hat, turned down his collar and removed his tinted spectacles.

"Look at me!" he said, leaning forward.

Mercoeur looked at him. At first, he did not have any clear comprehension of what he was seeing, but his hesitation was brief. He took stock, and shivered, amazed.

"But...you look like me," he said. "The resemblance is prodigious."

It was true. The resemblance was so complete that the two men seemed to be replicas of one another. Not only was there an identity of features, complexion, and evening expression, but an identity of build, of corpulence, and very nearly—the unknown man was slightly taller—of stature.

"It's unimaginable," Mercoeur murmured. "I must be looking into a mirror. But yes! There's one difference. I knew it! You have a black moustache and eyebrows!" The exclamation was sudden, as he discerned the detail that had perhaps, without him realizing it, prevented him from recognizing that perfect resemblance at first.

The unknown man smiled.

"Yes, they're black...for the moment. But I'm blond, you know—as blond as you are. Except that I thought it more prudent...so, a little dye, you see...which can be put in and removed with a little brush, in a matter of minutes...."

After a pause, he continued: "I didn't lie, you see, when I told you in my letters that you'd understand immediately...."

"I don't understand anything!" Mercoeur interrupted. "You resemble me in a bewildering fashion, it's true, but...."

"Give me time to explain," the unknown man interrupted in his turn. You have to give me an hour of your time! Now that you've seen me, you can't refuse...and I can assure you that you won't regret it...."

"All right," said Mercoeur. "I don't know what you have to say to me, and I don't know who you are...."

"I'll tell you. Anyway, my name is of no great importance, and don't believe for an instant that I have any intention of telling you some secret regarding your family or mine. It's simply a matter of material and undeniable fact that we resemble one another in an extraordinary fashion. But we can't chat at our ease in this square. I think you'll be willing to accompany me home. I'm staying close by, in a nice hotel...."

"Well then, let's go to your hotel," said Mercoeur, without hesitation. The unknown man's straightforward and frank manner had impressed him favorably. The adventure was becoming curious, and its singular and mysterious aspect no longer displeased him. He was increasingly intrigued, and, wondering what the unknown man wanted of him, he followed him.

Five minutes later, they went into a hotel of respectable and pleasant appearance. The unknown man took his key, gave his name—which Mercoeur did not quite catch—and opened his door on the ground floor. He switched on the light, invited his companion in and offered him a chair, and lit a log fire that was already prepared in the grate.

Sitting down in a red armchair, Mercoeur gazed mechanically at the room, which seemed well-kept and perfectly banal.

"This room is isolated and we can talk here without being overheard," the unknown man remarked, going to the washbasin. He passed a damp cloth over his eyebrows and moustache. He came back to stand beside Mercoeur, and the latter could not help shivering again, inasmuch as the man, now that he could see him without a hat, his hair and moustache as blond as his own, resembled him even more than he had a little while ago, in the half-light outside.

"Come with me to the wardrobe mirror," said Mercoeur, abruptly.

"If you wish."

Side by side, they stood in front of the full-length mirror for a few moments, slightly troubled.

"It's prodigious," Mercoeur murmured, finally.

"You know, if I seem slightly taller than you, it's because I've put false heels on my boots," the unknown explained, tranquilly. As with the dye in my moustache, I did it as a precaution. I don't want to neglect any detail...."

"Very well," said Mercoeur, returning to his seat. "Now explain yourself. What is this about?"

"This."

The unknown man sat down facing him. He took a wallet from his pocket and a folded piece of newsprint from the wallet, which he handed to Mercoeur. "First, would you please take the trouble to read this."

Mercoeur took the piece of paper and unfolded it. It was an article that had been clipped—quite some time ago, it seemed to him—from a periodical whose title was missing.[6] He read it.

Miscellanies.

A HUMAN DOUBLE FACTORY

This factory exists in America, and supplies the entire world. It is directed by Mr. J. C. Turkey, an honorable gentleman who founded it several years ago and has been able to give this important creation the energetic and intelligent direction that the complete development of such an important venture requires.

The products of this peerless company are utterly superior and defy all competition. It is impossible to do better work of this sort. Mr. Turkey has created his industry from scratch and had taken it to the extreme limits of perfection. The admirable subjects whose collaboration he assures for a high price are capable of assuming the most difficult characters, confronting the most visible situations, and playing the most delicate and complicated roles, without one having to fear the slightest weakness on their part. They are able to double the most well-known individuals, the most eccentric personalities as well as the dullest, without being distinguishable from the real thing by the most intimate friends or the most vigilant enemies of those they incarnate.

Mr. Turkey is a gentleman in the prime of life, distinguished, phlegmatic and clean-shaven.

"I cannot tell you precisely," he explained to me in answer to a question, "I really cannot tell you. It's a long time since I had the original idea. Do you remember a story by a French

6. The cited passages are taken, in an abridged form, from the opening pages of a story by Boutet published in *Le Français* in 1903 and reprinted in *Histoires vraisemblables* in 1908; a translation of the entire story appears in the second volume of the present set.

writer, Jules Verne? I can't remember the title, but it was set in America before the war for the abolition of slavery, and there are two brothers who resemble one another perfectly and take advantage of it to commit all sorts of crimes, each time creating for one another an apparently-indisputable alibi. Well, perhaps that only gave me a part of the idea, and I had the rest on hearing the complaints of people in the public eye who were unhappy because they don't have a minute's peace. I thought of all the advantages one could get out of the two things, and immediately set to work. It was long and difficult, I can assure you. It required a considerable financial investment to set the business up on a suitable footing, to carry out discreet advertising and to be able to respond in a perfect fashion to the initial orders. It was necessary, above all, to procure reliable, devoted, honest and intelligent collaborators....

"The clientele was created, I must say, very rapidly, almost of its own accord. People are so overstretched by social obligations, excursions, dinners, chores of every sort that they don't dare refuse, out of human respect, that the majority of them have welcomed the offers of my representatives enthusiastically. A few people were suspicious at first, but when they understood how worthy my employees are of confidence, when they have seen, in a drawing room, one of their friends come to sit down beside them and talk about familiar matters, without suspecting for an instant that it was a double that I had furnished, they were won over. And as all the employees I procure are discreet, zealous and delicate, and as all my clients—who are, moreover, from the top drawer of society—maintain complete silence regarding our relationship in their own interest, well, my enterprise is flourishing...."

"Might I ask how you operate?"

"How? It's very simple. Here's a new client who comes to me, asking for his double. Naturally, he's a very rich man, and generally, given that I'm now established in solid manner in society, he's an ambitious man. You get my drift? He's found himself in the public eye, in some fashion. Then, it's necessary *for him to go out, to show himself, to go to society occasions, to dine out. That's the only means, according to popular opinion, to sustain one's glory and increase one's renown. Whether it's true or not, people believe it. But work suffers, and health too, in consequence of the permanent fatigue and the dietary excesses that go with grand dinners. It's then that it's necessary to think about having a double. The newly famous man contacts me and I put him in touch with one of my artistes, who is almost the same height and build. If I don't have what he needs to hand, I carry out a search and find it. And after two month—three at the most—my employee, who has been in touch with my client throughout that time, has gradually acquired his external characteristics; he has adopted his mannerisms, his gestures, his manias. Naturally, he has similar clothing. He represents him very adequately at official ceremonies, weddings, funerals, even solemn dinners, and, in the meantime, the other works in peace at his fireside, in his dressing gown and slippers.*

"We can contrive to replace anyone at all, believe me—but it requires an enormous amount of work and money to achieve a perfect result. I've always achieved one, however, and no failure has tarnished my reputation. Some of my old subscribers have their own double, who only works for them, and who has succeeded in getting into their skin to such a point that even I can't tell them apart. I've obtained amazing results, I can assure you.

"Well, now you have an idea of the immensity of our enterprise, eh? You see that we can answer any demand. Our agents, I tell you, are superior men. Just think that we have had the honor of supplying crowned heads and Heads of State...yes, naturally, Heads of State.... But let's pass on; that's touching on diplomatic secrets. Simply know, my dear sir, that we supply the entire world, and that one never knows to whom one is talking...."

The article continued in the same style of humorous whimsy, but Mercoeur stopped reading and threw the yellowing piece of paper on the table. It folded up again of its own accord.

"And you disturbed me to read that?" he said abruptly.

"Yes, that's why I disturbed you," his guest replied, in the same tone. And his voice, now that he allowed it to assume its natural timbre, was so similar to Mercoeur's that he could have believed that an echo was repeating a sentence he had just uttered. And confusedly, that authoritarian voice, which really was his own and to which everyone around him was obedient without any thought of hesitation—to which he was accustomed—imposed its authority on him, in coming from the mouth of that strange double.

Reluctantly, he was unable to admit the possibility of a labo-riously-contrived trick; he was unable to get irritated and walk out immediately. Calmly, he stared at the unknown man during a long interval of silence.

Finally, he said: "But *that*'s not what you want to propose to me, is it?"

The other nodded his head affirmatively.

"I don't believe it's a practical joke on your part," Mercoeur went on, calmly, "and you appear to me to be a being endowed with reason. In any case, without my being able to help it, the astounding resemblance that exists between us absolutely forbids me to consider you a stranger. It's illogical, but there it is. Tell me, frankly, what you're getting at. You can't reason-ably expect to put into practice that amusing item of humorous fiction you've just given me to read, which is only a fantastic invention, admittedly ingenious...."

"One sometimes finds the seed of a useful idea in the most frivolous fantasies," the other said, coolly. "I understand your astonishment. But...yes, that really is what I'm getting at—and only that, I assure you. Come on, look at us! One obvious ques-tion arises before anything else. Yes, before even asking whether what I'm proposing to you is possible or not, let's ask that ques-tion: would it be useful to you? You understand: *useful?* Would your work, your career, your entire life be made easier by it?

"I think that it would, and, according to what I've been able to learn about you, from articles in newspapers, hearsay and the anecdotal details that create, for the general public, of which I am a member, the personality of men in the public eye, I don't think I'm mistaken, and that you are, doubtless even more than me, of the same opinion.

"Think about it. You can reply, if you want to, later. But now, permit me, in a few words, to tell you who you're dealing with. I'll tell you right away that I'm not of any passionate interest, but I'm a respectable man and it's preferable, in case we can reach an understanding, that you know me. I'm thirty-nine years old—a year younger than you, I believe—and my name is Raoul Berjean. It's an acceptable name, don't you think? My father was a road-inspector in the Dauphiné, but our family is Breton in origin, from the Brest region."

"I too have Breton ancestors," said Mercoeur, who had lit a cigarette and was listening attentively.

"Yes, I know, and perhaps our resemblance can be explained by distant alliances of which you and I are inevitably unaware. Anyway, that's not important. There are cases of extraordinary resemblance between people who are completely unrelated to one another, for which no explanation is necessary. An old legend says that every man on earth has his double. I'm your double, that's all. I'll continue my biography. I went to school in Grenoble, and then studied law. Having no fortune, my father only left me ten thousand francs, his savings, so I went into service in the legal department of a big company in the region. That's it. I'll add that I'm not married.

"That's my life: a dull and quiet provincial life. As I don't have a taste for card games in the café or départemental intrigues, however, I started reading to occupy myself—reading every-thing: newspapers, magazines, novels, history books, every-thing! When I encountered something that amused me in a periodical, I clipped it. That's how I came to keep the article I've just had you read, which appeared fifteen years ago in some humorous publication or other. It made an impression on me. I have a marked predilection for the romantic and plausible fantasies. The question of resemblance fascinated me at the time, and I made a study of it, to the limited extent that I could with the meager resources I found out there in libraries. Recently, I've become preoccupied with it again.…

"It was last year, during the holidays, about fifteen months ago. One morning, on opening a newspaper, I was amazed to see my picture on the first page—which is to say that I had an unthinking impression, which only lasted a second, that it was my picture. In fact, it was yours; your name was underneath it Three days before, you had become a Minister, and the entire press was occupied with you. You know that as well as I do. However, I remained stupefied because of the perfect physical identity that I observed between us. I ought to say that no one around me noticed it; in those days, I wore a pointed beard, very short hair and yellow-tinted spectacles because my eyes became tired—but I realized it, and I compared that photograph of you, reproduced in the newspaper, with a photograph of me, taken four or five years before, when I was clean shaven. There was a perfect similarity, and I saw it even more clearly when I procured a better photograph of you.

I ought to tell you that you already interested me because of your exceptionally brilliant career, and everything that was said about your energy, your capacity for work and your remarkable qualities as a statesman. At first, I frankly confess, I was naively and a little stupidly proud of resembling a superior man; then, on reflection, I was gripped by a cruel bitterness, and I was ashamed of being nothing but a modest employee with no other prospects than the tiresome routine of a banal and paltry existence. I told myself that in other circumstances, perhaps I too would have been a superior man. Then, by a curious sort of duplication, it seemed to me that I was sharing a little in your triumphs, which I was passionately following in the newspapers. As I told you, I have imagination, and it had the time to exercise itself freely while my tedious everyday labor was carried out....

"Then I remembered the fantasy that had once struck me, which I had cut out and kept. And finally, I said to myself, why not? Yes, why shouldn't I replace Claude Mercoeur, in certain cases, in order that he might have, in the meantime, time to work, to rest or to amuse himself...?"

He paused. Mercoeur looked at him curiously, his cigarette in his fingers. "Go on," he said, finally.

"The first thing I wanted to do," Berjean went on, "was to see you with my own eyes. I went to Lyon when you were there on an official visit to unveil a monument to some great man or other. I saw you; I heard your speech. I observed our perfect physical resemblance and the analogy there was between our voices. At that moment, however, I was a little thinner than you—but I remedied that with a few months of dieting. At the same time, I improved my English, having learned that you were very fluent in that language. I knew it quite well myself, thank God, my mother, who had been brought up in London, having taught it to me as a child. I studied the political movements of recent years just as carefully, and tried to acquire some knowledge of Japanese art, since, it appears, you're an expert on the subject.

"That's not true," said Mercoeur. "I've been given that reputation, but it's usurped. I have a taste for it, to be sure, but I lack the time to occupy myself with it, and I don't know anything about it."

"So much the better," said Berjean, "for it's very difficult. In brief I prepared myself as best I could—and, take note, without being at all sure that I would ever make the decision to come to find you in order to propose such an unlikely collaboration....

"At times, I told myself that I was simply mad, and I would no longer think about it for a few days, or at least try not to think about it any longer...but it kept coming back, obsessively. I became ambitious—for you! My life seemed increasingly dull, bleak and sterile. It seemed to me that, by not coming to offer you my aid, I was betraying a cause that we had in common. What I just said is confused and bizarre, but so were my thoughts.

What do you expect? Our situation is so extraordinary.

"Finally, a month ago, I came to a decision. I asked my employers for a leave of absence, on health grounds, and I left. When I arrived in Paris, I took up residence here. I knew the quarter, in which I'd stayed during a few brief visits I made to Paris, the most recent of which was four years ago. I arrived at night and, determined to have a meeting with you as soon as possible, I shaved myself, in order that you would be struck by the resemblance between us at the first glance. Then I dyed my moustache and eyebrows, in order that the resemblance wouldn't be obvious to everyone—and it's for that reason, too, that I made myself taller with the aid of built-up shoes.

"Then I wrote my first letter, and it was only then that I suddenly realized that it would be very difficult to meet with you. I couldn't go to see you, or ask for a normal appointment with you, or explain to you in my letters what it was about. If anyone but the two of us knew our secret—it was still entirely my own secret—it would no longer be possible to realize any plan. What I was asking of you was extravagant, I know, and that distressed me. My two previous sessions waiting at the church railings seemed interminable, but a singular sentiment encouraged me. Would you like to know what it was? Well, I said to myself: 'If I were him, I would come....' And after all, I was right, since you came this evening...."

There was a momentary silence.

"Then that really is what you're proposing to me?" said Mercoeur, slowly. "You've been able to convince yourself, momentarily, that I might agree to discredit myself, to make myself ridiculous, to risk my career by lending myself to the practical realization of that implausible fantasy, which, if I were crazy enough to try it, would come to light immediately? It's vaudeville, my dear Monsieur, and it's also melodrama...it's anything you like, except something realizable." And he could not help adding: "Unfortunately...."

"Unfortunately, you say?" observed Berjean.

"I do say unfortunately, yes. Of course I say unfortunately! If your offer were acceptable, I'd accept it. That's perfectly evident. And it would be the greatest service that anyone had every rendered me. I can't, in spite of my efforts, in spite of working very rapidly, in spite of only allowing myself the most indispensable repose, do by myself all that I'd like to do. Absorbed relentlessly by dogged labor, I have no life. I don't have a minute in which to live! That's the one thing that caught my attention in what you made me read just now: that slavery of the well-known man who no longer belongs to himself. Certainly, it would be admirable, inestimable, to be duplicated, to have another self who can incarnate your person when all that's necessary is to appear, to be there, to be represented.... I've often dreamed of being rid of the drudgery of protocol, which exasperates me and absorbs such a great portion of my time, uselessly...."

Berjean was smiling.

"Well, I'm offering you just such a means...."

"You're offering me an insanity, which you've taken delight in imagining in your idleness and isolation. You've convinced yourself of the possible realization of a chimera. Our extraordinary resemblance is your excuse.... I sense that you're an honest man, and that you're sincere—otherwise, I could almost believe that it's one of my adversaries, or one of my rivals, desirous of replacing me, who has contrived this fantastic story in the hope that I might let myself be taken in and sink myself...."

"That would be very Machiavellian," observed Berjean, still placid. "I don't think you understand the situation...."

"Don't persist," Mercoeur interrupted, rising to his feet.

"I shall persist. Sit down. Since you've listened to me patiently thus far, listen a little longer. I've wanted to have this conversation too much to let it end like this. You'll allow yourself to be convinced, because what I'm proposing is possible. Really, I don't believe you're seeing the situation as it is. Doubtless, if I were the agent of some enemy, and I betrayed you myself by revealing our pact as soon as I took you place, that would do you harm. But that's not what's happening. You do me the honor of not judging me thus, and you're right. The truth is sometimes a force in itself, which imposes itself....

"I'm not a traitor; you know that. Besides which, everything I've told you about my life is easily verified. Thus, one sole dread is preventing you from accepting my collaboration, which might be of inestimable value to you, as you've confessed: the dread of being found out!

"Think about it: first of all, the apparent extravagance of the substitution. No one would ever dream of suspecting the truth, because it's so audacious. Then again, I shall only replace you at official ceremonies, at least in the beginning. And you will reappear yourself the following day, or even a few hours later. If any suspicion—impossibly, I assure you—should ever arise, you'd be able to destroy it instantly."

"But in sum, how can you imagine, in spite of the extraordinary similitude there is between us, that you wouldn't be immediately identified and unmasked? I repeat, as a literary means, perhaps it's ingenious...."

"Forgive me, but I've studied the question a little, as I told you. Agreed, it's a literary means that has served well, but it's not only that. One finds a number of authentic and very surprising historical examples of extraordinary resemblances. I can cite, can I not, Pliny book VIII chapter 23, and Valerius Maximus book II, chapter 15, reporting that Sura, the proconsul in Sicily, found a poor fisherman there who resembled him perfectly. They both had precisely the same features, the same height, the same gestures, the same voice, the same laugh, and they both had a stutter. According to the same Pliny, book VII chapter 13, Strabo, the father of Pompey the Great, had a cook who was his very image, and who he was able to have pass for him. There are numerous analogies. The most typical is that of Martin Guerre in the sixteenth century. You know the case?"

"Vaguely," said Mercoeur.

"This is it, in a nutshell. Martin Guerre was married young to Bertrande de Rols and lived with her in a village in the Midi. He was twenty-two when having committed an insignificant larceny, he left the region, without telling anyone—even his wife—where he was going. There was no news of him for eight years. After that time, a man appeared who said that he was Martin Guerre and who had every appearance of it. Everyone recognized him without hesitation, including his four sisters and Bertrande de Rols, his wife, who resumed conjugal life with him. A few years passed; there was a quarrel over money between Martin Guerre and one of his uncles. The latter affirmed that the man who had comer back was not really his nephew, and tried to constrain Bertrande de Rols to disavow as her husband the man with whom she was living—but she replied that she knew better than anyone else, and that it was either him or 'the devil dancing in his skin.' And yet it wasn't him! One day, a man with a wooden leg appeared, who said that he was the real Martin Guerre, that he had come back from the army and had lost his leg at the siege of Saint-Laurent. He laid claim to his name and his property. The two Martin Guerres were brought together. They were prodigiously similar and treated one another recip-rocally as impostors. The four Guerre sisters and Bertrande de Rols were summoned. With no more hesitation than the first time, when they had recognized the man who had come back as Martin Guerre, they recognized that they had been mistaken and that it was the second man who was the true Martin Guerre, their brother and husband. Then the first Martin Guerre—the one who had come back first—admitted that he had lied and that he was really Arnauld de Thil. He was hanged.

"You, Claude Mercoeur, won't come back to reclaim your identity, since, if I assume it, it will be with your consent. Do you want other examples? A number of historical enigmas and *causes célèbres* are based on cases of resemblance. There's no need for me to list them all. There was the false Dimitri;[7] there was the affair of the necklace, with the resemblance between Marie-Antoinette and the girl Nicole Leguay.[8] In England there

7. There were actually three "false Dimitris" who claimed to be the Russian Tsarevich Dimitri Ivanovich, one of whom actually became Tsar in 1605-6.

8. The reference is to the famous "affair of the necklace" in 1785, in which Cardinal de Rohan was swindled out of huge sum of money with the aid of

was the extraordinary Tichborne affair, in which a cunning butcher's boy succeeded in passing himself off as the heir of an old family lost at sea. Until the last moment, and even after he had been sentenced by the judges, the mother of the vanished boy persisted in affirming that the impostor really was her son. And it was in England again that the astounding Druce Portland mystery unfolded,[9] based on the resemblance that existed between a great nobleman and a furniture-seller. It was a sensational story, with all the apparatus of the most effective novel: a double existence, sometimes a merchant, sometimes a duke, subterranean tunnels, false beards and wigs, a supposed burial, a coffin loaded with lead, a clandestine marriage, all sustained by a limited company....

"You can see that I've studied the question! All these examples prove that what I'm proposing to you is entirely practicable. I too hesitated at first, wondering whether my plan was anything but a puerile folly...."

"Admitting that your plan might be realized," Mercoeur interjected, "I can understand the advantages that I might obtain from it—but what's in it for you?"

"It's obvious that you don't know what it's like to get bored in a small provincial town," said Berjean, with a hint of bitterness. "My life had become absolutely intolerable since I began to think about this. I was devoured by the bizarre second-hand ambition I mentioned just now. I'm nothing in myself, but by involving myself in your existence, your celebrity, in this fashion, I'd become...I'd become something...an understudy of an illustrious man...only an understudy, it's true, but for a few hours, I'd have the satisfactions of self-respect that I can't obtain or myself, since I have neither a name, nor a fortune, nor a position, nor any ability, nor any energy....

"I'm a mediocre individual, I know...but a mediocre indi-

---

a Marie Antoinette lookalike named Nicola Leguay d'Oliva.

9. A *cause célèbre* that ran from 1897-1908, some thirty years later than the equally famous case of the Tichborne claimant.

vidual who resembles you physically. That's my only chance; all I have going for me is my resemblance to you, and having imagined that I might make something of it. Take note that I believe I'm intelligent enough not to commit any denunciatory gaffes...."

"You haven't mentioned the question of money," Mercoeur said, looking him in the face.

"It wasn't worth the trouble. I know that you'll do what's necessary. You'd have to pay the expenses of my existence here—which will be your existence too. Then again—but I assure you that it's secondary, because I'm entirely tranquil on that score—you're rich. I'll profit from your wealth, and if everything goes as we wish—and it can't go otherwise—you'll give me enough, won't you, to grow old tranquilly?"

He went on, with a hint of excitement that made his voice tremble: "You accept, then? I swear to you that we'll succeed. I repeat that I'm certain of it. That's what permits me to believe that I can talk to you with so much assurance. It seems to me, a little, that I'm talking to myself...and I'm not embarrassed; I have no timidity...you'll excuse me, won't you? And it's agreed: you accept."

"I...I don't know," said Mercoeur. "Frankly, I'm tempted. Even if it's only because of its extreme audacity, I find your project seductive. I like taking risks when it's for something worth the trouble. I'm precise, clear and considered, but that doesn't mean that I refuse to admit the romantic into my life and my plans. You've obviously imagined and refined all the details of the project. Would you care to explain them to me?"

"Well, here it is: first of all, it's necessary for us to 'rehearse' together for some time—a fortnight, perhaps three weeks, in order that I can completely assimilate your mannerisms and habitual gestures. You'll give me an hour or two whenever you have the time to spare. It's also necessary that you indicate to me exactly what attitude you strike in public, how you conduct yourself with those who are by your side in official ceremonies, the kinds of words you usually employ. I thought that I might perhaps make my debut at some banquet or other—one of minor importance, of course. There are doubtless numerous people at these official feasts who don't know you, or hardly know you...."

"Yes. I don't know any more odious way of wasting one's time. It's part of the ensemble of gestures, perfectly unnecessary so far as I can see, imposed on a man in government by what I call the representative error. You're then the center toward which fifty, sixty or a hundred private ambitions converge, which all adopt overtly the same name: devotion. Under every protestation, every eloquent formula of disinterest, one senses the same submerged phrase, which ends up coming to light, either brutally or cleverly veiled, according to the temperament of the interlocutor: *I want this!*"

"My God, you're a skeptic," said Berjean, a trifle alarmed.

"I'm skeptical with regard to people, not with regard to ideas, when they're worth the trouble...but as you see, I'm already thinking aloud with you.... It's bizarre, but I repeat, I can't help treating you as an intimate acquaintance. That extraordinary resemblance absolutely forbids me to treat you as a stranger. As it gives you assurance, it gives me confidence. I'm talking to you as if to myself, unable to help myself. That kind of confidence isn't habitual to me, however. Until now, I've only had it with one man...the only friend with regard to whom I'm not skeptical. You say that you'll begin with a banquet. So be it!"

"It's just that I too want to habituate myself. I'm not very timid, but after all, I'll certainly be less so facing a hundred people than one or two, given the particular circumstance.... I'll learn what has to be said. Do you talk much?"

"No," said Mercoeur, "I'm taciturn." He laughed, and added: "Don't forget that I don't eat very much and I only drink water."

"My appetite is ordinary," Berjean observed, "and I drink wine...not to excess, but with pleasure, Bah! I'll deprive myself, don't worry. And I see that it's necessary for me to take up smoking. A physician made me give it up it because of palpitations, but I can easily start again.

"I'll resume my explanation: I don't think we can continue to reside in this hotel; it's not comfortable enough for you, and will present grave practical difficulties. I'll rent an apartment, preferably on the ground floor, and I'll mention a brother I have, who travels a great deal, and sometimes comes to see me. That brother will be the other of us. To begin with, I won't be much use to you, but with practice, I'll eventually be able to double for you whenever you don't want to be 'mentally present.' I'll get to know my role quickly, depend on my zeal—and if any unforeseen difficulty comes up, I'll avoid it. The mechanics of substituting ourselves for one another won't be complicated. You don't live at the Ministry, do you?"

"No, I live alone, and simply, served by a single domestic, in a small apartment in the Rue de Lille, where I've lived for fifteen years."

"Perfect. When you have need of me, you leave your house, and take a cab some distance away to come to our apartment. I'm waiting for you, dressed like you, Claude Mercoeur: same black overcoat, same bowler hat, same correct cravat. I go take your place. You stay at home; you're free; you're me—and if it's for a long time, if you want to go out on your own behalf, you blacken your moustache and eyebrows, change your hairstyle, with a central parting, for instance, instead of brushing your hair back; you put on high-heeled shoes, yellow-tinted spectacles, a check overcoat, a soft hat, a Lavallière cravat. That will be my habitual costume. And you'll be Berjean while I'm Mercoeur....

"Soon, I hope to be able to give you several successive days of liberty and tranquil work. It will be necessary, as soon as we begin, to dismiss your domestic. He's certainly too familiar with your habits. Some detail of your behavior would surprise him when it's necessary for me to play your role at your home. A new domestic, who will see us alternately, will accept our mannerisms as a whole without realizing that they are those of two individuals. He might perhaps think you capricious, but that's all. For you to become Mercoeur again and me Berjean, the operation will simply be reversed...." Animatedly, he concluded: "Well…that's agreed, isn't it?"

Mercoeur shivered as if he were waking up from a dream. "Well, no. No, not yet! I want to think about it. I'm not refusing… why should I refuse, after all? Why not by tempted by this chance that will give me faculties that no other man has…incomparable possibilities! Listen, Berjean. I haven't decided anything. I want to consult a friend—the man I mentioned to you just now.…"

"But think—if anyone at all knows.…"

"Not him! He's reliable, as reliable as I am. I refuse to deceive him, and besides, we can't do anything if he's not in on it. He knows me too well. And then, I want him…the risk's mine, not yours!"

He became the authoritarian, almost brutal Claude Mercoeur again, whom no one thought of resisting.

"Good," murmured Berjean. "I understand…perhaps you want to take a precaution against me. I have nothing to say, and as I've told you everything with perfect frankness, I no longer have any hesitation, since you're sure of your confidante.…"

"It's half past midnight," Mercoeur said, suddenly. "I'm leaving. You'll have my response in three days."

He left.

Berjean remained pensive. He felt that he could not sleep.

Suddenly, he noticed Mercoeur's cigarette case on the table, which the latter had forgotten. He took out a cigarette and lit it, in order, at any rate, to get used to it.…

On Sunday morning, a letter arrived for him, which he opened with his heart beating rapidly. It contained the simple words: *I accept.*

He shivered profoundly; his face cleared; it seemed to him that he had been reborn. His stagnant years as a poor employee, riveted to his quotidian labor, devoid of hope, devotion of emotion and devoid of the unexpected, he discarded with the gesture of a man shrugging off a burden. He went to the murky mirror on the wardrobe to look at himself…to look at Claude Mercoeur, beneath his features.…

He went back to the table, took a piece of paper and wrote a letter, addressing it to his distant employer in the provinces:

Monsieur le Directeur,

I have the honor of asking you to accept my resignation. Reasons of health oblige me....

And the excitement that animated him did, indeed, make his hand tremble like that of an invalid agitated by fever.

III.
The Rehearsal

In a quiet old house on the Île Saint-Louis, on the quay facing the left bank, at the corner of a solitary little street, Raoul Berjean, after a second meeting with Claude Mercoeur, had rented a modest ground-floor apartment consisting of three small rooms, accessed by a narrow corridor, and a kitchen. The apartment door, under the arch of the house, was situated before the concierge's lodge; in consequence, one escaped the latter's professional curiosity, at least partially. The windows of the first two rooms overlooked the quay; the window of the third, which formed the corner of the house, and the kitchen window overlooked the side-street. As the windows were low and not barred, but only fitted with shutters, one could, if the need arose, make use of them to go out at night without asking for the door to be opened.

Berjean, whose imagination was somewhat romantic, as he had confessed himself, had been seduced by these details, all of whose advantages he had envisaged with satisfaction. They were truly the best possible circumstances for keeping the secret of his audacious pact with Claude Mercoeur very comfortably. They constituted a surplus of precaution, a guarantee of security that had filled him with enthusiasm.

Mercoeur, although he had initially thought the Île Saint-Louis a little too far away from the habitual center of his public existence, had finally come round to that opinion. Berjean had therefore rented it in his name, supplied with money by Mercoeur, had furnished the three rooms simply and comfortably, and had taken up residence a fortnight after the first meeting by the railings of Saint-Germain-des-Prés.

And it was there, in the middle room—the largest of the three, which Berjean had made into a kind of study-cum-living-room, that Mercoeur, Berjean and Dr. Vautier met one evening in December.

When Mercoeur had told him about the strange proposition of the man who resembled him, Dr. Vautier, after the initial moment of surprise, had reflected for some time. Then, looking at Mercoeur again, he had said: "Why not? Yes, why not? It's necessary to be wary of rejecting the strange and extraordinary out of hand simply for the reason that they are strange and extraordinary....

"What is being proposed to you is perhaps the means for the superior man that you are to become something more than a superior man...yes, to acquire a quasi-miraculous power...the power of duplication, of having, perhaps not twice as much time as other men, but at least a third more time. All the useless aspects of your existence will be suppressed, since someone else will take them on for you. He will help you to bear your burden by taking on the part that you don't need to bear yourself. Thus, you'll be able to last....

"I say last advisedly. You're exhausting yourself. However much strength, energy and faculties of resistance you have, you can't go on indefinitely if you don't get some rest; your labor is crushing you. It's a banal but absolute verity that human strength has its limits. Hours of respite are necessary, and without them, there might perhaps—probably, even—be an obligatory, brutal and diminishing halt imposed by illness and exhaustion. By demanding too much of yourself, you risk no longer being able to obtain anything at all one day or another. Hazard, and this man's ingenious idea, are offering you the possibility of that respite: an exceptional, prodigious, incredible chance.

"Take advantage of it...or, at least, try to take advantage of it. It's an unusual artifice that's being offered to you...unusual, yes, but one that has nothing base or vile about it, which does no harm to anyone. It's a protest—which will remain unknown, it's true—that you're making against the hours that your position obliges you to waste for society's sake. Anyway, in my opinion, a man of your value is the sole judge of what he ought to do. In order to do your work well, you're at liberty to adopt the means that are necessary."

"Then your opinion is that I ought to accept?"

"Yes. Besides which, if I were to say no, you'd accept anyway. Your decision is made. My advice is precious to you, I don't doubt, but it doesn't count by comparison with your own opinion. My dear friend, I'm telling you what I think, as always...I'll add that if you were not like that, you wouldn't be Claude Mercoeur....

"However...however, it's very evident that your opinion, and mine, are based on the express condition that this singular substitution is logically possible—I mean that it's necessary that the resemblance between this Raoul Berjean and yourself be perfect, absolute...and that's a question that only I can resolve, since I alone am in the confidence of your plan.

"Does this man really resemble you as much as he believes, and you believe? Only someone other than you, seeing you side by side, can decide. The experiment of the mirror that you carried out is encouraging, but insufficient. There are matters of bearing, attitude, mannerisms, the gestures that cannot, in spite of the closest resemblance, be identical. Will Berjean be able to copy them exactly?

"Experimentation will tell us that. I'll guide him, rectify his errors and indicate details to him of which you're certainly unaware yourself. During the weeks that separate us from his debut and my departure, I'll bring him up to speed, so to speak—

and if we don't achieve perfection, well, it will be necessary to give up. Based on what you've told me about this man, however, I hope that he'll succeed. Anyway, for the very reason that it's so unusual, your plan defies suspicion; it would require some gross imprudence on the part of your double, or a determination to betray you...."

"Neither of those things to be feared," said Mercoeur, swiftly. "He's an intelligent and serious fellow, and he'll do anything in the world to satisfy the ambition to be me for which he's turned his life upside-down without hesitation. And, on due reflection, it's worth the trouble for him. Consider his existence in the provinces, and consider the existence he'll have here.... As for betraying me, truly that's impossible, given that it would be so contrary to his evident interest. Then again, if he betrays me...well, I'll admit it—yes, frankly. I'll explain the motives that drove me to the deception...and my authority will increase, I'm sure, for having dared to do it."

"Perhaps. That's not absolutely certain. It could be that the scandal would be enough to sink you....but there are means of taking precautions in advance. Let's leave that aside, anyway; treason is improbable if the man has told the truth about his antecedents."

"I'll find that out. It's easy for me to obtain information about him by a roundabout route. No, no, he's sincere—you'll see. I sense it. I can be proud of him, as of myself."

Vautier made no reply. He promised himself to study Berjean, not only from the point of view of his resemblance to Mercoeur, but also from the moral point of view.

It was after that conversation that Mercoeur wrote to Berjean: *I accept.*

The double green velvet curtains were carefully drawn over the window; a coal fire was burning in the chimney and three large unshaded lamps were illuminating the room. Dr. Vautier, sitting in a leather armchair, was observing Mercoeur and

Berjean, who, similarly dressed and standing in front of him, were chatting together.

"It's perfect," he murmured. "Or at least, it soon will be." Aloud, he said: "You've made extraordinary progress, Monsieur Berjean. This is our fifth rehearsal, and you've already identified with your model almost completely. Yes, we're almost there. Don't forget, however, that characteristic gesture of Mercoeur's, when he suddenly shrugs his shoulders slightly and puts his head back, furrowing his brows slightly…and the hands in his jacket pockets…yes, like that—you've got it! Don't forget to make that gesture from time to time while listening to an interlocutor. Then again, get into the habit of being a trifle more abrupt in your movements—Mercoeur's always abrupt. He doesn't gesticulate much—look out for that; you have a tendency to do it a little more than he does—but his gestures are sudden and curt. Pay attention too, while speaking, to emphasize the words a little more. Your voice has a tendency to become softer, almost more musical, than his."

"Very well, Monsieur," said Berjean, meekly.

Mercoeur took a cigarette and lit it. Berjean did the same.

"Very good!" Vautier approved. "The two gestures are identical. Now, would the two of you care to sit down facing me, so the three of us can chat. Take note of your model's movements, Monsieur Berjean; he crosses his left leg over the right and inclines his body slightly to the right.… You haven't quite got it; the gesture is more abrupt.… That's right, this time! And don't forget that he always wipes his nose with his left hand… they're details, but nothing is negligible. Perhaps there'll be a meticulous observer among the people you meet.…

"Come on, I swear to you that success is certain. I'm a good observer; it's almost impossible to tell you apart. For me, evidently, the difference exists; perhaps it would be visible to anyone who studied you side by side, as I'm doing now—it's not absolute identity—but on seeing you successively, no one not forewarned would be able to doubt that they were seeing the same person. I'm not sure that, even forewarned, the dissimilarity would be discernible....

"Monsieur Berjean! Don't adopt that dreamy expression. Come on! Claude Mercoeur never has a dreamy expression. He's frequently silent, especially in the milieux in which you're going to replace him, and in that case, it's true, he has an absorbed expression, but his eyes are never vague and he never has that almost amiable half-smile that softens your features too much. When he's bored, he's aggravated and hides it, which doesn't give him a pleasant expression. Be careful, won't you? Excuse these perpetual lessons, but...."

"I'm infinitely grateful to you, Monsieur," said Berjean, deferentially. "My sole desire is to be worthy of the honor that Monsieur Mercoeur is doing me in accepting my modest collaboration...."

"What if we were to discuss this banquet a little," Mercoeur interjected. "I've given you the guest-list, Berjean, and described those to whom you'll be obliged to say a few words."

"I know it all by heart," said Berjean, "and I'm in the process of learning the speech I have to make. I'll recite it for you next time we rehearse, and you can rectify my intonations...."

"Be careful during the meal to cough sometimes," Dr, Vautier put in. "That will explain the slightly muffled tone that the excitement of your debut might perhaps give you...."

"And if anyone asks you any questions that are outside the range of those that I've indicated to you, just say: "We'll talk about that another time.""

Vautier started to laugh. "Do you hear that clear, curt intonation, which sends the tiresome or indiscreet person back to their seat? *We'll talk about that another time!*"

"Speaking of bores," said Mercoeur, "you'll certainly be assailed, Berjean, by a fellow name Bourfémont. You know him, Vautier—our old school friend. He'll be there because he gets in everywhere. He's a fat clean-shaven chap with rosy cheeks, a black moustache and a shiny skull, decorated, elegant and self-important, who has a mania for reminding me of all kinds of childhood memories that are utterly indifferent to me and that I have, in any case, completely forgotten. It's true…I have so many things of immediate interest in my mind that they've chased all the petty details of the past out of my head—I can't even remember the names of our teachers.…"

"You've cleared a space in which to lodge everything that's presently useful," said Vautier. "It's an excellent thing to forget; one doesn't notice oneself growing older as much. But as for me, my friend, there are things about the past that I haven't forgotten.…" Mercoeur interrupted him with a gesture, but he concluded: "Don't worry, I don't want to talk about my gratitude again—but you know that I've told Monsieur Berjean. Yes, the other evening while we were waiting for you…I wanted him to know in order that he could have confidence in me, as in you.…"

He had also done it in order that Berjean would know that he was being observed and studied by someone who had the most absolute devotion for Claude Mercoeur.

"That imbecile," Mercoeur continued, "by which I mean Bourfémont, has a habit of heaping me with excessive eulogies and protestations of friendship. Among all our former comrades, he's forgotten those who've succeeded. He positively bores me to death. Treat him coldly. He'll address you as *tu* repeatedly. Don't reciprocate. He'll make allusions to a certain promise. Tell him that he has to be patient. In any case, it's a promise I never made, but he hopes to make me believe it. It's a matter of the rosette he covets, and won't get, at least from me, for it would be unjust, since he had no entitlement to it and would be taking the place of some worthy fellow who has, to whom the distinction would be useful in his career and who yearns for it to the point that it makes him ill. So, be cold and cut short his flatteries, which are usually so excessive that it would make me look positively ridiculous if I seemed to be listening to them.…"

"I'll tell him that an incense burner ought not to be used as a club," said Berjean.

"Not bad, for a minor provincial employee," Vautier remarked. "Let's see—we still have a few minutes before we part. Let's chat together about something trivial—the weather, the political situation, the latest play that none of us has seen...."

"There's going to be a gala at the Opéra in February, to mark the visit of the Emperor of Japan," Mercoeur said. "You can take my place, Berjean."

"I'm under your orders. But tell me, Monsieur Mercoeur, since you want me to spend the night at your home after this dinner, which will be my debut, and only come to find you here tomorrow morning so that you can go to the ministry, whether it will be necessary to make a preliminary visit to your apartment."

"Of course. You can come one evening with your spectacles and your moustache dyed black. You can come up without speaking to the concierge—my domestic will be out...and I'll dismiss him in order to replace him with another, as we said, on the eve of your debut...."

"Monsieur Berjean, Monsieur Mercoeur never smoothes his moustache the way you're doing at present," Vautier put in. "But I beg you, let's not talk business any more. Let's chat—let yourselves have a familiar conversations. Let's see, Mercoeur, do you think a woman—I mean an honest woman, naturally— ought to be flirtatious or not, or to what extent? Give us your opinion—Monsieur Berjean and I will respond."

Mercoeur burst out laughing, and all three of them began to chat, initially with the hint of awkwardness that hinders and contrived conversation, but then in a more relaxed manner. Vautier, while making an occasional contribution to the conversation, observed the two men. As usual, Mercoeur was brusque and trenchant, not only in his tone but also in the thoughts he expressed. Berjean, whose opinions differed from his, gradually became animated, and the nuanced reserve of respect that he had maintained at the outset dissipated. He contradicted Mercoeur with a certain verve.

"We can leave it there, if you like," Vautier said, finally. "It's time to go. Monsieur Berjean, I have one serious observation to make to you: be careful. You're witty, and you show it; you let yourself shine easily. You're spontaneous and clever, and you say amusing things. Avoid that with care...."

There was a brief silence, Berjean had smiled lightly, and seemed a trifle embarrassed.

Mercoeur, initially surprised, looked at Vautier without benevolence. "My dear friend," he said, finally, trying to adopt a detached tone. "Is it really true that I lack wit to that extent?"

Vautoer looked him in the face. "I don't say that you lack wit, but you don't have that much—or, at least, you don't show it. No, old chap, you can take offence if you want, but you know full well that I'm not inclined to flatter you idiotically. You're never witty when you talk. You say what you mean, clearly, and, when necessary, eloquently. You have forcefulness, bitterness, irony, but you don't have what people call sparkling conversation. You know that as well as I do, and you've told me a thousand times that in your opinion, a sparkling conversationalist is the worst kind of bore.

"That opinion is vexing for Monsieur Berjean, who has the propensity to be a sparkling conversationalist himself, and would make you, if he were to let himself go, a reputation for wit that doesn't correspond at all to your personality as it's known. That's all...now, don't either of you hold it against me. Let Monsieur Berjean take care to moderate his sallies and darts...and let's go, because it's late. My carriage is outside and I'll drop you at home, Mercoeur."

They took their leave of Berjean, put on their overcoats and left. Light snow was falling. They shivered in the bitter cold and quickly climbed into the carriage that was waiting for them, which moved off along the dark quay.

"Well?" asked Mercoeur.

"Don't worry—it will work."

"And you no longer think there's a possibility of a denunciatory gaffe, or some treason?"

"A gaffe—he's incapable of that; he's too clever. And he's equally incapable of any treason. Yes, I'm sure of it. The other evening, when I was alone with him, he handed me a piece of paper…it was a signed confession that he had stolen from me. *This way*, he said, *you'll no longer have any doubt about my sincerity. I'm putting myself in your hands by accusing myself falsely. I know that Monsieur Mercoeur trusts me, but your friendship is more suspicious than his self-interest. You have a weapon against me that should now inspire every confidence in me."*

"And what did you do?" asked Mercoeur, after a pause.

"I burned the piece of paper. But now I trust him. The man's sincere.…"

"Everything he told me about himself has been completely verified by the information I've obtained," Mercoeur observed. "No, there's nothing to fear…that was always probable…definitely, then?"

"It will work," said Vautier. "Don't worry."

"Finally, I can live a little," murmured Mercoeur, leaning back in the carriage.

And, indeed, for him, as for Berjean, a new life was opening up, in which neither of them—the one in spite of his powerful intelligence, the other in spite of his ingenious flexibility and inventive mind—was able to recognize that there was a danger.

IV.
Gilberte Heurlize

Throughout the time that the strange pact proposed one foggy night by Raoul Berjean to Claude Mercoeur lasted, no one had the slightest suspicion. None of those who approached the Minister Claude Mercoeur had any clue that it was not always the same man who occupied that eminent position. Perhaps someone occasionally remarked that the statesman's capacity for work was more astonishing than ever. A few flattering echoes published by the press and one or two caricatures representing Mercoeur as Atlas supporting the world of politics were the proof of it—but none of the other members of the Government, none of his political or social acquaintances, and none of his most immediate collaborators at the Ministry realized that "the most visible of politicians" had been duplicated.

Berjean stuck to his role unfailingly, with an incomparable composure, presence of mind and tact. That humble provincial employee, transported almost instantly to the top of the social ladder, was able to adapt himself to the situation with perfect mastery. He did not allow himself to be caught off guard by anything unexpected, and was as much Mercoeur as Mercoeur was himself, with an incontestable genius. And the situation was, in any case, so extraordinary, so far beyond anything that anyone might suspect, that it was shielded from suspicion by that very fact.

At first, Berjean, in accordance with the agreed plan, only took Mercoeur's place for fairly short periods of time, when the Minister simply needed to be somewhere to represent his high office. Then, quite rapidly, success made both of them bolder, and Berjean became Claude Mercoeur with increasing frequency. He had assimilated the latter's mannerisms to ultimate perfection; he worked hard on imitating his handwriting, and rapidly succeeded—and, on Claude Mercoeur's specific instructions, signed documents on his behalf. After a few weeks, having been initiated into current affairs and administrative procedures, he was even able to take charge almost entirely of the official life that the man whose double he was had previously borne on his own. Mercoeur's uncle—his only relative, a magistrate in Algeria—came to Paris, saw Mercoeur twice and Berjean three times, and left again without suspecting anything.

Claude Mercoeur's life while he was Raoul Berjean was largely unknown. Prudently, he only described it in vague and indirect terms in the rare letters that he addressed during that period to Dr. Vautier, who was then in America. He had always been rather uncommunicative in epistolary terms, and he only allowed himself, in writing to that intimate friend, to indicate a few impressions and relate one or two incidents. In order to comprehend, it was also necessary to be aware of the situation.

That the hours of solitude and liberty thus acquired by the man who had previously been a slave to his public life quickly became very dear to him is beyond doubt. While he worked reflected or relaxed in the little ground-floor apartment on the Île Saint-Louis, with his moustache blackened, clad and coiffed like the man whose identity he was assuming, he experienced a serene satisfaction whose value he appreciated more every day. During the day, he generally avoided leaving his dwelling or, at least, the quiet island. He liked it, so ancient, silent and solitary. He liked its gray stones, its trees, its large houses dormant in their solemnity, its streets along which no one passed, and its quays, to which he went at dusk, surprised by so much calm, leaning on his elbows into order to watch the mute water flowing down below, sparkling with reflected light. He laughed at himself a little, in discovering these joys and taking delight in them. His thoughts acquired more amplitude there; repose renewed them; he had never felt more himself than in plying that humble role of an obscure unknown living without ambition. In the evenings, quite often, he left the island to go and dine in a modest restaurant in the Latin Quarter. Sometimes, after dinner, he sat in one of the cafés on the Boulevard Saint-Michel, where there was light, gaiety and noise—and he thought about Berjean, taking his place in the meantime at some official reception.

One evening, on a table next to his own, Mercoeur heard three young men talking about him, with regard to a speech on general politics that he had made two days before in Parliament, and which had attracted considerable attention.

"Mercoeur's very good," one of them said. "He's determined—he knows where he's going. He's the only Statesman we have."

"Perhaps," said another. "I'm not so sure. He's succeeded too soon. I don't trust these young prodigies. Everyone praises his capacity for work, yes, but he works too hard. He has no life. He has no experience. To be a leader of men, it's necessary to know life." Having said that, he struck a pose. He was blond and handsome. He was not yet twenty. A young woman came in and sat down next to him. She was pretty.

Mercoeur thought that it was true, that he had never lived, never having had the leisure to do so, absorbed for twenty years exclusively by his work, his ambition, his career. As he had said to Vautier, he had not even had time to love. No youthful memory, tender or cruel, loomed up in his past; he could not see any female face in his long, austere existence. It occurred to him that he had, in all probability, already lived more than half his life; he thought that in ten years he would be fifty, and then it would be too late…and for a few moments, he wondered whether he might have been mistaken, whether the meaning of life might not be where he believed that he had found it.…

A bright and beautiful face came into his mind, with luminous gray eyes, a fresh mouth and a white forehead gripped by a heavy mass of black hair. It was the face of Gilberte Heurlize.…

Mercoeur was astonished. Was he in love with that woman, whose image imposed itself on him in that fashion? He had not encountered her for some time, since Berjean was now replacing him at the official soirées to which she often came. The daughter of a senator whose had been a Minister, and for five years the widow of a diplomat, she had maintained all her connections in the political world.

He shrugged his shoulders slightly, though. Was he becoming sentimental? The role of juvenile lead hardly suited him, and he certainly ought not to risk it with regard to a woman who affirmed that she had no wish to remarry, and who had never shown any interest in him other than that one takes in a man in the public eye, even if he is old or ugly. He would never dare to say anything to her, he knew full well; a fearful timidity and a suspicious pride that could not bear the idea of a rejection had always prevented him.…

With a slight effort he expelled the image and overcame his emotion. He left the brasserie and, along the solitary streets, in the starry March night in which there was a premature hint of spring, he went back to the Île Saint-Louis.

*

Dr. Vautier had left Paris at the end of December, fully reassured on the subject of the consequences of the Mercoeur-Berjean association. He knew that Mercoeur had nothing to fear. Indeed, during the months of January, February and March, the association functioned without a hitch, to the satisfaction of Mercoeur, who was free, and Berjean, who tasted the joys of self-esteem, doubtless of a somewhat artificial nature, but keen nevertheless. Compared with his present existence, his former life seemed to him to be a dull nightmare. He plunged delightedly into the new world that Mercoeur was fleeing with no less equal delight.

It was on the third of April that the great charity sale organized for the flood victims of the Midi was held at the Ministry of Marine, in the large red and gold drawing rooms with the famous tapestries, which the Minister, Admiral Lestangle, had put at the disposal of the organizing committee.

Madame Gilberte Heurlize was a member of that committee, and was manning one of the most important counters. Like all the other ladies, she had obtained lots from all her relatives, had sent invitations to all the people she knew, and was counting on the attendance of a large number of people in the world of politics. She was counting especially, and above all, on the presence of Claude Mercoeur, who, at the last soirée at the Spanish embassy, had made her a formal promise to come.

Would he keep that promise? Would he even remember it? He was absorbed by so many preoccupations of every sort, which took up almost every minute of his time...and yet, deep down, Gilberte was sure that he would not be content to send his contribution, but that he would come in person, that he would come for her sake....

For several weeks he had not been the same, with regard to her. Now, every time he encountered her, he seemed glad, and in her company he seemed amiable and attentive, showing her a sympathy and admiration—very discreet, of course—that she could not help but notice....

He was no longer the brusque and reserved Claude Mercoeur,

absorbed and indifferent, who, for such a long time, had disconcerted Gilberte while interesting her so keenly....

From the opening of the sale onwards, she waited for him,
a trifle emotional. She knew that she was beautiful, and was
careful of her beauty—for herself, until now, but today, for
Claude Mercoeur. She was wearing a dark blue, satin dress with
subtle pleats, decorated with scintillating embroideries; a capacious tulle capeline, also blue pressed her black hair down over
her forehead. She was particularly pretty; she caught glimpses
of herself in mirrors; she knew it by the gazes that rested upon
her. At thirty she had retained a girlish complexion, as she had
retained the perfect lines of her slender figure....

She was astonished to find herself so emotional in waiting
for that man. Was it because of his position, more powerful
with every day he occupied it? Because of his popularity and
power? She wondered...but no; someone else in the same position, having the same power, would not have inspired the same
emotion in her. No dream of ambition played any part in it; she
did not like ambition. Was it, then, for himself? Why only now,
when she had known him for such a long time?

A murmur ran around the drawing rooms. There was a stir in
the crowd. "Mercoeur...it's Claude Mercoeur!"

He appeared, the image of physical and intellectual strength,
with his solid build in his simple clothes, his powerful head, his
aquiline features and his penetrating eyes, dark and shining. A
group was forming around him, of people avid to greet him, to
show themselves beside him. Rapid and abrupt, but always courteous, and almost smiling today—which rarely happened—he
advanced, shaking countless hands.

He went to greet the chairwoman of the committee, who
was not selling, and who was Madame Delaherse, the wife of
the President of the Council. On seeing him, she felt a slight
constriction in her heart; she knew that Mercoeur would replace
her aging husband at the first opportunity. Without allowing
any of the resentment of those who are on the way out for those
who are up and coming to show, however, she was charming,

thanking him effusively, and escorting him personally to the counter of the vice-chairwoman, the beautiful Madame Vonat, a resplendent redhead whose complexion, hair, teeth and costume brightened that entire side of the room. He paid a hundred francs for a hideous little engraving, which he put in his pocket without the embarrassment of wrapping.

Then, finally, he had the leisure to go to Gilberte Herlize's counter, in another room.

She was waiting for him, very calm now, having quickly overcome the flutter of emotion that she had experienced on seeing him go past the entrance of the drawing room at a distance. He bowed over the hand that she offered him.

"Thank you," she said to him. "I scarcely hoped...."

"Oh," he murmured, "I would have neglected anything"—he dared not say *for you*—"in order to come."

People were listening to them. Two young women, one in mauve and the other in pink, who were selling at Gilberte's counter, impressed by the great man's presence, were neglecting the fruitful commerce that they had been undertaking until then with such zealous grace and the determination with which they had been dredging the purses of all their visitors.

Mercoeur drew nearer to the long counter encumbered by an incongruous mixture of bazaar items and works of art, piled up pell-mell, strewn with the inevitable crop of pincushions that make every charity sale blossom.

"With your permission, I'll make my choice," said Mercoeur, after a short silence—and Gilberte detected a very slight disturbance in his voice, which, undoubtedly, she alone perceived, and which pleased her while also disturbing her.

She set about cheerfully showing off her wares, like a shopkeepers keen to make a sale. "We have objects of great beauty, tinplate, porcelain, wallets, cigarette cases...."

"Yes, perfect—a cigarette-case. That's the thing...."

He extended his hand toward an embossed leather case, which the young woman was touching simultaneously with her ungloved hand; their fingers touched. Mercoeur repressed a tremor, at the same time as his gaze met the large gray eyes that looked at him and did not immediately turn away.

"No, no, don't take that one," said Gilberte, rapidly, her voice perhaps a little less calm than usual. "It doesn't have a mono-gram—we've certainly got one with your initial...."

"Yes...precisely...here's one," he replied.

She looked at the object he was holding and started to laugh. "I don't think your name begins with a B, Monsieur Claude Mercoeur. Admit that you're distracted and that your thoughts are a long way from our poor sale." She was laughing to hide her disturbance. She was touched, and also rather proud, to have made an impression on such a strong man sufficient to make him flustered.

He shivered and collected himself. The cigarette-case he had picked up was marked with a B. What a mistake, indeed! Was he mad, to have suddenly made such an error? Was this young woman troubling him to the point of making him forgetful? Fortunately, the incident, over in a flash, had passed unnoticed by the public, who were flooding toward the room where a concert was about to begin.

"Undoubtedly!" he exclaimed. "What am I thinking? An M...and here's one!"

He had picked up another cigarette-case; again he looked at Gilberte, hesitated, and said, softly: "I can assure you, however, Madame, that it wasn't because my thoughts were far away from here...."

This time, she could not help blushing, but she made no reply. She accepted the folded banknote that he handed to her.

"What are you going to do over Easter?" he said, after a pause, in the tone of man making casual conversation. "Are you leaving Paris?"

"Oh yes, I've had several invitations. I haven't accepted any of them yet. I'm hesitant. I expect to be leaving soon, but I don't know where I'm going. One friend has asked me to go to Touraine, another wants to drag me to Biarritz, and my cousin Desmazis is insisting that I go and spent a few days with her on her estate at Fontainebleau…but I don't know yet.…"

"Ah!" he murmured. "You haven't decided. I regret that, for I have to leave, the day after Easter for Auxerre, for an inauguration. On my return I'll take advantage of the fact that the Chambres are on vacation to grant myself a little liberty, to stay in the country for a few days lest I end up making myself conspicuous by never taking any time off…I have the appearance of a good pupil zealous in his studies. As I'll certainly choose Fontainebleau perhaps I'll have the good fortune that my sojourn will coincide with yours.…"

He interrupted himself. A huge lady wearing too much make-up precipitated herself toward them in a whirlwind of variegated silks, exuberantly.

"How late I am. Kiss me, my little Gilberte! Very happy to see you, Monsieur le Ministre, illustrious man…oh, your last speech! What a marvel! I was in the public gallery, folding myself up so as not to applaud. That poor Frappel, you certainly nailed his trap shut! Gilberte, my dear, I'm sick with shame. I promised you to be early! I was stupidly delayed, my seamstress turned up…but we'll make up for lost time. And tell me, it's agreed, isn't it? You're coming to Touraine! We're counting on you. I'll pick you up in the car on Tuesday."

Gilberte Heurlize assumed a despairing expression. "I'm so sorry, my dear friend. You know that my cousin has already invited me to Fontainebleau; she was so insistent that I ended up giving her a formal promise…just yesterday. Family obligations, alas! I was just saying exactly that to Monsieur Mercoeur. I have to leave the day after tomorrow.…"

Once again she looked at him, and saw all the joy and gratitude in his eyes; she smiled imperceptibly, very cheerfully, very softly. He bade her farewell and left. Around him, as at his entrance, he heard the crowd whispering: "Claude Mercoeur… that's Claude Mercoeur."

For the first time since he had imagined the pact that made him into someone else, which he had put into practice with so much mastery, he saw the downside. A sudden, bitter pain compounded out of jealousy, humiliation and rebellion, took possession of him and made him go pale....

His carriage was waiting for him outside the Ministry. He sent it away, and Raoul Berjean walked along the quays, in the mild freshness of the April evening, toward the Île Saint-Lois, where the real Claude Mercoeur, whose double he was, was waiting for him.

To calm the new emotions that were agitating him, Berjean walked for a long time. Deep in thought, struggling against contrary sentiments that were assailing him by turns, he went alongside the river without taking any account of where he was going. Suddenly, he realized that he had reached the Pont d'Austerlitz; he crossed over, went back down the Quai Saint-Bernard on the left bank, and, in the falling dusk, reached the Île Saint-Louis by means of the Pont de la Tournelle.

Mercoeur, whose role he had been playing for three entire days, was waiting for him, reading. On seeing the man who was the reality of which he was only the appearance, Berjean undoubtedly experienced the bitter jealousy to whose first attack he had fallen prey even more cruelly. He was able, however, to conceal it. The authority that emanated from Mercoeur resumed its empire over him. With the habitual, respectful and familiar tone of a trusted employee making his report, he gave Claude Mercoeur a detailed account of what he had done, and the news that he had received during the three days that he had been taking his place.

Mercoeur listened attentively, interrupting from time to time with a question or an observation.

"My dear Berjean," he said suddenly. "I forgot—I have a small observation to make to you. There's mention once again of my wit in the morning papers. It appears that I was very witty at yesterday's reception at the Hôtel de Ville. What have you been saying? I beg you not to forget the advice of my friend Dr. Vautier...." With a hand gesture, he cut off the reply that Berjean was about to make. "Let's leave it at that," he went on. "Just don't forget that I don't have the reputation of a man of the world. What about the charity sale that you haven't mentioned?"

"I went to it," said Berjean. "I was getting to it. You've received the thanks of Madame Delaherse. She told me that her husband, the President of the Council, isn't suffering as much from his asthma today. Madame Vonat desires your protection for a young cousin who wants to go into the diplomatic service, and she reminded you about a decoration promised to her brother-in-law. She was looking very beautiful. You bought his engraving from her for a hundred francs."

"It's frightful," said Mercoeur.

"And you bought this cigarette-case from Madame Heurlize...."

Had Berjean's voice changed when he mentioned Madame Heurlize? Or had Mercoeur, on hearing the young woman's name, experienced a visible excitement? Something passed between them: a kind of brief, indefinable, imprecise sensation that, for the duration of a lightning-flash, was like a revelation of mutual hostility.

"Madame Lalandelle arrived very late," Berjean went on. "She congratulated you for having nailed Frappel's trap shut—her words. She was in the gallery. That's all, I think. Oh, I forgot. As you instructed me to do, you've told several people that after the inauguration at Auxerre, you're going to take a few days off, probably in the vicinity of Fontainebleau. When am I leaving?"

"Soon. It's a trifle excessive never to grant myself the slightest respite. People are mocking my relentless labor. And thanks to you, that respite—relative, at least, for annoyances are no more lacking in the provinces than in Paris—will give me a good week of liberty here....although it might, perhaps be a little imprudent. What if something unexpected crops up, or if, by chance—it's improbable, but even so—you were to fall ill out there?"

"My health is perfect." Berjean protested, swiftly, "and I'd still have the strength to take the train or an automobile to return here and become Berjean again. I'll do the same in case of some unexpected event—that's already happened, remember, on two or three occasions, and it won't be any more difficult for me in Fontainebleau than in Paris."

"Yes, undoubtedly. However, I confess that those few days in the country are tempting me, I'm not sure why, and if I didn't have so much work to do…but all things considered, it's impossible.…"

Mercoeur had risen to his feet. He changed his clothes in the next room, in a matter of minutes, and removed the dye from his moustache.

In the meantime, Berjean had resumed the appearance that the other was abandoning.

"Until Saturday evening," Mercoeur said to him. "I have a Council meeting tomorrow, parliamentary questions the day after—I have to be there for those two days.…"

Mercoeur went out rapidly. He crossed the bridge, stopped a carriage at the corner of the Boulevard Saint-Germain, and gave his address.

He was thoughtful. A dull irritation, whose cause he could not contrive to discover, was agitating him. Abruptly, he perceived that it was with Berjean that he was irritated. A resentment had arisen within him with regard to the man who was so often, and with so much success, himself. Was it such a trifling thing to be Claude Mercoeur, then, that this petty provincial employee could so easily put on the appearance? Certainly, it was conditional on that extraordinary physical resemblance, but it was not in his physical appearance that the powerful personality of Claude Mercoeur resided.…

He lit a cigarette and, offended, wounded and humiliated by the fact that he had been duplicated so easily, he meditated on the vanity of glory.

V.
Love

That evening, in the elegant bedroom of the small apartment he was occupying in a luxury hotel, Raoul Berjean dressed with particular care. With the naivety of an adolescent eager to please, who thinks that a neatly-tied cravat and well-groomed hair will contribute to impressing a woman with whom he is smitten, he spent a time in front of his mirror that Claude Mercoeur, had he known about it, would have thought ridiculous. That, at least, was what Berjean said to himself as he put on his smoking jacket. He also said, it is true—and with some irritation—that the opinion of Claude Mercoeur was a matter of perfect indifference to him.

For a week, at Fontainebleau, he had been Claude Mercoeur. He had seen Gilberte Heurlize every day, and often twice a day, for, in addition to the visits he had made to the home of the young woman's cousin, Madame Desmazis—who was entirely delighted to welcome the great man—he had often encountered Gilberte by chance: by a chance so fortunate and repetitive that it was doubtless favored by one or other of them, and probably both of them, that they met in that fashion.

He was now in love with the young woman: a profound love full of delight and bitterness, which he had not even tried to resist, so irresistibly did he feel it. He had not dared thus far to make any direct confession or to implore a response, but only two days separated him from his departure and he knew that he had to speak before leaving Fontainebleau.

He went out at half past seven in order to go to Madame Desmazis' house. She was hosting a dinner in his honor. She was exhibiting him with a triumphant ostentation to all her relatives. She had invited friends from Paris expressly so that they could see her in familiarity with the illustrious statesman. Berjean lent himself to it with a generosity that Claude Mercoeur, in his entire career, had never shown to anyone whatsoever, but

Berjean would have done much more in order to get close to Gilberte. People thought that Claude Mercoeur was being humanized, becoming less distant and less cold, acquiring a pleasure for worldly pleasures. Berjean was not at all worried about betraying the person he was playing on that point.

Personally, moreover, he did not have the lofty savagery with which Mercoeur, before their pact, had defended his time. He liked society, and he believed in high society; he was happy to appear there, to be admired, fêted, all-powerful—him, the poor little provincial employee who had never known anything but dinners at the cheap eating-house and dismal soirées at which, disgusted with the paltry attractions of a local café-concert, he had run aground in his solitary lodging, drunk on ennui and impotent aspirations.

At Madame Desmazis' house that evening he found a dozen people for whom Bourfémont, Mercoeur's former comrade at school, had shamelessly solicited from Gilberte the favor of being invited. He hoped to take advantage of the intimate gathering, in which his illustrious acquaintance would certainly be more accessible than elsewhere, to conquer the red rosette that he coveted with an ever-increasing ardor, now inordinate and almost morbid.

Maneuvering with guile and audacity, he succeeded, after dinner, as soon as they had gone into the drawing room, in trapping the minister in a propitious corner. With a few banal phrases of obsequious admiration, he made allusions, veiled at first, to the object of his desire. Berjean, inclined to mockery, feigned not to understand. Bourfémont persisted and, animated by the despair of seeing the distinction without which life was devoid of charm for him, drawing away yet again, he risked a direct request.

With sweat on his brow, so tremulous with emotion that he stammered and only succeeded in pronouncing inconsequential phrases in which the informality of their former camaraderie was mingled with pompous formulas of official politeness, he spoke about the coronation of his career, his wife, to whom it would give so much pleasure, the services that he would be capable of rendering if encouraged, the rights of a friendship that dated from the happy times when they had been side by side of the school benches—yes, those childhood friendships were the only sure and durable ones!—and he recalled with pride a punch in the eye that Mercoeur had landed on him when they were both in the sixth. He talked at length about that entitlement of glory, then talked about his wife again, his children who would be so proud....

Suddenly, Berjean, aggravated, remembered Mercoeur's habitual phrase, and with the latter's cutting voice, he said: "We'll talk about that another time"—and turned his back.

The unfortunate Bourfémont, who knew what that meant, twitched in agony. He thought he had almost attained his goal......

At that moment, as Bourfémont drew away, crushed, Berjean saw Gilberte Heurlize nearby. She was looking at him with a hint of astonishment.

"Oh, what a harsh tone!" she said to him. "I scarcely recognized your voice. That's the Minister's voice, isn't it?"

He blushed slightly, and, troubled—as he was every time he was in the woman's presence—he could not find anything to say but: "I didn't know that you could hear me...." And after a momentary pause, he added, while trying to smile: "There's no Minister here. Before you, there's a man who...."

He did not finish his sentence. "Yes, yes," said Gilberte. "Ask that unfortunate Bourfémont, who was imploring you, whether or not there's an all-powerful Minister here."

Berjean shrugged his shoulders. "He persists in trying to obtain what it would not be just to grant him."

"My God," she said, "I believe I know what he was asking of you, and truly it would be a charity. He'll certainly fall ill if he doesn't get it. His wife is one of my friends; I like her very much. And you know, when an injustice does no harm to anyone, and might cause so much joy, I find it excusable."

"Well, it's done," he said, forgetting that he was disposing of a power that was not his. "Since you desire it, it's done. I'm only too happy...."

He had manifested so much joy in obeying her, in putting himself under her orders, in proving to her how much power she had over him, that the young woman blushed, and did not know what to say.

Without transition, he continued in a low voice: "I'm leaving the day after tomorrow, you know, and you're going to return to Paris too, I need to talk to you before then; I need to see you in private. Can I do that tomorrow? Please, it's necessary that I talk to you...."

Her eyes lowered, she replied in a low voice: "Very well, come at three o'clock. I know that my cousin won't be here."

Before moving away, she looked up at him. A glance was exchanged between them that left them quivering—and both of them knew that their interview the following day would not tell them anything more. Hearts beating, however, they thought about it incessantly until it took place.

The next day, when Berjean rang the bell at the gate of Madame Desmazis' villa, the door of which was opened to him by an old domestic, who immediately went away, he saw Gilberte appear on the front steps. She came down lightly and lithely, and came to meet him.

"Let's stay in the garden, shall we?" she said, in an unsteady voice. He was experiencing an emotion of his own that tightened his throat and made his hands shake.

They went along one of the pathways.

It was a large garden, half-wild. In the vicinity of the house flowering bushes surrounded a square pond on which swans were swimming. Statues separated the green thickets. Further away, under the large trees, the grassy paths plunged into the shade of unkempt syringas. It had rained in the morning, and droplets were still trembling on the leaves, but the April afternoon, moist with water evaporated by the blazing sun, was as warm as summer.

Side by side, silently, Gilberte Heurlize and Raoul Berjean

moved through the solitary shade of the pathways. Berjean was dominated by a force superior to his will. He was clearly aware of the folly of his actions, and into what abyss of bitterness, suffering and humiliation he was about to throw himself, but he also knew that no power of Earth could prevent him from telling the woman that he loved her....

He hesitated, however, retained by the sole dread that she might suffer, later, when she learned...for how could he not tell her?

But she was there, beside him, already his, since she loved him—he had no doubt about that. The world, and life, were contained for him in the present moment, in the imperious surge of his passion, in the proud intoxication of conquering the confession of that love....

Gilberte saw that he was troubled. She attributed it to the only cause she was able to suspect, and was deliciously moved by it. Was not that timidity, in such a man, the striking proof that he loved her?

Finally, he spoke, in a low voice, brusquely, without daring to look at her.

"You know why I've asked you for this interview? You know, don't you?" And without waiting for a reply, he went on: "I'm troubled, and I'm not used to that. Excuse me...I can no longer find the words that I wanted to say to you. With you, I no longer feel myself. I can no longer find myself. I'm absorbed in you. I no longer have any presence of mind. I must seem ridiculous to you, during these minutes that I'm walking, silently, by your side. However, I said to you, I swear, eloquent words when, alone and thinking of you, I dared to speak to you...now here I am, like a timid child. Tell me, can I speak? You know what I want to say to you. For your sake, and mine, prevent me from saying it if...if you disapprove...."

They had both stopped at the entrance of an old bushy arbor. She raised her eyes. He found once again the gaze that she had directed at him the previous evening. He forgot Mercoeur and Berjean. He was a man facing a woman.

"I love you, Gilberte," he said, in a voice that was almost hoarse with emotion. "I love you with every fiber of my being. I love you to the point at which life without you would no longer have any meaning for me. I love you...."

She was in front of him, standing up straight, in the soft and vaporous light. He had never seen her so beautiful. She had not turned her bright eyes away, but a slight blush rose to her cheeks and her breast was rising more rapidly.

"I love you too," she said, simply.

"Then you consent too share my life?" he stammered, trembling with joy.

"Yes. I did not know you before. Now I know you, and I love you."

"I've loved you since the first day I saw you...."

She smiled gaily. "And you waited such a long time to tell me."

"Such a long time! But...."

"But it's at least five years, perhaps six, since we first met. I don't say that we knew one another...."

"Five or six years...."

He had shuddered, stupefied. He remembered, shivered in horror, and stammered: "Oh yes...yes...five or six years...but indeed, we didn't know one another. That's what I meant."

"No, it's true," she went on, pensively. "I would never have suspected that there was inside you...." She stopped.

"That there was inside me...?" Berjean queried, a crazy hope making him go pale.

"Well...you. Yes, the person that has been revealed to me... and that many others don't know. A new, more human Claude Mercoeur, more alive, capable of loving, of making himself loved. I would have thought, before that...revelation...that nothing in the world could interest you but your work and your career."

"Let's leave my work and career to one side," he interjected, almost violently. "It's not for that reason that you love me, is it? Forget that I'm Claude Mercoeur. Don't you love me for myself?"

She smiled again. "But your career is you. Come on, I can't forget who you are! I'm only a woman, you know, and I'm very proud to be loved by a man whom all the world admires, and I've long admired myself. There's a confession that proves my frankness…and my vanity, no?"

"However, if I were unknown, obscure, devoid of power or reputation, wouldn't you love me?" said the unfortunate man.

"But then you wouldn't be who you are. Your intelligence, your energy, your genius are as much a part of you as your facial features. What a singular question!"

She looked at him in astonishment. He trembled, at having gone too far. Once again the delicious intoxication of the moment overwhelmed him. Again, at length, he told Gilberte that he loved her, that he had never loved anyone but her.

She listened, charmed and palpitating, to his words of love. He gazed at her ardently. He gazed at her supple figure, the shape of her breasts beneath the silk of her corsage, the voluptuous line of her lips, slightly parted over her pure teeth. He thought that he had conquered true glory, since it was for him that she was quivering with love. He took her in his arms, ardently, and leaned toward her—toward her mouth, which she gave him.

It was only when he had left Gilberte Heurlize, after that kiss, and also after having agreed the month of June for the date of their marriage, that Berjean began to appreciate in all its frightful plenitude the awfulness of his situation. Until then, the enchantment of loving and being loved had intoxicated him. Now, reality gripped him again: the strange and cruel reality that he had foolishly created.

He thought about the future. An anguished sweat chilled his forehead. He shivered in shame, horror and anger.

He loved Gilberte; she loved him. Who did she love? Who would she love when she knew?

And he understood that he felt an invincible hatred for Claude Mercoeur.

VI.
The Mystery of the Île Saint-Louis

It was the nineteenth of May, and some weeks had passed since the trip to Fontainebleau.

Early that morning, in the vast and severe ministerial study in which Claude Mercoeur, six months earlier, had opened the third letter written in green ink—the one that had been efficacious—in the presence of Dr. Vautier, the usher was unhurriedly assuring himself that everything was in order when Claude Mercoeur came in, abruptly and rapidly, as was his custom.

He silenced the usher with a gesture when the latter, excusing himself for being late, respectfully remarked that Monsieur le Ministre was earlier than usual.

Mercoeur glanced at the clock. "Do I have the newspapers?" he said. "Good. Leave me alone. Don't disturb me for any reason. When Monsieur Rivel gets here, tell him that I'm waiting for him.

"I won't forget, Monsieur le Ministre, "and Monsieur le Chef du Cabinet certainly won't be long. He's very punctual, and...."

The usher, an old servant, experienced and faithful, who had seen many ministers come and go, was incurably loquacious. Dismissed by an imperious wave of Mercoeur's hand, he hastened to disappear.

Alone, Mercoeur sat down at his desk. From the pile of daily newspapers he selected a broadsheet, which he unfolded with a slightly feverish motion.

He shivered slightly. At the top of a column a headline had struck his eyes. It read:

A MYSTERIOUS DEATH

A tragic event has caused a disturbance among the placid inhabitants of the Île Saint-Louis. Last night, shortly after midnight, two policemen of the Boulevard Sully section were approached by a man who seemed simultaneously prey to drunkenness and great excitement, who told them that a crime had certainly been committed in a ground-floor apartment on the quay near the Pont de la Tournelle. He explained, somewhat confusedly, that he had been walking along peacefully when he had heard, a short distance ahead of him, gunshots coming from the ground-floor apartment in question. He had approached in haste. Someone that was running in the direction of the Pont Saint-Louis, and whom he had tried to stop as he passed by, had knocked him down violently. Then he had run in search of help, in the opposite direction.

To begin with, the policemen, given his obvious state of drunkenness, had refused to believe his declarations, but in the presence of his insistence, they had followed him on to the deserted quay to the house he pointed out.

They had arrived just in time. On the ground floor, smoke was pouring out of the gaps in the shutters, and the glow of flames could be seen inside. They immediately opened the shutters, which were not locked, climbed through the rather low window, and extinguished the fire that had broken out in the room, but had not yet taken hold, without overmuch difficulty. On the half-burned carpet, in a pool of blood and amid the debris of an oil lamp whose glass reservoir had been broken, lay the inanimate body of a man. He was dead. His oil-soaked clothing had been consumed on his body; his hair and moustache were burned and he had large burns on his face. Near the right eye there was a terrible wound, which had shattered the skull. A large-caliber revolver, from which two shots had been fired, was on the floor beside the body.

The alarm had, of course, been raised. The concierge, who got up in haste, recognized the victim, in spite of the wounds disfiguring his face, as the tenant of the ground-floor apartment, Monsieur Raoul Berjean, who had been resident there since last autumn.

The initial observations suggested that the fire had been started by the fall of the victim, who collapsed, shot dead by himself or someone else. The lighted lamp, set on a little table, had broken and its oil, set alight, had spread out.

What happened? Was it murder or suicide? The investigation will tell us. A search is being conducted for the unknown man who was in the vicinity of the house where the drama unfolded and knocked over the passer-by who raised the alarm.

A note at the end of the article redirected Claude Mercoeur to the Latest News section.

The Île Saint-Louis Affair

The investigation has been actively pursued all day without yet producing appreciable results. If it was murder, robbery was not the motive, for nothing had been stolen from the victim's home. But the police do not seem to believe that it was murder, various indications opposing that hypothesis, and they do not seem to be lending much credence to the existence of the enigmatic individual who knocked over the only witness to the affair. The latter, a worthy cabinet-maker from the Faubourg Saint-Antoine named Prosper Boltin, is categorical in his affirmations, which he has repeated to us very forcefully, but he does not know exactly where he was when he was bowled over and would be absolutely incapable of recognizing the person who knocked him down; he does not even know whether it was a man or a woman. Indeed, he admits himself that he had dined that evening with his brother-in-law, a wine-merchant with a shop near the Pont-Neuf, and numerous libations had rendered him so cheerful that when he went across the Place du Parvis on the way home that police had cautioned him for singing too loudly.

It should be noted that no one in the house where the drama occurred heard anything. It is, admittedly, an old house with solid outer walls and thick partitions. In addition, the apartment situated above the ground-floor apartment is occupied by an old lady who is completely deaf. By a singular coincidence, the young maidservant who also sleeps in the apartment, suffering from toothache that evening, had stuffed her ears with cotton wool impregnated with camphorated oil and wrapped her head in a chin-strap, which rendered her as deaf as her mistress.

We have been able to interview the concierge, Madame Flein. Although still upset by the night's tragic event, she kindly informed us regarding her unfortunate tenant. He had rented the ground-floor apartment last November. He came, he said, from the provinces and wanted to recuperate and work in Paris. He represented him self as a rentier and gave the impression, according to Madame Flein, of someone who had just come into an inheritance and wanted a quiet life. He was also a taciturn man, although very courteous, and led a very orderly existence. The concierge saw little of him, because he could go in and out without passing her lodge. He did his own housekeeping and took his meals in local restaurants, without being a regular patron of any one in particular. No one ever asked to see him, and she believes that he had no visitors except, occasionally, that of a relative in the evening; Madame Frein could not specify whether it was a brother or a cousin.

Let us note that this relative, who is, it is thought, a commercial traveler, will doubtless only learn about the tragic death of Raoul Berjean from the newspapers. He is invited to make himself known as soon as possible to the Law, which hopes to obtain information from him capable of casting some light on this mysterious affair.

Having read that, Claude Mercoeur dropped the newspaper. He was pale, a bitter expression hardening his features. His eyes were staring straight ahead, unseeing. Mechanically, he took out a cigarette and struck a match. Suddenly, he started and shook his hand; he had not lit the cigarette and the dying match had burned his fingers.

He opened another newspaper, and then another. They all reported the Île Saint-Louis affair at some length under various headlines: *A Mysterious Affair; The Mystery of the Île Saint-*

Louis; Murder or Suicide? Tragic Enigma; Nocturnal Drama....

The interpretation of the facts differed, the details given sometimes being contradictory, but no item of information was revealed other than those contained in the first article.

A few papers hostile to the government insinuated that the police were pretending not to believe in the unknown man seen by Prosper Boltin in order to be able to conclude that it was a suicide, with the aim of not having to search for a criminal they would not be able to find—and they cited a number of examples of criminals who remained unpunished, commencing with Jud and Walder.[10]

Mercoeur pushed the papers away. There was a knock on the door. It was Rivel, his chief of staff, a tall, slim, dark-haired young man, decorated and elegant, with an intelligent, efficient and determined manner. In a few clipped words he apologized to the minister for having kept him waiting. He had been obliged to see the President of the Council before coming. He paused, and looked at the heap of open newspapers.

"I see, my dear Minister, that you've taken the trouble to read the reports that our friends and enemies have given of your latest speech on the subject of our economic future."

Mercoeur, who had not yet said a word, looked up at his interlocutor. "Our economic future?" he said, slowly, as if astonished. "The reports?"

Rivel seemed politely surprised. "I see that your thoughts have already passed on to something else, my dear Minister."

Mercoeur had already collected himself. "Evidently," he said, as authoritarian and abrupt as ever, "when a question is exhausted, and when one has got to the bottom of it as best one

---

10. Charles Jud, suspected of having committed at least one murder on the Paris-Mulhouse railway line, was sought by the Parisian police between 1860 and 1864, but evaded capture and thus acquired a reputation as a master of disguise, which inspired a good deal of crime fiction. "Arnold Walder" was the name attributed to a Swiss suspected of a double murder in the Faubourg St. Honoré in 1879, who was never arrested, apparently having left the country for New York.

can, it's necessary to forget it immediately and pass on to something else. Otherwise one wastes time needlessly. The President of the Council you said?"

For five whole days the Île Saint-Louis Affair excited the public. Favored by a lack of other events, and, in consequence, given considerable space by both the morning and evening press, it was possible to think that it might become a *cause célèbre*. The partisans of the murder hypothesis and those of the suicide hypothesis launched equally fervent polemics. Crowds of curiosity-seekers flocked to the old quay on the Île Saint-Louis to contemplate the house where the drama had taken place.

The concierge and the cabinet-maker were interviewed many times over, and know the proud joy of seeing their honest faces reproduced by all the national papers. Then they went back into the shadows. The Île Saint-Louis Affair was no longer interesting. Dr. Larmy, the medical examiner responsible for the autopsy of the man found dead concluded that it was suicide. The trembling hand of the despairing individual must have fired two shots before succeeding in hitting the target. It had also been proved that the revolver belonged to him, an armorer who had sold it to him testifying to that fact. In consequence, the drama became banal, and was replaced in the public interest by the excitement stirred up by a theft of antique jewels committed by a negro chauffeur, to the disadvantage of Mademoiselle Claudia Traive of the Comédie-Française. Only the policemen responsible for the investigation before the file was closed retained the memory of the mysterious relative who sometimes came to see Raoul Berjean while he was alive, and who had obstinately neglected to make himself known to the Law. They continued to search for him for some time to acquit their conscience, and then forgot about him.

On the twenty-fourth of May, the same day that Claude Mercoeur learned from the newspapers that the inquest opened on the Île Saint-Louis affair had concluded that it was suicide, he received a letter with an American postmark, which was from Dr. Vautier.

I'm finally returning, said the latter. *I'm eager to see you again, my dear friend. When you receive this letter, I shall be on my way, and will arrive in Paris at the end of the month.*

VII.
Who?

In spite of the calmness of his character and his habit of disciplining his impressions, when Vautier, on his return from America, heard about the mysterious drama of the Île Saint-Louis, he experienced an exceedingly violent and complex emotion. Anxiety was dominant therein—an anxiety all the more ardent because he only learned about the affair in the first instance from a brief article that simply announced the tragic death of Raoul Berjean.

Upset, to the extent that a man like him could be upset, Vautier lived through veritably nightmarish hours during the final phase of his return journey. All his personal concerns were effaced by comparison with that preoccupation. Mercoeur, the friend for whom he had an affection all the more profound because it was an exceptional sentiment for that cold heart mastered by intelligence, was never out of his thoughts. Perhaps Mercoeur had need of him, as the only person who knew about his connection with Berjean....

Vautier suffered in thinking that he had not been able to give his devotion to the man who must need it so badly. He examined the tragic event relentlessly, about which he now knew everything that the public knew; he applied his rigorous methods of scientific investigation to it, and imagined all the causes and effects that were in the domain of the possible, studying their implications one by one.

When he learned that the investigation, without discovering anything about the victim's double life, had concluded that it was a suicide, those of his anxieties that had been concerned with a public scandal afflicting Mercoeur were erased, but only in part. In the train from Le Havre that brought him to Paris he examined once again all the admissible hypotheses that he had already examined a hundred times over.

In Paris, when he arrived home, he found a note from Mercoeur.

My dear friend, I too will be very glad to see you again. Drop in at the Ministry as soon as you arrive; you'll either find me there or they'll tell you what time I'll be back.

The note appeared to Vautier to be written in a more nervous and negligent fashion that was Mercoeur's habit. He went to the Ministry right away, but Mercoeur was at a Parliamentary committee meting and Vautier was obliged to come back at the end of the day.

He was immediately introduced into the Minister's study. The latter came toward him, and shook his hand effusively.

"Well, my friend, was the voyage satisfactory? I've had echoes of it from your letters and the press. French science owes you a great deal of glory, my dear Vautier. I congratulate you officially and personally."

"There were times when I almost regretted having gone," said Vautier. In a significant tone, he added: "I dreaded that I might be needed here."

Mercoeuir drew nearer and lowered his voice. "You've heard, haven't you? I want to talk to you about that, as you can well imagine. I can't now; it's late and I have an official dinner this evening. I'm tied up all morning tomorrow; in the afternoon I'll be in the Chambre, and the next day too, undoubtedly. The political situation, as you've seen in the newspapers, is agitated. I don't know whether Delaherse is going to step down....in that case, it will be me...but that's not what I want to talk to you about, Vautier, as you know. Come to my house in the Rue de Lille early on Sunday morning. We'll be able to talk...."

"Agreed—but tell me right away whether there's anything for you to fear. My dear friend, I've never felt so much anguish as at the idea that you might perhaps need me, and that I wouldn't be able to prove my devotion."

"I had no need of you materially, Vautier. There's nothing to fear...but I needed my only friend morally.... Until Sunday, no?"

"Yes, until Sunday. And we'll also talk about your health—you don't look well...."

"I've been working very hard, but I'm quite well...."

Vautier withdrew, anxiously. Mercoeur seemed thin and pale, apparently afflicted by a contained nervousness—which might be explained by overwork, but in which Vautier thought he could detect the action of a torment, perhaps imperceptible to an observer who did not know the Minister as well as he did, but certain. Was Berjean's death, even if it had had no other consequence than imposing on Mercoeur all the obligations eluded during the existence of his double, sufficient explanation, after a fortnight, of that singular anguish and disturbance in such a strong man?

After his conversation with Mercoeur, Vautier was more agitated than ever by doubt. The delay imposed on his desire to know seemed to him to be immense.

He was unable to shake off his preoccupations until Sunday; they dominated all his actions. On Saturday, yielding to an irresistible impulse, he went to see Dr. Larmy, the medical examiner who had carried out the autopsy on Berjean and concluded that he had committed suicide.

Larmy, who had been Vautier's comrade during their internship, was flattered by the visit of his illustrious colleague. Having talked to him about his official functions, Vautier had the satisfaction of hearing him raise the subject of the Île Saint-Louis case himself. Without revealing his own interest in the affair, her obtained the most minute details from the medical examiner.

When he eventually left him, the opinion he had always had of Larmy seemed more well-founded than ever: that Larmy was the most incompetent of physicians and that his investigations had nine chances out of ten of reaching the wrong conclusion.

Once again, Vautier examined all the imaginable aspects of the mysterious drama, including the most extraordinary.

It was nine o'clock on Sunday morning when Dr. Vautier rang the doorbell at the door of the entresol in the Rue de Lille.

"Announce Dr. Vautier," he said to the domestic who opened the door. Astonished by the man's bewildered expression, he added: "Why, what's the matter?"

"Monsieur le Docteur will excuse me, but I'm wondering how he was informed that Monsieur is ill...."

"Ill? Your master is ill? What is it?"

"Oh, nothing serious, surely. But just now when he got up, he had a fit of dizziness."

A door opened. Mercoeur appeared. "If you gossip like that, Julien," he said to the domestic, "you'll be leaving my service." To Vautier, he said: "It's nothing at all, my friend—just a slight vertigo due to overwork. It's happened twenty times before."

"No matter—before anything else, I want to examine you."

"No, there's no need. Come on, Vautier, we need to talk. What's the point of wasting time?"

"It will only take two minutes. You can't refuse me that. It's for my own sake that I'm asking. I'll be able to listen to you more tranquilly afterwards...."

Mercoeur could not suppress a gesture of annoyance. He hesitated, looked at Vautier and saw that he was resolute. "All right, then, if you absolutely must!"

They went into a small drawing room, furnished very simply. Mercoeur took off the indoor jacket that he was wearing. On his right arm, a little above the wrist, Vautier noticed an irregular scar several centimeters long and very recent.

"How did you get that?"

"Oh, it's nothing. A little accident. I'll explain...."

When Vautier had listened to his chest with his stethoscope, he asked: "Well? There's nothing wrong, is there? You're satisfied? We can talk now? Hang on, though—I have to give an order."

He rang, and the domestic appeared.

"I don't need you here any longer," Mercoeur said. "Take the letter I gave you to Auteuil right away."

"I'll go immediately, Monsieur."

The domestic left the rom. Mercoeur went to the window, and after a few moments, having seen him leave the house, he came back to sit down facing Vautier, who was waiting for him silently, in an armchair.

"Now," he said, "no one can hear me but you. I've developed a prudence that astonishes me—but think of the consequences of anything being overheard. I never knew before how burdensome it is to have something to hide...." He paused, then resumed, abruptly: "The truth about Berjean's death isn't what the official investigation concluded. Berjean killed himself, but it wasn't deliberate....and I was mixed up in it."

"I feared so," said Vautier. "The passer-by knocked down on the quay immediately after the drama, that was...."

"Yes, it was me who bumped into him—but the quay's poorly lit, our sudden encounter only lasted ten seconds, and, fortunately, the man was so drunk that he hardly knew what was happening. He was incapable of giving my description; the police didn't believe his story and there was no clue that could reveal the pact that I'd made with the dead man."

"Why is he dead?" asked Vautier, in a slightly muffled voice.

Mercoeur looked him in the face, and then said, curtly: "Because he was in love with the same woman as me."

Vautier shuddered.

There was a brief pause; then Mercoeur went on: "I'll tell you everything. You know that you're myself, and from the first moment, I suffered from being unable to confide in you. Yes, the same woman: Gilberte Heurlize. I love her. I've always loved her, I believe. Haven't I talked to you about her before? I loved her, before even realizing it. She's the only woman thanks to whom I've understood the meaning of the word love. Before her, love hadn't had any place in my life. I love her to the point of abandoning for her my ambition, my career, everything that has been until now my reason for living…when one falls in love, at my age, for the first time, one loves completely.…"

He had been speaking with apparent calmness, in a low voice, but it had become tremulous. After a few moments of silence, employed in mastering his emotion, he continued: "Why had I not understood sooner what she was to me? Why, for so long, did I not admit to myself that I loved her? I don't know, exactly. It's doubtless because I didn't have time to examine my sentiments, because my ambition absorbed me, driving away everything that might have disturbed the line of conduct that I'd mapped out, because I was afraid of allowing myself to love…to love too much.… Then again, my pride feared a refusal. Me, Claude Mercoeur in unrequited love—no!

"All that disappeared, magically, the moment that I thought I perceived that Gilberte was in love with me. It was at a semi-official dinner at which I had to appear in person, because there had been a session of parliamentary questions that evening and I had to be in a Council meeting the following morning. Gilberte was sitting next to me. I hadn't seen her for several weeks, Berjean having taken my place at the receptions to which she was invited. She seemed to me to be changed—no less beautiful, I'd never seen her so seductive—but changed in regard to me. I could scarcely talk to her, being obliged to take part in the general conversation, but her manner, especially the expression in her eyes…it was indefinable…it was the kind of animation that makes you understand, better than words, that one is no longer, to a woman, someone indifferent. When I said goodbye to her as we left, her hand remained in mine for a moment, and her eyes met mine.…"

Once again he stopped, and then, in a lower voice, he said: "I didn't know then that Berjean.… Listen, Vautier, it's not him that she loves, it's me, Claude Mercoeur! It's me that she loves. It's me that she's going to marry in a few weeks. After that dinner, I thought about her incessantly. I tried at first to fight it, to get a grip on myself…but it was hopeless, and I knew it.…

I didn't see her for some time, but my love grew. In the meantime, Berjean met her at a charity sale to which I'd promised to go, but didn't because it was during the days when I was struggling against what I was experiencing. Then, at Easter, when I thought it appropriate to give myself the appearance of taking a few days' vacation, Berjean went to spend ten days at Fontainebleau. She was there too. I only found that out later...I found out one evening last month...the evening when Berjean died.

"I had gone to meet him at nine o'clock on the Île Saint-Louis. He was supposed to come to sleep here in the Rue de Lille and take my place for two days. I had important work to finish...but I was preoccupied with something else. The day before, as I left the Ministry, I'd met Gilberte. A friend was with her and we only exchanged a few banal remarks, but when her eyes fixed on me, there was now love in them...and I thought that she could see in my eyes how much I loved her....

"I'd never been so happy in all my life as during that brief conversation brought about by chance. She had understood my love; she loved me...and with what exquisite delicacy she had been able, without words, to tell me so.... Not for a moment did the idea occur to me....

"When I met Berjean the following evening, I already knew that I had to break off our arrangement because I was certain that I was going to marry Gilberte. His behavior had changed some time before, and it displeased me. That evening, he was afflicted by an ill-contained agitation.

"All of a sudden, he said to me: 'I need to talk to you. I've wanted to do so for several days. Now I can't wait any longer.'

"We were in the middle room. The shutters were closed but the windows were open, because it was a mild evening. Berjean closed them, and came back toward me...and he talked. He told me that he loved Gilberte, and that she loved him. He told me that he had confessed it to her on the day he had left Fontainebleau. He told me that she had agreed to marry him....

"Retained because her sister was ill, she had stayed in the

country for a month, but she had now returned to Paris; he was going to see her again. He told me that he had abandoned himself recklessly to an irresistible sentiment, that he was desperate, and that his role with regard to me was torturing him. He talked for a long time; I was scarcely listening. Only his first words counted for me: he loved Gilberte; Gilberte loved him!

"Suddenly, though, I started laughing. 'It's not you she loves, I said to Berjean. 'It's Claude Mercoeur.'

"For some time, there had been a latent hatred between the two of us. It burst forth. He dared to tell me that I was lying, that it was him she loved, and that I was also lying when I claimed to love Madame Heurlize. I tried to stay calm, to make him see the reality, to bring him to his senses, but he became delirious, talking to me about his love, his suffering, what he called the bitterness of his destiny. He wanted to tell Gilberte, and for her to choose between us. I stopped listening. I took the papers that belonged to me out of the desk, put them in my pocket and headed for the door.

"Berjean barred my way. 'I won't let you leave!' he said. 'Once you're out of here you'll have escaped me. I'll no longer have any proof. Who'll believe me when I say that I've been Clade Mercoeur's double—that I've been Claude Mercoeur? You'll have me charged with blackmail, or locked up in an asylum! No! No! People need to know. The Claude Mercoeur that Gilberte loves is me! Everyone needs to know! It's necessary that you be found here. There has to be a scandal!'

"He was shouting. I was astonished that he didn't wake the whole house. Outside, on the quay, I heard the voice of a man singing, drawing closer, who was also going to hear…I made a dash for the door.

"Berjean launched himself to block the way, grabbing my arm. At the same time, he brandished a revolver. I freed myself. At the same moment, he fired. I don't know whether it was at me, but he didn't hit me. I grabbed his wrist; there was a struggle. There was a second shot, and Berjean fell backwards on to the table, and on to the lamp, which broke. By the light of the oil, which caught fire, I saw that his skull was shattered. I opened the window. A pane broke and cut my wrist. I leapt outside, pushing back the shutters and fled. It was then that the man coming along the quay tried to grab me. I knocked him over, and ten minutes later, in the Boulevard du Palais, I stopped a cab, which took me to the Place du Théâtre-Français. I got out, walked a short distance, and took another cab, which brought me to the Rue de Lille.

"No clue permitting me to be identified as the so-called relative who came to visit Raoul Berjean could be discovered in the ground-floor apartment on the Île Saint-Louis. There were clothes that I had worn, but no one could have any suspicion that they didn't belong to Berjean. About the discovery of the drama and the progress of the investigation I don't know anything other than what was published in the newspapers...."

There was a long pause Vautier had listened very attentively to Mercoeur's story without saying a word. Now, grave and a little pale, he looked at Mercoeur.

"What about Madame Heurlize?" he asked, finally.

"I've seen her again several times since the drama."

"And her sentiments?"

Mercoeur started in surprise, almost indignantly. "Still the same, of course! She loves me! A woman like her isn't fickle. When she gives her love, she gives it forever. Her reserve, which she has difficulty vanquishing, renders that love more precious. Our plans are made. In our recent meetings, isolating ourselves from the crowd surrounding us, we've talked at length. It has been noticed—but that's not important. Soon, everyone will know about our impending marriage. Gilberte has asked me to wait for a few more days before publishing the exact date, which she wants to fix herself...."

Abruptly, Vautier stood up. He was very pale. Looking his interlocutor in the eyes, he said: "You're not Claude Mercoeur!"

The other stood up too, as if in a start of amazement. "What are you saying?" he stammered, after a brief tragic silence.

"You're not Claude Mercoeur. You've killed him in order to

take his place. You're Raoul Berjean."

"Vautier! You're mad!"

"You're Raoul Berjean. You've killed Mercoeur. I suspected as much, confusedly, from the first time I heard about the drama. Without wanting to believe it at first, rejecting the frightful idea…but the suspicion never let go. It was exacerbated. None of the objections I tried to oppose to it stood up. They fell, one by one, and a horrible certainty imposed itself upon me, in spite of my resistance: Berjean has killed Mercoeur in order to take his place! It was the only logical explanation of the drama: the explanation that no one but me could suspect. It was also the fatal consequence, the inevitable conclusion, which you were doubtless preparing, from the very beginning, in the pact that you imagined, which your victim was foolish enough to accept, and which I was blindly culpable in advising him to accept!"

"Come on, Vautier, get hold of yourself! Recognize me. This is insane! The unfortunate Berjean died in the circumstances I've just described to you.…"

"Yes, if it was Berjean who died, that is the way he would have died. If Mercoeur were telling me that, it would be the truth. But why should Mercoeur have killed the man that he could, at any time he wished, expel from his life without risking anything but attempted revelations so incredible that they would have passed for the delusions of a madman? Berjean must have killed Mercoeur in order to take over his identity definitely.…"

"But that's crazy! How can you think that a man, even one as intelligent as Berjean, could hope to supplant another completely? Especially when that other is me, Claude Mercoeur. My association with Berjean was only able to succeed because, hour by hour, so to speak, I indicated to him what he had to do… and it was only for official representations. Once again, Vautier, I beg you, come back to reality. Ultimately, it's not possible that you don't recognize me, your friend. It's not possible that you seriously believe in the novelistic twist of Berjean playing the role of the murdered Mercoeur for the last fortnight, without anyone perceiving.…"

"Yes, I believe it, since it's so! Perceive the substitution? How could anyone perceive it? Not by means of physical appearance—it's already proven that Berjean could duplicate Mercoeur. Intellectually, by virtue of the decisions, actions and speeches of the usurper being inferior to those of his victim? Get away! An intelligent man—and you were right just now, Raoul Berjean, you are very intelligent—is able to adapt himself to a situation and play his role without committing any gaffe especially when he had already been initiated!

"Then again, there's acquired momentum. The reputation of a superior man is attached to Mercoeur, and it's as difficult to destroy a reputation as to make one. The man who is Mercoeur is, so far as the world is concerned, a superior man. He doesn't act like a man of genius? Bah! Certain adversaries, certain competitors claim, perhaps, that he's declined...but on the other hand, his admirers say that he's sage and disciplined and as strong as ever. Besides which, I repeat again, you're an intelligent man, remarkably intelligent, Raoul Beerjean—not a man of genius, like Mercoeur, but more intelligent than the majority of the officials that surround you.

"I'm more than ever convinced of your abilities having listened to you since I've been here. The accuracy of your tone and the verity of the emotion are extraordinary. The story you told me just now to explain the drama of the Île Saint-Louis is a marvelous invention. Everything holds together, everything is perfectly logical, especially this so-called love experienced by Mercoeur for Madame Heurlize...whom, in reality, you alone have, perhaps loved, but at any rate seduced into making your wife, because she's rich, after having made her your mistress because she's beautiful...."

Vautier stopped. A hand had seized his arm; a voice growled: "Shut up! Shut up! Gilberte has not been Berjean's mistress! He hasn't even kissed her fingertips. He told me so himself."

Vautier detached his arm, without violence, and uttered a brief ironic snigger.

"Very good! You're remarkable, Berjean. You're playing your

role to the full. I expected that: the indignant revolt of Mercoeur, who ought, according to your story, be torn with jealousy with regard to the dead rival who was himself...."

"You're mistaken, Vautier. I'm not jealous. I have no reason to be jealous...but let's leave that. Listen once again; it's necessary that the misunderstanding be cleared up. It's necessary that you cease to believe in the reality of this melodramatic and crazy story that you've concocted on hearing, far from Paris and from me, of the death of that unfortunate man. You don't lack imagination, for a man accustomed to the rigor of scientific investigation...although one can't be a great scientist without imagination. Until now, I wouldn't have believed you capable of such romantic excesses...but I can't let my old Vautier go astray any longer because of...because of his friendship for me—for that's the origin of these insane suspicions, which are going to dissipate, isn't it? It's the alarm of your profound friendship for me. Let's see—what proof can I give you?" He burst out laughing. "Truly, it's unimaginable! Proofs, so that my best friend will recognize that I'm myself."

"Proofs? What proofs? Childhood memories? Mercoeur admitted himself to being so absorbed by his work that he didn't retain any memory of trivial incidents. You know that, Raoul Berjean; he said so in front of you—so a failure of memory wouldn't be evidence against you, any more than a detail you could cite would be evidence in our favor...for Mercoeur must certainly have told you many things precisely in order that you wouldn't give yourself away when you took his place. But there's something else, Berjean...first of all, your behavior, in which, when I came back the day before yesterday, as well as today, I no longer recognize the behavior of my friend."

"It's almost six months since you last saw me. You arrived with the preconceived idea of discovering a tragic mystery. Besides which, what's surprising about the fact that a man who has been subject to the anguish and emotions to which I've been subjected recently should remain nervous and preoccupied?"

"I examined you just now, after that fainting fit the domestic told me about...."

"It wasn't a faint, just a slight vertigo...."

"Mercoeur never had anything like that. He was in perfect health, even though he was overtired. Berjean had heart flutters several times, as he told Mercoeur and me. Well, when I listened to your chest just now—I had to insist; you didn't want me to—I observed that you had an irregular, intermittent heartbeat...."

"But couldn't the excess work that I'm imposing on myself more than ever, and the torments and anxieties I've experienced, have caused that?"

"Strictly speaking, perhaps...but that injury you have on your right wrist. Mercoeur had a slight mark on that exact spot."

"Yes, made by an acid burn during a chemistry experiment at school...."

"Exactly—you're well-informed. It was easy enough to ask Mercoeur what it was. Well, doesn't that recent wound to your wrist very conveniently prevent it from being ascertained that the mark on Mercoeur's wrist is absent? Yes, yes, I know—the window broken on the night of the drama.... That adds up to a lot of difficult explanations. So many singular coincidences are equivalent to a certainty."

The person he was accusing made an abrupt movement. For a few seconds he seemed to be having difficulty containing himself. "I've had enough!" he cried. "I've just spent the most anguishing hours that I've ever known...I've been mixed up in a drama that could have turned my life upside-down, destroying my career, disrupting the love that is now the most precious thing of all to me, and when you come back—you, the only person in the world in whom I could hope to find a sure confidant, a faithful friend—you stand up before me as an accuser! A man like you can't in good faith persist in such an aberration! You can't believe what you're saying—do you hear me, Vautier? You can't believe in this evidence that isn't, this extravagant story....

"Have you, too, become one of my political adversaries? Do you want to prevent me from becoming President of the

Council? What interest do you have in trying to dishonor me?"

"It's quite obvious that you aren't Mercoeur," said Vautier, coldly. "He would never have suspected me of such things, in any circumstances. You're Berjean, and you've killed him."

"Well, denounce me then!"

There was a pregnant silence. Vautier, on his feet, remain motionless, his hands behind his back, frowning, his eyes fixed, looking straight ahead without seeing anything.

His interlocutor was pacing back and forth in fits and starts. Finally, he stopped in front of Vautier. "Why haven't you denounced me already? Why have you been arguing with me for two hours, if you're sure that I'm Berjean and that I've killed Mercoeur? Just now, I was exasperated by your obstinacy, by the fatality that has caused you to imagine this bizarre idea, by my disappointment in finding you an adversary, instead of a friend! But you know full well that I know your sincerity. Come on, this isn't Berjean who's talking to you! Look at me! Recognize me, Vautier. You know very well that I'm Mercoeur!"

They were face to face, eye to eye.

"No!" cried Vautier, with a kind of despair that tormented his thin and grave face. "No, I don't know anything! I'm in doubt! Yes, I'm in doubt! Otherwise, my duty would be very simple. Yes, at moments I believe...I believe that I'm with Claude Mercoeur, that it's his voice, his face...but that voice and face are also Berjean's In the former case, I'm betraying the friendship of the man to whom I owe every gratitude, every affection, every admiration! I'm betraying him with extravagant suspicions at the very moment when he needs my friendship. In the latter case, it's his murderer that I'm favoring in keeping silent, it's his murderer whose accomplice I'm making myself—me, the only man who can unmask him, and who, for want of decision and clear-sightedness, might leave him free to profit from his crime...."

"For whom are you explaining that? For Mercoeur or Berjean?"

"For whichever of the two is listening to me," said Vautier, dully.

"It's me, Claude Mercoeur, who's listening to you, Vautier. I understand your anguish, but al that is, for me too, the worst of torments. Be sure of that. Listen, Vautier—find a proof; reflect, discover some means of certainty. We have to get out of this impasse. You have to recognize me. And hurry...I need your friendship. I'll try to think myself of some demonstration by which I can convince you. Come to see me at the Ministry in the morning."

"I'll come," said Vautier.

"And it will be my old friend that I'll find, won't it?" He held out his hand.

Vautier sketched a gesture, stopped, looked him in the face, and said: "I can't."

Vautier went out. One o'clock was chiming. In the street heading toward the Boulevard Saint-Germain, he turned his head to look at the windows of the apartment in which he had left the enigma that he could not solve, and which was torturing him: Claude Mercoeur.

VIII.
The Evidence

"Monsieur le Ministre, it's Dr. Vautier," the usher announced.

The Minister, Claude Mercoeur, who was alone in his office, sitting at his desk working, got up and took a few steps toward his visitor.

The latter had not seen him since the visit he had made one Sunday to the apartment in the Rue de Lille, and more than a week had gone by since then. Even more than at the moment of his return, he found Mercoeur thin and pale, his face marked by worry. A kind of fever appeared to be agitating him, and shining in his somber eyes.

Mercoeur looked attentively at Vautier too. "Don't say anything!" he exclaimed, abruptly, before his visitor had even opened his mouth. "I can see by your attitude and your gaze that you haven't yet abandoned your folly. No, don't reply, I beg you. This morning I couldn't listen to you, control myself, argue. I'm annoyed and I don't want to get annoyed with you...it's for a different reason that I had a telephone message sent asking you to come. Just tell me—have you thought of a satisfactory proof that I could give you in order to convince you?"

"No," Vautier replied, coldly, "but in spite of the judgment I formulated the other day regarding public blindness in matters of reputation, I've heard it said in political circles that Claude Mercoeur has seemed fatigued for some time, that he no longer has that rapidity of decision, that clarity of judgment, the simultaneously audacious and practical intelligence that was able to resolve the most difficult problems as if miraculously. He's deemed to be below par. And I'm the only one who might know why...."

"Shut up, I beg you, shut up. Yes, I'm below par and I can't recover my habitual lucidity or my energy—but it's because all my faculties are absorbed by other preoccupations, more poignant than political concerns. I've seen Gilberte Heurlize twice in the last week. My love for her is stronger every day, but her love...."

He paused momentarily. "I've asked Gilberte to fix the date of our marriage; she hasn't yet done so, but she's promised to make a decision before our next meeting. That meeting was to have taken place this morning. Gilberte has just telephoned me to ask if she can come to see me here, which she has never done...."

Seeing Vautier heading for the door he cried: "No, stay! I want you to stay. I want you to witness this meeting. That's why I had you summoned. I want you to be hidden here. I want you to be able to hear us. Look, here, in the deep bay of the window, the curtains will hide you...."

Vautier look at him in astonishment, and he went on: "You might perhaps obtain, in the course of our conversation, the proof that I'm Claude Mercoeur."

Vautier hesitated. Someone knocked on the door. He made up his mind and went to hide behind the vast curtain.

"Monsieur le Ministre," said the usher, coming in, "it's the lady you asked me to announce immediately." He looked around, astonished not to see the first visitor, but concluded that the latter must have gone out by another door, which led to the secretaries' office.

"Have her come in."

Gilberte came in. Mercoeur hurried toward her. She had never seemed more seductive to him. He met her gaze, and the expression he saw there made him pale with a cruel emotion.

"Gilberte, Gilberte it's you...."

She took away her hand. She was very emotional, but she fixed a firm and sincere gaze upon him.

"I've come because I wanted to speak to you," she began, in a rapid, slightly tremulous voice, which grew gradually firmer. "Yes, I need to speak to you. To wait any longer would be wrong, unworthy of you and of me. Listen: what you have hoped for, and what I, too, had hoped for momentarily...cannot be. Our marriage cannot happen...."

Livid, he stepped back, and his hand sought the back of a chair on which to lean. For an instant, he wondered whether Vautier, in the obstinacy of his suspicion...but he rejected that idea. "Why?" he stammered. "Why?"

"Because...my God...but it's necessary that I tell you the truth.... Because I was mistaken when I thought I loved you.... I have admiration and sympathy for you, but I don't have love, and I'm incapable of marrying without love...."

"But you told me, you admitted...."

She blushed, but did not lower her eyes. "Yes, I told you that I loved you...at a moment when it was true.... It has ceased to be true. I cannot yet understand what has happened to me...and to you.... Yes, to you.... For several years we have known one another and there has never been anything between us...."

"But I've always loved you!" he said, violently.

"No, don't say that—it isn't true. When you began to love me it was this winter; you were no longer the brusque, distracted, indifferent Claude Mercoeur that you had been before. You were no longer the man absorbed exclusively in his career—I don't say ambition, you're too superior to have ambition. In order to talk to me you left serious conversations. That never happened to you. Then I had the revelation within you of a charming intelligence, cheerful, spontaneous and whimsical—an intelligence that you had previously hidden completely. I found in you a sensibility, a poetry that I had never suspected. You ceased to be an eminent politician, in order to be simply a man beside a woman. And I loved you...yes, I loved you as I had not believed it possible to love. At that charity sale, you remember, you committed that inadvertency—because you were only thinking about me, I understood—of mistaking the initial in choosing a cigarette-case. Well, I was profoundly moved and troubled myself. It was for you alone, you understand, that I went to Fontainebleau. Between ourselves, it's a memory that will always be very dear to me...and to you too, I'm sure...an exquisite memory, was it not?"

"There wasn't only Fontainebleau!" he exclaimed, with a jealous wrath that she did not understand, and which offended her, for she was emotional. "Since our return to Paris, every time we met, we talked to one another...."

"No! And you know that full well, since you haven't been the same. You've gradually become the Claude Mercoeur of old. I can no longer find the man that I knew for a few weeks...and certainly, that's because the love that you believed you had for me has faded away...don't protest! If you had remained what you were for me for too short a time...well, I too would have remained the same. I've been married, you know, and unhappy. I never wanted to marry again before...before...the day when I thought I was sure of loving you....

"You remember: we were in the sunlit pathways, still moist from an April shower. You spoke to me with so much delicate and reserved tenderness. You were so sure of what to say to move me...and I was already so ready to be moved by you...and when you talked about getting married I said yes, frankly…with the greatest joy in my life.… I suffered when you left.

"Then, when I saw you again in Paris, at first you hadn't changed…but then…then…the other Mercoeur came back, the one from before.… And like a dream from which one awakens, the charm that was between us vanished…you know that, don't you? Confess that you expected that I was going to say to you what I've just said.…"

"But no, I love you! I love you more than ever…it's me who loves you, Gilberte, it's me who loves you!"

"If you love me, it's no longer as you did in those brief weeks of spring. I'm no longer a child to be mistaken about my sentiments. I did love you…I no longer love you. I have the impression when I'm with you of being with a stranger…an unknown. Why? It's all so singular and confused…but it's necessary to give up. I could never marry a man that I don't love.…" She hesitated. "…That I no longer love."

She bowed her head and remained pensive. "And yet I'm suffering from no longer loving you," she murmured. "It seems to me that someone very dear to me is no more. I search for him in you…but I can't find him. It's him that I would have married. It's him that I loved, and whom you no longer are…because our love has died…yours as well as mine…yours before mine, certainly.… Adieu."

She turned away. He tried to stop her.

"Gilberte, don't leave me like this! You're mistaken! I'm the same! Work is absorbing me, it's true, but for you I'll give it up…if I must…I love you."

She looked at him almost harshly, and repeated: "We no longer love one another!"

He saw her, lithe, rapid and graceful, go through the door, which closed behind her, separating her forever from Mercoeur. And Mercoeur, his eyes fixed on the door, remained motionless, overwhelmed, almost haggard.

A hand was placed on his shoulder. He saw Vautier.

"Well!" he cried, furiously. "Well, do you still doubt me now?

You recognize me, don't you? She doesn't love me! I really am Mercoeur! For several days, I've felt that she was drawing away from me...that her confidence and tenderness were diminishing. I glimpsed the truth, without wanting to believe it: it's Berjean that she loved! It's him that was able to make himself beloved—yes, he had the intelligence, superior to any other, to be able to make himself beloved! It's him that she thought, for a moment, she loved in me, before perceiving, instinctively, without understanding it, that I wasn't him!

"She's not mistaken! She hasn't, like you, mistaken Mercoeur for Berjean! A friend like you was mistaken; an intelligence like yours wouldn't believe the truth that I cried out! But a woman who is no longer in love is more clear-sighted. She didn't hesitate. You heard her: 'The other Mercoeur has come back and the dream has vanished....you no longer love me and I no longer love you!'

"She no longer loves me! But that's because she never loved me! I no longer love her! But that's because I can't, in spite of loving her, give her the love for which she's looking in me—the love of Berjean, who's dead!"

He let himself fall into a seat in front of his desk and hid his face in his hands. Vautier drew closer to him slowly and put his hand on his shoulder again.

"Forgive me, Mercoeur, for having added to your torments by my error...."

Mercoeur shrugged his shoulders indifferently, and made no reply.

"Pull yourself together," Vautier went on. "Be strong. Overcome your emotion. It's necessary that no one perceives it. You owe it to your work...."

Claude Mercoeur raised a ravaged, tear-streaked face toward his friend. "That no longer interests me," he replied.

In the large severe office, where Gilberte Heuirlize's perfume still lingered, the two men remained silent.

THE MAN WHO
HAS BEEN MAD

It is never very agreeable to encounter a man who has been your comrade at school but has subsequently been interned for several months in an asylum, doubtless offering all the modern comforts combined with all the amenities of medical progress, but exclusively reserved for lunatics.

Lucien Canalle, however, gave every appearance of being cured when he found himself face to face with me on the boulevard. Apart from a suggestion of sadness and exceedingly premature old age, he seemed quite normal, and I strove to treat him as such. We stopped on the terrace of a café and I spoke cheerfully about memories of the school where he and his brother had undertaken their studies at the same time as me.

After a little while, however, he interrupted me.

"You're very polite," he said. "You're talking to me *as to anyone else*, aren't you? But I know, you see. I'm the man who has been mad! For you, as for others, for my entire life, I'm troubling. People watch me without appearing to do so. People are too free, too cheerful, too amiable, too agreeable…I'm the man who has been mad!

"Well, no—I haven't been mad. I've never been mad. I need, for once, to tell the truth, and it's no longer of any importance now: the harm is done, and the good too. It isn't me that has been mad, it's Louis, my older brother. No, I beg you—let me tell you everything before believing that I'm not cured!

"Louis went mad seven years ago. He was twenty-eight and

I was twenty-six. He wasn't mad all the time. He had fits. They gripped him from time to time. He took his clothes off; he thought he was surrounded by enemies; he argued with items of furniture and fought them. We had a family history of mental illness and, given that, Louis kicked over the traces too much between the ages of eighteen and twenty-five. He did too much mathematics and too much drinking. The two don't go together.

"When his illness started we were in the country at our family château. As you know, our parents had been dead for some time. I was alone with Louis in the depths of Morvan. He got worse and worse. His fits became more frequent and more intense. The rest of the time, however, there was nothing evident, and he didn't retain any memory whatsoever of his crises. He was a good fellow, as always, cheerful and content with life. I persuaded him to return to Paris.

"I'd already consulted Brunier...you remember Brunier? He was also at school with us and he's still—he was still, I should say—my best friend. He'd just presented his thesis then. He was a pupil of Professor Cave, the celebrated alienist, and I couldn't do any better than address myself to him. He knew Louis well, and examined him with care without alerting him to the fact, without worrying him, as a comrade.

"Eventually, he told me that it was serious, but curable, and with care, constant rest, fresh air and hydrotherapy, he could be brought out of it in less than a year, on condition that he was confided to Cave himself, who has a sanitarium in the suburbs—the best of everything, in terms of modern methods. You can take my word for it—that's where I was interned....

"I hesitated. It seemed horrible to me. As I said, outside of his fits, Louis was relatively reasonable; he managed his business affairs, and did his work in physics, directing it, however, toward implausible problems, scientific follies impossible of realization...but in sum, he lived like anyone else: lived too such, in fact, for he went out every night, exhausting himself in excesses of every sort.

"I was obliged to accompany him to all his places of pleasure. God knows that was hard on me, for I've always been serious-minded, as you know—but I scarcely dared leave him alone. Besides which, no one suspected anything. In the house where we had an apartment, in the Rue de Villiers, everyone certainly found him more amiable than me. His fits never took hold of him outside and I did my best to hide them from the domestics, shutting myself up with him in order to try to calm him down and conceal his cries.

"It couldn't go on, though. He was becoming violent. Brunier gets annoyed and tells me that I'm culpable, that Louis is in danger, that he's aggravating his condition every day by the life he leads, and that it's necessary to intern him without delay if we want to avoid a catastrophe, a public scandal and furious madness. Brunier also tells me that he's leaving himself for America, to make an important study in the asylums over there, and that he wants to be tranquil about the two of us before he leaves.

"Finally, he insists with all his might. Then again…listen to this: I wanted to get married. I was very much in love and I dreaded that some eccentricity, or worse, on the part of Louis, who knew the girl I loved—Yvonne Martier—as well as I did."

"Yvonne Martier!" I said, astonished. "But that's.…"

"My brother's wife, yes." Lucien Canalle laughed wearily. "It's like this," he continued. "I loved her. Louis loved her too, it appears, but I didn't know! We'd all known one another since childhood, we had the same right to be loved by her. Still, at that time, I wanted to ask her to marry me, and I was only prevented from doing so by Louis' illness. I couldn't abandon him…but that didn't affect my decision. No, I swear to you! Brunier is a serious physician, isn't he? And it was him who insisted on the internment of the sick person who was becoming dangerous. The necessary steps and formalities had had been taken discreetly and rapidly, because Brunier was expected in America.

"On the very day of his departure, he arrived at our place and told me that everything was ready and that Cave's nurses would come for my brother two hours later. At that point, Louis came in, and Brunier and I daren't say another word. Just then he was perfectly reasonable and he started teasing Brunier about his trip to 'loony-land.' That sent chills down our backs. Brunier said his goodbyes and went, warning me, in a whisper, that the warders were on their way.

"Louis went back to his room—to work, he said—and I shut myself in mine, on the far side of the apartment, anguished and desolate, wondering whether I was really doing my duty. I'd told the domestic to take the people who were coming to my brother. I preferred not to be present. You'll understand, I think....

"The doorbell rang. I heard voices, footsteps going toward Louis' room. I listened, expecting shouting, protests, a battle... but the footsteps came back. There was a knock on my door; someone came in. A very polite man said to me, in a quiet voice: 'Monsieur, Dr. Brunier is waiting for Monsieur downstairs. If Monsieur will be so good as to come down...'

"I tell myself that Brunier has forgotten something important and that he didn't want to alert Louis by coming up with the nurses. I run downstairs as I am, without my coat and hat. The man follows me. Downstairs, I see a large van. The door's open. Carried away by my assumption, I think I see Brunier inside and I stick my head in. It isn't him. I try to draw back but the man inside grabs me. The one behind me shoves me. They bundle me into the vehicle, the door closes and the van drives off. I try to struggle, shout, explain—futile! The van's padded top to bottom, the men are holding on to me, politely but solidly, and they're talking to me like a child of four, doubtless to calm me down. I do nodded calm myself down, telling myself that there's been a ridiculous mistake and that it will be sorted out as soon as we reach the sanitarium. Three quarters of an hour later we arrive...and I stay there for fifteen months!"

After a pause, Lucien Canalle continued: "I never found out exactly how the nurses had been so grossly deceived. To begin with, the domestic took them to my brother. He was in his right mind for the moment, writing equations on his blackboard.

They never imagined that that scientist was the madman. They had a discussion with him, doubtless asking for the Monsieur Canalle that they were supposed to take away. Louis, at first, must have been amazed, for he immediately thought that it was me that the men were talking about. He doubtless told himself that Brunier had taken measures, without telling him, to have me cared for, and that a mental illness was the cause of my sadness and my distraction—which, in reality, stemmed from my anxieties about him. Then again, madmen always sense madness prowling around them, and always want to attribute it to someone else, perhaps with the obscure fear of it being attribute to them.

"In brief, Louis, with his sick imagination, was perfectly willing to believe that I was mad. Perhaps he even thought that he had undertaken the necessary formalities himself, as he was told. He pointed out my room to the nurses, and watched my abduction from his window. That gave him a great deal of pain, moreover, for he loves me with all his heart—but as he said later, it was for my own good. Our domestic, who had heard his cries in the course of fits when I was trying to calm him down, and who attribute them to me, since I'd been shut away, confirmed him in that opinion....

"I'd rather not talk about my life in Professor Cave's sanitarium. No one would ever admit my mental equilibrium. Brunier had provided details of my—which is to say, Louis'—alienation and my lucidity did me no good. On the contrary: they were expecting fits. They lavished the most devoted, and the most exasperating, cares upon me. They promised to cure me, and they also promised my brother, to whom they send regular news of me, or who came to obtain it himself, without his being permitted to see me, because I was entirely and totally isolated. That was part of the Cave system. You can't imagine how much I've suffered....

"Perhaps I was mad, during the hours of despair and rage in which I saw my life lost, broken by chance, by a stupid error.... It's necessary, you see, never to speak of impossible coincidences; in this affair, everything fitted together perfectly for my irremediable ruin, and the improbable triumphed all along the line. For do you know what Louis was doing in the meantime? He was getting better and getting married! Just like that! He married Yvonne, the woman I loved, and whom, it appears, he loved without my ever having suspected it.

"My brother had had a violent shock when he had seen me taken away. He'd changed his ways completely. He'd abandoned his crazy research and his drunken nights. Alone and sad, he returned to the affections of childhood and perceived that he loved Yvonne. He married her, and the power of their mutual love drove his crises away forever—or, at least, if he's had any relapse, his wife hasn't said anything.

"As for me, I ended up getting out anyway, liberated by Brunier, who came back from America and experienced a rather sharp surprise, believe me, when Dr. Cave introduced him to the Monsieur Canalle he'd been treating for fifteen months, and when I explained to him, moderately—for I'd become very prudent—what had happened and how I came to be there instead of my brother. But Brunier's resilient, you know; he wasn't disconcerted and proved to me like $a + b$ that I couldn't make any complaint, couldn't say a word, without being a wretch. My brother was cured, married, and a child was on the way. With what right, with what objective, dare I break up that family? One of the two of us had been mad; it was me instead of him, that's all!

"I kept silent, naturally. But I had to leave, escape to the far side of the world, to distract myself, to be able to forget...to escape the pity, the terror, the mistrust of everyone I knew, for whom I was—and still am—the man who had been mad. Then again, listen, truly, Louis was too happy with Yvonne....

"I've become a nomad. I'm just passing through Paris. I'm leaving again—I don't know where. That's it!"

He left.

"Get away!" Dr. Brunier said to me, a few days later, when I went to see him for further information. "All that's just fairy tales! Don't be silly. If an alienist of the quality of Dr. Cave keeps a man locked up for fifteen months, there has to be a reason, hasn't there?"

THE INGRATE ISLAND

It was in the South Seas, around 52° South latitude and 47° West longitude, that the illustrious Monsieur Pluvinage, sociologist, hygienist, statistician, member of all the scientific societies and first-rate lecturer, was shipwrecked.

No one knew better than him how to discourage his contemporaries by informing them infinitely about things they did not want to know, in order to "raise their mental level," and no one knew better than him how to establish statistics proving, in a futile and contradictory fashion, anything one wished. Thus, his glory was universal.

Abut forty years old, gorged with honors and boiling over with propagandistic ardor, he had set out on a great voyage of study and investigation, throughout the vast world. He had given lectures in several languages that his vigilant parents had made him learn, and he had collected statistics everywhere in Asia, in Africa, in America; those three continents were as favorable to him as Europe—but Oceania betrayed him. Meteorological brutalities tenaciously assailed the vessel transporting him, drove it far off course, and finally into injurious corals, with the result that one morning, after various violent emotions, Monsieur Pluvinage found himself, clad only in pink-striped pajamas and embroidered slippers, hanging on to the extremity of a yard-arm, tossed forcefully back and forth by a not-very-pacific ocean.

Monsieur Pluvinage had saved his photographic apparatus, equipped with plates, and his statistics, forming three stout files. He also had a tin of licorice. The other end of the yard-arm was occupied by a Chinaman. Everyone else had been drowned.

"Do you know if there is any land in the vicinity?" Monsieur Pluvinage asked the Chinaman, as soon as he was able to speak.

"Sixty meters away," said the Chinaman.

"In which direction?" asked Monsieur Pluvinage, quite content.

"Downwards," replied the Chinaman. "I took a sounding before we hit the reef."

Monsieur Pluvinage did not appreciate the feeble joke.

For two mortal days, things remained the same, with the fear of sharks and cramp, dying of thirst and insufficiently nourished by his nauseating licorice. At the end of that time, the Chinaman said that he had had enough and let himself sink. Monsieur Pluvinage clung on harder to his yard-arm and his life.

It was not until the next day that he saw that the Chinaman had made a mistake, for the tide carried the yard-arm and Monsieur Pluvinage tranquilly on to a beach of black sand, where a few obliging human beings picked up the exhausted castaway, dying of hunger, fatigue and cold, and did their best to care for him.

For five whole days Monsieur Pluvinage was solely occupied in eating, and sleeping after having eaten, like a boa constrictor. At the end of that time, having recovered his strength and his lucidity, he was able to cast a glance around him usefully.

There was a little island, rather desolate and completely isolated from the rest of the world. There were penguins there, wild goats and imported pigs, cabbages, potatoes and onions in abundance, not many trees, a little stream and fourteen inhabitants in total: nine men, three of whom were colored—escaped convicts for the most part, or improbable adventurers who had done everything in life before running aground there, and now no longer had a name, an origin or even a profession—and three women from Tahiti or thereabouts, with two children. They had no communication with the rest of the world, and did not desire to have any.

Every two or three years, a ship that had dropped anchor in the vicinity, at the hazard of a fishing expedition, vaguely transmitted news of wars, revolutions or cataclysms, at which they laughed, and traded with them, in exchange for sealskins and oil, a few objects of primary necessity—most importantly a few barrels of rum, thanks to which, every Sunday, the worthy individuals held a small amicable feast. The rest of the time, they grew their potatoes and their onions, fattened their pigs and fished for cod with a line. The women sowed skins to make clothes.

For a very long time they had lived happily like that, healthy and cheerful, in virtue and innocence, having forgotten morality, crime and money. Then Pluvinage arrived, full of modern theories, fixed ideas about everything, convincing statistics and urgent lectures. He was, in addition, very grateful to those worthy people who had saved his life and cared for him so well, and desired with all his heart to do them good.

The first thing he did—and the only harmless one—was the photograph the little colony, whose members put on their best sealskins for the occasion and gathered in a group on the beach. It was a pleasure to see those twelve worthy people and two children, all bursting with health, strength and contentment with life. They were delighted to be photographed, but it was a Platonic satisfaction, because Monsieur Pluvinage only had his camera and his sensitive plates. He told them, however, that he would have great pleasure in accomplishing his duty by making them happy, and that he would get busy on that right away.

He began be revealing to them, with the aid of his diary, that they did not know the exact date, and that the day they took for Sunday and celebrated as such, with rum and repose, was in fact Wednesday. That seemed to be trivial, but it vexed them profoundly and upset their lives by making them want to remedy such an unforgivable error.

Then Monsieur Pluvinage launched himself resolutely on the path of progress and lectures. In a matter of days he acquired such an immense influence over them by informing them of a host of items of general knowledge, to which he accustomed them to listen without falling asleep. He talked to them about hygiene—in terms of both clothing and habitations—rational alimentation, calories, functional gymnastics, the education of children, intensive and extensive agriculture, chemical fertilization, guano, crop rotation, fish-farming, animal husbandry, leprosy, trichinosis and abdominal phlogosis.

He demonstrated to them peremptorily that they were living in wretched conditions utterly contrary to modern civilization. He made them disgusted with themselves and their surroundings by incessantly indicating to them everything they lacked. He humiliated them by comparing them with powerfully-organized European nations and saturated them with the necessity of bettering themselves. All of it was accompanied by citations, precise facts, peremptory figures and overwhelming statistics.

The unfortunates, dominated by the idea that he was prodigiously superior to them and, convinced that he knew everything—which was, unfortunately, true—listened to him with great respect and did their best to comprehend his theories and apply them. They dared not show themselves to be refractory to the civilization that had just come to them, with all its advantages, and Pluvinage became their benefactor and their guide.

Monsieur Pluvinage then cut loose. He had the cabins demolished and reconstructed in accordance with terrifying hygienic methods, with a hospital hut "in case of contagion"—although they had never had any—built a dike, a causeway and a lighthouse, all monstrously useless.

Every morning he gathered his victims on the beach and obliged them to undertake improved Swedish gymnastics and all kinds of grotesque contortions. He condemned them to boiling their water before drinking it, because he had found microbes in the stream. He banished meat almost entirely from their diet, because he was a vegetarian, and stuffed them with insipid flour-products that were very difficult to manufacture.

He fixed the hours at which they got up and went to bed, and a work-schedule that tired them out, and obliged them to abandon everything that they had done before in order to no longer to do anything but what he, Pluvinage, thought good for them—and was, in fact, to the highest degree, from the theoretical viewpoint, but not at all from the practical viewpoint.

The pigs, subjected to the most scientific methods of rearing, almost all perished; the cod, frightened by the work on the dike, fled out to sea, and the seals emigrated. The cabbages and the potatoes ceased to grow, as did the onions.

As for the fourteen inhabitants, they were purely and simply agonized. Fourteen neurasthentic skeletons, exhausted by labor and lack of nourishment, tormented by the fear of disease and death, devoured by ambition, jealousy and mutual rancor— Monsieur Pluvinage had revealed to them the necessity of a political organization in order to establish their human dignity in the eyes of nations—replaced the joyful Herculean individuals of yore.

Thus, in less than a year, Monsieur Pluvinage mastered the little colony. He did not see his ravages. He was content with himself and others. He was healthy and grew fat.

On the anniversary of his arrival, Monsieur Pluvinage arranged a public celebration, which he called a "Festival of Temperance"—a significant name, for the philanthropist was resolved to perfect his work.

He gathered them together in the morning and, as he had done on his arrival, he photographed them. Then he gave them a stern lecture on alcoholism and its ravages and announced to them that, in order to celebrate that auspicious day, he had taken it upon himself to break open the last remained barrel of rum and empty its contents into the sea, to the very last drop.

Those people, who had borne everything, could not bear that. Without any discussion, they marched upon Pluvinage, knocked him down and tied him up. They carried him to their little boat and rowed with all their strength to a little islet, entirely desolate, that was in the sea about eight hundred meters from their island. There, they built him a little cabin, provided him with provisions, and, having untied him, took to the sea.

"A whaler will probably come by in a few months," one of them said to him as they left. "Between now and then we'll bring you food, but we don't want to see you any more. If we do, we'll kill you." With a hateful smile, he added: "Isolation is also a curative method."

Monsieur Pluvinage never understood what had happened to him. Four months later, the whaler appeared and he embarked, after having cast a last distant glance at his victims—who, liberated from him, had forgotten all their torments and gradually returned to life.

Monsieur Pluvinage's return to Europe was a resounding triumph. The hero was much in demand and his lectures were packed out. He related his astonishing adventure, but, doubtless in good faith and in the ardor of his convictions, he left out the final unpleasantness and only talked about the generous and useful work that he had been able to do so well in twelve months.

Slides of the two group photographs illustrated his speech: on the one hand, the joyful Hercules overflowing with health, and on the other, a few lamentable and emaciated skeletons.

"Before my arrival!" said Monsieur Pluvinage, pointing to the skeletons. "At the moment of my departure!" he said, indicating the Herculean figures.

And the enthusiasm was indescribable.

THE AMERICAN'S MURDER

The affair began on the twelfth of November, with a sensational item of reportage:

A MYSTERIOUS DRAMA IN THE PLACE DU THÉÂTRE-FRANÇAIS

Yesterday, Saturday, at daybreak, the rare passers-by who were hastening through the cold fog were alarmed by a loud horrible scream. At that moment, a human body had just come crashing down on the sidewalk in front to the Cosmopolite-Hôtel at the corner of the Avenue de l'Opéra.

People ran to help the victim, who was lying there with his head split and his limbs broken, but death had been instantaneous. The hotel employees recognized the cadaver as that of an American, Joshua Wilson, who was resident on the fifth floor with one of his cousins, Thomas Wilson.

The police immediately went up to the apartment of the latter, whom they found half-dressed, extremely over-excited, bearing several wounds on his head, which he was bandaging at the moment when they came in. He refused to give the slightest explanation of the drama that had just occurred but declared himself to be "innocent of any murder." He was nevertheless placed under arrest.

The investigation revealed that the two Americans had been resident at the Cosmopolite-Hôtel for about two months.

Thomas Wilson, who speaks French perfectly, is about forty years old, seemingly rich and very fond of pleasure. His cousin, the unfortunate victim, was seven or eight years younger and seems to have fulfilled the subaltern functions of a "poor relative" in his regard. He only spoke English, was very hard of hearing and of an extremely taciturn and unsociable character. He spent the greater part of his days shut in his room, smoking, reading or looking sadly out into the street.

Only one person seems to have succeeded in obtaining some slight intimacy with him: a young English maidservant named Edith Campbell, who is in charge of the linen at the hotel. With regard to the young woman, Joshua had overcome his timidity, and it is probable that a vague romance had begun to blossom between them, for the young Englishwoman, on learning about the American's frightful death, was seized by a violent nervous crisis. She had to be carried to her room, and a doctor was summoned.

Monsieur Églantine, the distinguished Commissaire of the district police, has searched the apartment of the two Americans, who were, it seems, occupied in science, for the policeman discovered several electric piles and accumulators in a locked cupboard, as well as an apparatus presenting some analogies with those used in wireless telegraphy.

Monsieur des Angles, the well-known magistrate, has taken charge of the examination of this rather enigmatic affair.

Thomas Wilson was transferred to a police cell after his wounds—which do not seem to be serious—were dressed. It is said that he had chosen Maître Cabrolle, the illustrious advocate, to represent him at the assizes.

The victim's body has been transported to the Morgue, pending the autopsy.

STOP PRESS

According to information received, which we are only reporting with all reservations, the American charged with murder, the pseudo-Thomas Wilson, is none other than a celebrated doctor who has acquired great renown in scientific circles in the United States and Europe by virtue of his sensational discoveries. We shall abstain from publishing the name of the individual thus implicated, but in view of this, the affair will cause an immense sensation.

The American's murder, thus presented, interested the public keenly, all the more so because the news reported "with all reservations" was confirmed. The evening newspapers all printed the real name of the so-called Thomas Wilson. He was the celebrated Dr. Jeffries of New York. His picture was published, along with his biography and the history of his discoveries. As for the victim, no one had any information about him, or about the causes of the drama.

As it was Sunday, the investigation did not move forward. Young Ethel Campbell felt better; she got up and was able to resume her service, but she seemed profoundly upset and opposed a stubborn silence to all the questions put to her on the subject of the dead man.

On Monday, Dr. Gaspard, the medical examiner, presented himself at the Morgue in order to carry out the autopsy of the victim. At the same time, the accused American was interrogated for the first time by the examining magistrate in the presence of his advocate, the illustrious Maître Cabrolle, who had taken the trouble to come in person.

Monsieur des Angles cast a perspicacious eye over the American, whose clean-shaven and willful face was still entirely surrounded by bandages of a dazzling whiteness, and opened his mouth to begin the interrogation.

At that moment, the accused began to speak. "Monsieur le Juge," he said, "I don't want to allow French justice to proceed any longer along an erroneous path. In the presence of the illustrious Maître Cabrolle, who has consented to lend me his inestimable support, I ought to tell you, honestly, that I am innocent!"

"I'm entirely ready to believe you," replied the magistrate, with perfect courtesy, "but all the appearances accuse you of murder."

"There has been no murder," the foreigner affirmed.

"Yes, I know—a suicide! That's your thesis! But the blows that you've received, the fact that you were alone with the man who died...."

"There is no dead man!" the astonishing American interjected, with a forceful accent of truth. "The body that was found in the Place du Théâtre-Français under the windows of the Cosmopolite-Hôtel—through one of which I had thrown it, I freely admit—is not the body of a man.... No, no, I'm not feigning madness; I'm simply telling the exact truth, which is very easy to check. What I threw out of the window is an automaton, a machine with a human face, an android that I constructed myself last year!"

There was a dazed silence.

"Come on!" the magistrate finally murmured. "That's crazy...it's impossible...it would be perceived...."

"Don't go on, Monsieur le Juge," the American went on, with frank amusement. "No one has ever perceived anything—to my astonishment, in fact, for I did not think that my work would be so perfect. Have you read *L'Eve future*?"[11]

At that moment there was a kind of tumult at the door of Monsieur des Angles' office, and Dr. Gaspard, who has already been mentioned, burst in.

"It's incredible!" he cried. "Do you know what has been submitted to me for autopsy? A manufactured entity! A kind of electrically-operated doll! My laboratory assistants were terrified! They had perceived it without daring to say anything when the body was frozen, for the thing was at human temperature, it appears, when it was functioning. It's a man, I tell you! It's marvelous! Everything is there! The heart, the brain, the lungs, the blood in the arteries! There are receivers, doubtless for

11. Villiers de l'Isle Adam's novel in which Thomas Edison constructs a female android for a French aristocrat disillusioned with the perfidies of women of flesh and blood, first published in 1886.

picking up signals at a distance! It's amazing!"

"Your admiration is deeply touching, my dear colleague," said the American.

"Dr. Jeffries! You're Dr. Jeffries! My dear Master! My illustrious colleague!" Dr. Gaspard could not contain his enthusiasm.

"You'll excuse me for having disturbed you," said the American, urbanely, to Monsieur des Angles, "but I affirmed in vain that I was innocent—no one believed me. Besides which, I liked all that. I needed a complete, resounding affair, in order to launch my invention. In America I'm too well-known; people would immediately have suspected something—while here, with a sensational crime, an arrest, newspaper articles, and the truth exploding like a bomb…it's the most magnificent publicity, you see!

"Can you imagine that I've been working on the idea of automata for twenty years, and that I constructed five machines that I demolished before succeeding with Joshua. Whenever I'd solved a hundred problems, I discovered a hundred more, even more complicated.… The accumulators gave me infinite trouble; we know so little about electrical matters. But I'll explain all that in detail. My paper is ready to be communicated to the scientific world. I'll present it at the same time as the body.…"

"Forgive me," Monsieur des Angles suddenly interjected, "but what about the wounds on your face, Dr. Jeffries. How did they come about?"

"My wounds?" The America hesitated momentarily. "Well, it was *the thing* that inflicted them. I had decided as I told you, to make people believe that there had been a murder, to stir up a sensational affair in order to launch my creation. But I waited, I hesitated…it displeased me to destroy the thing that had cost me so much work, which was my first success, and which, moreover, seemed so human. When *that* looked at me with its great shiny eyes.…

"Anyway, on the night of the murder"—he caught himself up, smiled and resumed—"the night of the adventure, I took one glass of whisky to many to brace myself, I came back home rather late, overexcited and fully determined...and...I don't know exactly what happened—the whisky, no doubt—and must have forgotten to switch the machine off before throwing it out...at any rate. It must have defended itself...since I bear the scars."

"It defended itself?" asked the magistrate, astounded.

"No! I mean that I handled it clumsily!" A shadow had passed over the American's hard face. "I'd had too much whisky. Let's go to the Morgue—you'll see that it's just a machine."

"What about the young maid?" asked Dr. Gaspard, very interested.

"The young maid? Oh yes! That was an experiment. I wanted to ascertain whether my automaton really could fool someone. I could switch it on by means of electrical waves and then, naturally, tell it to do whatever I wanted. I left it alone with the girl three or four times, having shut myself up in the next room, ostensibly to work. Afterwards, I could scarcely help laughing, on seeing the girl look tenderly at the machine, with which, I truly believe, she was smitten...." He added: "It really was a fine machine."

"I demand that my client be set at liberty immediately," said Maître Cabrolle.

That sentence was the only one pronounced by the celebrated advocate in the course of the astonishing affair, but it was sufficient to confirm his reputation.

Dr. Jeffries' glory exploded like a firework. Overnight, he and his android became famous throughout the entire world. The newspapers were full of amazing details of the human machine. All the historical automata were recalled; Albertus Magnus was cited, Vaucanson, Maelzel, Hoffmann and Villiers de l'Isle Adam. Scientists lined up in chorus for or against. Financiers offered enormous sums, speculators proposed the launching of joint-stock companies for the manufacture of artificial domestics and animated statues. Dr. Jeffries became an honorary member of a host of scientific societies, received a large number of decorations, and his picture, in full face and in profile, ornamented hundreds of thousands of postcards, which also depicted the unfortunate Joshua Wilson.

The latter had been badly dislocated by the fall. In addition, Dr. Gaspard had mutilated him variously, in his initial surprise and astonishment, while attempting to achieve comprehension. As a result, the so-called cadaver, after having been paraded in the amphitheaters, had ended up being exhibited in public, and multitudinous crowds filed past the marvelous machine, contemplating the pitiful body with astonishment: a simulacrum of humanity with frightful wounds, a triumph of human creative genius.

Among these visitors was a pale and blonde young woman. The wardens subsequently recalled that she appeared to be in a state of intense and concentrated overexcitement. For a long time, she remained motionless and stuff, staring at the massacred thing intently. Then she uttered a sort of brief hysterical laughter, and went away.

The same day, at about midnight, as Dr. Jeffries was coming back to the sumptuous apartment that he now occupied on the first floor of the Cosmopolite-Hôtel—which he was about to leave in order to give a series of lectures in Europe, accompanied by an exhibition of the body of Joshua Wilson, while waiting for the construction of another Joshua Wilson to be completed—he suddenly heard the door of the antechamber opening.

A slender shadow in a white apron loomed up in front of him in the darkness of the drawing-room, in which he had just arrived. Then he remembered the young English maid.

He tried to say something, or to do something, but he did not have time.

"Liar! Liar! Murderer!" she said, in a low voice, through clenched teeth.

She raised her hand. Three gunshots rang out. Dr. Jeffries fell forwards, head first. He coughed up a mouthful of blood, and died.

LENOIR AND KELLER

In the dawn that had, as usual, woken him up, the man emerged from his hut, edified in a fissure in the inaccessible rocky cliff. He went down to the beach of sand mingled with crushed seashells, into which his feet sank. The sun rose over the somber sea, still agitated by the previous days' storms. In the distance, on the islet that was visible west of the island, of which it seemed to be the advanced sentinel, the colonies of penguins that roosted there formed confused white patches on the bare rock; the birds of the South Seas rose up in spiraling, screeching flocks over the surface of the waves.

The man studied the sky, the water and the birds with a mechanical interest. He sat down on a boulder. From a threadbare brown canvas bag slung over his shoulder he took a piece of a kind of primitive pancake, which he ate. He drank from a wicker-work gourd. He took a wooden pipe out of his pocket, the stem of which was consolidated with a piece of string, stuffed it and started smoking it slowly. That day—the second of May, 1899—he had decided not to work; it was the anniversary of his arrival.

He had now been living there for five years, isolated at the end of the world. His name was Lenoir, and he was thirty-two years old. He was a man of medium height, broad-shouldered, of vigorous and agile appearance. He wore heavy boots, trousers of crudely-sewn sealskin, an old striped jersey and a sailor's jacket, all of it full of grease, oil and soot. Beneath his battered hat, his black hair, badly cut and unkempt, descended jaggedly over his forehead. So much sun and rain had burned or lashed his thin face that a uniform sunburn masked it completely, in which his bright eyes seemed even brighter, and the teeth that he showed when he spoke whiter still.

For, from time to time, either in French or in English, which he could speak fluently, by virtue of speaking it for years, he talked to himself, aloud, in curt and ungrammatical sentences peppered with sailors' slang. Since the old American who had been his associate and companion during the first two years of his sojourn had died, he had acquired that habit, in order to remind himself of the sound of the human voice, which he did not want to forget, and in order to give himself the illusion of company in his solitude.

He reported, as he went along, what he was thinking and what he was doing. He talked about the seasons and the weather, the cod for which he fished, the seals that he killed, and the possibility that one day, one of the rare ships that he saw from time to time passing by far out at sea would stop—which had already happened twice—in order to communicate with him and take sealskins and fresh foodstuffs in exchange for tools, tinned food and a little money, which Lenoir carefully stored in an old biscuit-tin that served him as a safe.

He had just finished his pipe, while watching a seal that was advancing toward the shore beyond the mouth of the little stream when his gaze was attracted to an object visible on the water further away, above which the gulls where wheeling, and he shivered. He stood up.

"A launch...the current's bringing it in."

He looked again, shielding his eyes with his hand. "Is it empty? Why are the gulls circling around it?"

The floating object, driven by the tide, came toward the land. Lenoir took off his boots, went into the sea, took twenty paces, and waited, waist-deep in the water, for the current to bring what it was carrying to him.

A few minutes later, the man seized the prow of the little boat. He looked in, and went pale beneath his sunburn. The launch was not empty.

"Are they dead?" he asked. "Are they quite dead?" while towing the boat with all his might, with the aid of a rope that was hanging from the prow.

On the beach, he moored it to the large boulder on which he had been sitting. Then he climbed in.

Two men were lying, inert, in the bottom of the boat. One was old, lying on his side, his eyes open and vitreous, his mouth open within his gray beard, the breast of his seaman's jersey clutched in his clenched fist, with an expression of frightful suffering on his emaciated and convulsed face. One was young, thirty or thirty-two years old, blond, tall, sturdy but also emaciated, his face hollow and earthen, his eyelids closed.

Lenoir picked them up one by one, lifted them out of the launch and laid them down on the beach. Then, leaning over them, he examined them closely.

"They're dead," he murmured. "They're dead...."

As for the old one, no doubt could remain; he was cold and already stiff—but the other body was still supple and warm, and Lenoir set about fighting to pull the man back from the death that was about to take him. He rubbed him with all his might. Between the jaws that he unclenched with the blade of his mouth he poured a few drops of rum mixed with the water that his gourd contained. He was gripped by a powerful emotion.

He was neither impressionable nor sensitive; he had had too many adventures for that; too frequently, at sea or on land, he had seen his life and those of others in peril, from the elements, wild beasts or humans. But nothing—no personal peril, however horrible it might have been—had ever been as tragic and as affective for him as the mute and dogged combat for the life or death of another that he undertook on the sand of that tranquil shore, beneath the morning sky in which the birds were screeching.

With his sleeves rolled up as if for a fight, and a challenging expression in his resolute eyes, he redoubled his efforts against the invisible adversary that did not want to be vanquished. Above and beyond his instinctive sentiments of simple humanity, an abrupt horror of solitude had taken possession of him, and an anguished sweat moistened his brow at the thought of finding himself alone with two cadavers, now that another human existence had palpitated before him....

The castaway finally made a feeble little movement of his hand and opened his haggard eyes, which immediately closed again. Then, suddenly, in an imperceptible and hoarse voice, he began singing in a low voice.

"That's it...he's drunk sea-water...he's gone mad," Lenoir said to himself.

But the man was not mad; he did not die; and he was so strong that in spite of everything his savior lacked in order to care for him, he soon recovered his strength.

On the first day that he was in a fit state to emerge from the hut to which Lenoir had transported him, he went down to the beach, still a trifle unsteady on his feet. Lenoir was with him. They sat down on the sand and remained silent for a moment before resuming a conversation they had begun.

"So this is an island?" said the castaway, finally.

His voice was still weak. He spoke English with a guttural accent. He had not yet said anything about himself except that his name was Keller and that he had come from Australia.

"Yes," said Lenoir. "We're in the far south, lower down than Africa. Out there, a devil of a way to the west, is South America, Tierra de Fuego."

"What became of them?" Keller interjected.

"Who?"

"The others who were with me in the launch."

"There was only one—an old man with a gray beard. He was dead. I buried him at the foot of the cliff. What happened?"

"Fire on board. To begin with, we'd had a bit of wind and an accident to the rudder, and we drifted, and drifted...then the fire started, no one knew how. We took to the lifeboats. There were seven of us in the one I was in, and we lost sight of the others. We had almost no food; bad weather carried us away. When we got down to the last biscuits, there was a fight. Two men fell into the sea…and the sharks.…

"Another died; he became delirious and said that he could see his house, where he was expected for dinner. There were four of us left. We were dying of starvation. The wind was driving us God knows where. It was bad…I tried to eat a leather belt I had. We saw two ships, but they didn't see us. I don't remember any more after that.…

"The old man with the gray beard was called Olsen. He was a Dane. But for you I'd be where he is.…"

That was the first word of thanks that the castaway had addressed to Lenoir; the latter was satisfied with it. "It's not worth the trouble of talking about it," he replied, shrugging his shoulders. "I didn't risk anything, and I couldn't let a man die like that without trying to get him out of it. I'm glad to have succeeded.…"

"So it's an island?" the castaway went on. "And no one comes here?"

"It hasn't happened to me before," said Lenoir. "I don't expect anything. I've been here five years, at first with an old man, who died, and then alone. At one time there was some sort of station, or a port of call, if you like, something like the beginning of an establishment for fishing and seal-skins…at any rate, an American company maintained a few fellows here, on principle, to indicate that it was here. They still wanted to set up something permanent for seal-hunting. Then they went elsewhere, where they found something better. In brief, only two or three men were left…who only wanted to go back home. To come and live like that, it's necessary that one has a taste for it or good reasons for not wanting to frequent society. Finally, there was only one old American when I arrived. I was aboard a ship that belonged to the Company and which landed here; when they found that there was only one man left they asked if anyone wanted to stay…and I said that I'd like to.…"

"Why?" asked Keller.

Lenoir seemed to hesitate. "I don't know, exactly…perhaps

because I had nothing better to do…perhaps because I'd had enough of trailing around the world without ever being sure of eating the next day or the next month…I'd been doing that for nearly twenty years and I was sick of it. I'm from a little place whose name I no longer recall, a village near Dunkerque in France. I was twelve when I found myself alone, my parents having died, without there being anyone else to take care of me. I've done all sorts of things in my life: sailor, ferry-boat pilot, stevedore in ports; I've hunted monkeys and parrots in Borneo; I've been a bartender; I've worked in mines at the Cape…I don't know any more! I've been everywhere, I've seen everything… I've even done things that it would have been better not to do. In sum, I'm a *loupeur*, if you know what that means."[12]

There was a silence. Lenoir reflected, trying to extract himself from his confused memories and shadows of the past. He twitched his shoulders to signify indifference.

"My memory's not so good any more," he said, more to himself than his companion. "Anyway, now, I'm here, I'm tranquil, I'm used to it. When the American died, it was hard for me to find myself like that, all alone. There were times when I was afraid, would you believe it? There were times, in the first weeks, when I wept when I thought about what lay ahead. I repeated my name in order to be sure I'd remember it. It seemed to me—stupid, isn't it?—that there was no one left alive in the world but me.…

"Then it all settled down. I got used to it. I stopped worrying about it. I no longer have any desire to go, as in the early days, when I hoped to see a ship to take me away. One came, and I didn't go. Go where? To do what? Nothing good! I'm here, and here I stay. It's my home. Life out there, the past…unknown. When I think that I might not be able to find myself any more, I ask myself: 'What's your name, then, my lad?'"

12. In literal terms, a *loupeur* was someone who supposedly searched forests all over the world for exotic wood formations (loupes) to be employed by cabinet-makers, but the term came to be applied to any kind of vaguely purposeful vagabond.

After a long pause, Lenoir added. "There. I've told you that, I don't know why.... Because it's a long time since I've seen anyone, and I needed to talk. Then again, it's as well that we get to know one another, since we're going to be living together...."

He waited, expecting an analogous confidence, but none came. Keller remained silent.

"What about you?" Lenoir asked, squarely, to provoke the reciprocity that he felt he was owed.

"Me?" Keller shrugged his shoulders. "That's of no interest. What does it matter what one was before once one's here, where we are? If I told you that I'd had misfortunes and that I too have had good reason, for seven years, not to go back to Europe, what good would that do you? I no longer own anything but what I have on my back, and no one's waiting for me anywhere. Like you, I'm a citizen of the world, as the Americans say. The world, now, for me as for you, is here.

He stood up, looked around, and repeated: "Here."

Lenoir stood up in his turn. "In that case," he said, very gravely, "from now on, you and I are associates, for better or worse. You and me: it's the same thing. You and me are only one, now. It's said. We need to swear."

They swore, and shook hands with great solemnity. The pact was sealed.

From then on, their life unfurled, monotonous and various, in accordance with the seasons, the weather, their daily needs. They only made rare allusions to their earlier existence, which they had forgotten. Lenoir was content not to be alone and the fits of furious ennui that gripped Keller in the early days eventually eased. The two men had a perfect understanding, and throughout the months and years that followed, no dissent drove them apart. They saved one another's lives several times, and cared for one another when they fell ill. For the common good, to defend themselves against hunger and bad weather; they combined their efforts, with an untroubled accord, and without calculating whether one of them was sometimes doing more than the other.

At intervals of two or three years, it happened that ships on fishing expeditions or on commercial business in the South Seas stopped close to the island and traded with the firm of "Lenoir, Keller & Co."—as Lenoir had baptized their hut and their strand, insisting energetically on the "& Co." under the pretext that it looked good. But neither of the two associates seemed to think for a single moment of asking for a passage to return to the old world, which had become foreign to them, where they had known so much misery and defects, and doubt-less committed many sins, and much suffering, the memory of which, for them, had disintegrated in the peaceful solitude and the leveling shadow of passing time.

Neither of them knew any longer what they had been before. Slowly-created links bound them to that land, beneath that sky, beside that sea, in that savage and placid isolation, in which they now bowed grey hair over the same tasks that had occu-pied them in the distant days when, still young, they had come together there. Without understanding it very well, without even formulating it, they were vaguely happy, and when, after the day's work and the evening meal, they smoked their pipes sitting side by side under the smoky little lamp, they remained silent, having nothing to say to one another, existence having made their ideas identical to such an extent that they were only a single individual.

It was Lenoir who, on morning in June—it was then more than seventeen years that they had both been living there, and three years since they had spoken to any human being except for one another—first saw a ship moored a mile or so from the coast, beyond the reefs over which the sea foamed.

He turned toward the hut and shouted: "Keller! Keller!"

The other appeared and looked. A launch dropped by the ship and manned by a few oarsmen advanced toward the island.

"It's an American schooner," Keller observed.

He said no more. They both waited for the launch, which soon reached the sand of the shore. The ship's first mate was in command, an American about thirty years old. He offered them eau-de-vie, munitions, clothing and tinned food. He took aboard sealskins and fresh foodstuffs. Then, before the launch went back to the ship, which was heading eastwards, they drank some rum and chatted.

"Well, you're not curious, you two," the American said, finally. "Don't you want to know the news?"

"News? What do you expect us to do with that here?" said Lenoir. "News of what?"

The American seemed surprised. "News of the war, of course."

"What war?"

The two astonished associates looked at the American, who was initially bewildered. Then he turned to his sailors. "That's right...they don't know...."

"How could we know?" said Keller. "We haven't seen a ship for some time. So?"

The American told them the story of what had happened in the world since the beginning of August in 1914. He explained the facts clearly and succinctly, with neither passion nor partiality, occasionally appealing to one of his companions in order to specify some detail: the date and circumstances of a battle, an invasion, the capture of a town, the sinking of a liner, an aerial bombardment.

The two men listened, open-mouthed.

When he had finished, he took the launch back to his ship, which soon drew away.

It was getting late. Lenoir and Keller, side by side, went back to their hut silently.

"That's quite a story," said Keller, suddenly.

Lenoir did not reply immediately. Finally, he murmured: "That's true. We've been here, quite tranquil, and never suspected anything...."

"Yes, eh? And during that time, Europe....what a dance! Well, when we set about something, us, it's serious! It's for real!'""

"What do you mean, *us*? Good God—it's true. You're a German!"

"Yes, I'm a German. So what?"

They looked at one another. There was a new expression on their faces. Something had loomed up between them, which came from out there, from the other side of the world, from battlefields, ruined cities, devastated countries, burned villages, all the suffering, all the distress, and all the accumulated mourning. But a habit of friendship so old, so vivacious and so powerful bound them together that they were unable to comprehend the confused sentiments that welled up within them, from the depths of a past so distant, so completely abolished, ignored for so many years—and grew....

"It's worse than in '70," Lenoir suddenly murmured. "But this time...."

"Bah! All of that's all the same to us...." Keller affected a smile, to which the bitterness of his voice gave the lie, and he added: "If Germany crushes France, that doesn't prevent is from being tranquil here...."

"Shut up! It's you who'll be crushed this time!" cried Lenoir. "He said, so, the American!"

"That not true!" cried Keller.

Face to face, the two men measured one another with their gaze. Suddenly, a blind violence gripped them, a fury in which their will played almost no part, and hurled them against one another. Without another word, they wrestled savagely.

They fought with all their might, grim and mute. The outcome of the battle seemed to hang in the balance for a few moments, but Keller was knocked down. He got up again, resumed the struggle, then abruptly broke away, leapt backwards, and rummaged in his pocket. His adversary saw the gleam of a blade in his right hand and grabbed his wrist. The battle recommenced, even more ardently. They rolled on the ground, hoarse breath escaping their throats. The knife, having slipped from Keller's hand, was on the sand beside them. Lenoir made a furious effort and got the better of his opponent. He stretched out his hand and picked up the knife.

But he did not strike. Letting go of his enemy, who was choking, he got up, breathlessly, holding the weapon in his hand.

"I can't...." he murmured. "It's not for that that I snatched him from death fifteen years ago...."

He moved a short distance away, and then came back toward Keller. The latter stood up in his turn, slowly, and stood in front of him, head bowed; on his face, reddened by the struggle a little while ago but now livid, there was an expression in which there was rage and shame.

"Get out!" said Lenoir. "What we swore, you and me, is finished. Take half of everything; take the boat, go to the islet. You'll be as well there as here. I'll stay. I'll go to the west coast. That way, we won't see one another...."

While Keller made his preparations for the separation, he added, to himself: "And then again, that way, when ships pass, it'll be easier to see them. And now...I want to go back...I want to go back there...."

Vague memories resurfaced, outlined against the background of the shadow of the past: confused and familiar images...a village beside a gray road, a child running home for supper, toward a poor little house where his mother was waiting, a child that was himself....

He had the sound of oars in the calm waves. In the boat, Keller was going to the islet.

Lenoir shuddered, straightened up...almost called out....

But he did not, and he turned away, resolute....

Darkness fell, hiding the two separated men from one another.

ABOUT THE TRANSLATOR

BRIAN STABLEFORD has translated more than a hundred volumes of French prose into English. His principal interests are the French Romantic Movement and its Decadent/Symbolist aftermath, with particular reference to the evolution of the *conte cruel*, and the evolution of the *roman scientifique* from its origins in the eighteen-century *conte philosophique* to the aftermath of the Great War of 1914-18.